At the time of his untimely death in January 2005, K. Sello Duiker had published various short stories and two novels: *Thirteen Cents*, which was awarded the Commonwealth Prize for a first novel (Africa Region), and *The Quiet Violence of Dreams*, which won the Herman Charles Bosman Prize for English Literature. For many aspiring South African writers he served as a role model, someone who fearlessly tackled unconventional themes and explored new terrain. For an older generation of writers his work epitomised the best of post-1994 South African Black Writing. Duiker spent a large part of his childhood in Soweto, where he was born in 1974. He received a degree in journalism from Rhodes University.

The Hidden Star

K. Sello Duiker

At the time of the author's death on 19 January 2005, the manuscript of *The Hidden Star* was completed, but still in unedited form. It was posthumously edited by Annari van der Merwe, a close friend and publisher of *The Quiet Violence of Dreams*.

Published by Cassava Republic Press 2017

First Published by Umuzi, an imprint of Random House (Pty) Ltd 2006

ISBN: 978-1911115434

Cover design & illustrations: Graeme Arendse

Design and layout: Jibril Lawal

Printed and bound in Great Britain by Bell & Bain Ltd., Glasgow

CONTENTS

THERE IS A PLACE, far from the quiet suburbs where one knows one's neighbours only by name and never sees them. A place where children run idle in the streets while their parents labour in the big City of Gold to bring home food and hope for a better tomorrow. It is a place called Phola, a place with nothing much to brag about except that all the shacks face the morning sun and the inhabitants for the most part live together in peace. Until recently it was a very ordinary place to live.

For a while now, however, neighbourhood children have been disappearing from the midst of their families and friends, and no one knows what has become of them. None of the residents of Phola, however, want to talk openly amongst themselves about what is mentioned in whisper only.

Of late, Phola is no longer an ordinary place to live.

Chapter One
A CRY IN THE NIGHT

NIGHT has fallen. The moon bathes the tiny homes in a milky light, but the harsh bright lights of tall street lamps wipe the soft shadows from the dwellings at their feet. The air is still and warm, with moths whirring about in search of a light to dance around. Mamani, the woman who sells food, sits by an open fire outside her shack, roasting mealies. She swats at the mosquitoes that whizz about her neck, her arms and the sleeping toddler strapped to her back. The high-pitched buzzing irritates her. From the far end of Phola, music blares from a ghetto blaster and people can be heard laughing and dancing to the infectious rhythm of kwaito music. A pack of stray dogs has gathered near a rubbish bin. They are thin and their coats are mangy, and at any sudden movement they bare their teeth in vicious snarls. A black-and-white cat with half its tail missing struts in the moonlight, unaware of the danger. As it rounds a corner near the rubbish bin, the dogs stop sniffing for food and with wild yelps dash after it. In their mad chase they bump an old couple out of the way and knock over a basin with water that someone has left outside her door. Angry curses are hurled at the scraggy cat and unruly dogs. Finally the cat jumps onto the roof of a shack, leaps onto the next and vanishes into the night, leaving the disappointed dogs aimlessly sniffing about.

In the distance a police siren wails, but the children playing hide-and-seek in the maze of shanties do not hear it. Their only worry is not to stray too far from their homes, because of late their parents have become very strict about that.

In a nearby shack a girl is sitting at a small table, staring at an open book. Next to the open book an alarm clock softly ticks away the seconds. A short candle casts a faint yellow light on the cardboard-covered corrugated-iron walls and the lino floor. In one corner of the room there is a single bed, in another there is a table and two chairs. A small wardrobe and an old kitchen unit are propped against the wall opposite the door.

The girl sighs. She is tired, but she knows she can't go to sleep until her homework is done. She is also worried, because the candle is about to burn out and it is their last one.

Nolitye is short for her eleven years, with dreadlocks that fall to her shoulders, and big, shiny eyes that light up when she smiles.

Nolitye turns and looks to where her mother Thembi is asleep, curled up on the single bed with her back to Nolitye. Nolitye and her mother do not have much money, but their clothes, although old and a little tattered, are always clean, and they have tried to make the shack as homely as possible. The wall behind the bed is decorated with a poster of two hands joined together in prayer. The room is always neat.

Outside a dog suddenly barks. Nolitye knows who has caused the disturbance. It would be Ntate Matthews stumbling between the tightly- packed shanties. Every full moon Ntate Matthews drinks too much and when he's tipsy he's usually disorderly, his mouth quick to insult anyone or anything that crosses his path.

The dog barks more loudly. Nolitye pushes her book aside. It must be Rex, she guesses. Like most township dogs, he is a mixed breed, a big, sturdy black mongrel with hanging ears. He sometimes looks friendly, but mostly shows his fangs in a snarl. He is the leader of the pack of four strays that roam their area.

"Get away, you ugly thing! Hamba!" Ntate Matthews shouts. "Shut up, you ugly thing!"

Nolitye knows the shouting only makes Rex more vicious. She can imagine Rex moving closer, ready to attack, saliva drooling from his fangs.

Now Ntate Matthews is kicking an empty tin at the dog and growling like a mad animal himself. More dogs are barking outside.

Nolitye tries to forget about the noise outside. She pulls her Maths book closer. She must finish her homework before the candle burns out! Maths is her favourite subject. She likes the simplicity of playing with figures and the fact that, if she does the sums carefully, she always gets the answers right.

"I said, get away, you beast!" Ntate Matthews shouts so loudly that Nolitye peeps over her shoulder. Her mother is still fast asleep. She snores softly. Nolitye can't ignore the racket outside any longer. Now even the neighbours are yelling at Ntate Matthews. An irresistible urge overcomes her and she quietly gets up.

"You big drunk, why don't you go home and sleep!" someone shouts.

"Ag shut up." Ntate must have fallen over himself, because someone bursts out laughing.

"You won't be laughing when your kids start disappearing," Ntate Matthews says.

As Nolitye tiptoes to the door, a young man's voice asks, "What rubbish is this guy talking now?"

"Watch your mouth. You young people think you know it all today," Ntate Matthews grumbles.

Before Nolitye can turn the key in the lock, her mother stirs. "And where do you think you're going, young lady?" she asks sleepily.

Nolitye freezes. "I was just . . . uh going to get some water for the kettle, Mama."

"What? We filled the bucket together this afternoon."

"Oh yes . . . I forgot," she says, caught out.

"Nolitye."

"Yes, Mama."

"Don't lie to me. I know you wanted to go outside."

"Just one stone, Mama, please."

"You're always collecting stones. There's already a bucketful of your silly stones under the bed." Thembi sits up. "Is it that stupid name your granny gave you that makes you do it? 'Keeper of the Stone', 'Keeper of Knowledge'- where have you ever heard of such a name? I wonder who put it in her head."

"The stones are not silly, Mama. And my name is not stupid. Gogo said: you mess with a woman, you mess with a stone."

"But your grandmother didn't mean you should collect a stone every time you hear a noise outside. You know Ntate Matthews always does this and the following morning he just gets up as if nothing has happened."

"I know, Mama. But I just have to. Please."

She pulls a face that would make any mother's heart melt. Thembi sighs. "Okay, but don't be long. You still have to finish your homework and the candle is almost burnt out."

"Thanks, Mama! I won't be long. I promise."

Nolitye doesn't bother putting on shoes. She turns the key and closes the door quickly, before the candle can blow out.

Ntate Matthews is still staggering between the shanties, shouting at the top of his voice. Rex and the other dogs are circling around him, snarling.

"Get up, you lazy people, and kill these stupid beasts!" Ntate Matthews yells. "And what are you staring at?" he lashes out when he notices Nolitye watching him.

She turns her gaze away but from the corner of her eye sees Ntate Matthews trying to kick another empty can. This time he trips and falls on his bum. More people have come out of their shacks, some in their sleepwear. Everyone laughs raucously. Nolitye can't help but giggle.

"Shut up, you idiots!" Ntate Matthews slurs. "You don't know who I am," he says, pointing drunkenly at his chest. He burps and everyone pulls a disgusted face.

"Yes, we do," a young man answers back. "You're just a lousy no-good. Go home and sleep."

The man dismisses Ntate Matthews with the wave of a hand and saunters off. The other neighbours also disappear into their shacks and leave Ntate Matthews to his drunken state and the dogs.

Rex grabs Ntate Matthews's trousers at the ankle and doesn't let go.

Ntate Matthews swings his other leg and gives the dog a cruel kick that sends it moaning. But seconds later Rex returns, teeth bared. The other dogs close in around Ntate Matthews, ready to attack. Rex opens his jaws, growling ferociously.

"Rex, don't do it!" Nolitye tells the dog. "He's just a harmless old man."

"Who says I'm old? I can still give you a beating," Ntate Matthews is quick to say.

"He's got a big mouth."

"You little brat! What do you mean, I've got a big mouth?"

"I didn't say that," Nolitye says.

"I may be drunk but I'm not a fool," Ntate Matthews insists. "Then get up and go home, you stupid man."

Ntate Matthews, who has been watching Nolitye closely, frowns. He opens his mouth, but no words come out.

"What's the matter? The cat got your tongue?" Rex says to his face. The other dogs relax and mill around with wagging tails. Ntate Matthews rubs his eyes.

"What is going on? Who is behind this witchcraft?" he demands, surprisingly sober.

"So now he knows the secret. Big deal," one of the other dogs growls, an equally big dog, but brown with one pointy and one floppy ear and a dark ridge of wrong-way-round hair running down his back.

Ntate Matthews shakes his head. "I must be very drunk," he mumbles to himself.

"Don't worry, Ntate Matthews," Nolitye tries to comfort him. "But how can these strays talk?" he asks urgently.

"Hey, watch your mouth," Rex growls. "We're not strays, we live here." Ntate Matthews gives him a bewildered look.

"I don't know why you can hear them, Ntate Matthews. Only children are supposed to hear animals talk," Nolitye explains, a little furrow on her forehead.

"It's because he's drunk," Rex explains. "Freaky, but it sometimes happens like that with grown-ups. He'll probably wake up tomorrow and not remember a thing."

"But he'll have a stinking hangover and a headache," a tiny dog with a long body and long whiskers, a thin tail and ears like a bat's gleefully yelps.

Ntate Matthews stands with his mouth open. He feels a little dizzy. It is too much for him to accept that animals, dogs of all things, can talk. His face screws up in fright. He holds his cheeks in his hands and shakes his head.

"Are you alright?" Nolitye asks.

"I knew I was drinking too much. Now I can hear dogs talking. What's happening to me?" He starts wheezing.

"Relax, it's not the end of the world. You're drunk, remember?" Rex taunts him.

"Yes, I'm drunk," Ntate Matthews says, trying to calm himself. "I'm drunk and this is just a bad dream."

"That's right," Rex agrees.

"A very deep and very bad dream," Ntate Matthews mumbles.

"What were you drinking anyway?" Rex asks.

Ntate Matthews pinches himself hoping that he will snap out of whatever it is that makes him hear dogs talk. Then he gives himself a hard slap on the cheek.

"You can't like yourself very much if you do that," Rex comments.

"It's useless," Ntate Matthews sighs. "I've lost my mind."

With his shoulders hunched he starts sobbing. And then, in the middle of his tears, he lets out a long burp that sounds just like a growl.

The sound delights Rex and his pack. Nolitye too can't suppress a laugh. "It's not funny," Ntate Matthews says and wipes away his tears.

"That'll teach you not to drink more than you should. And you know what? I still want to bite you!" And Rex playfully bares his fangs.

Ntate Matthews gasps, straightens up and takes a step back. "Rex, be nice," Nolitye reprimands him.

"I was only joking. I just wanted him to stop crying."

"So if you're Rex, who are the others?" Ntate Matthews asks, embarrassed.

Rex keeps flashing his fangs to intimidate Ntate Matthews. "I'm Rex, and don't forget it. Half of me may be Labrador, but the other half is Rottweiler. I'm the big gun around here. All the neighbourhood dogs and cats know and respect me. Even Mandla, the donkey. So don't cross my path."

Nolitye smiles. Rex isn't always as tough as he makes himself out to be. Sometimes, when his fighter instincts take over, he is as mean as a hungry hyena; at other times, he is playful and likeable . But that doesn't happen a lot.

"Guys, introduce yourselves," Rex tells the other dogs.

"I'm Ticks. They say I am a true African dog, a cross between a ridgeback and something else . . . a Doberman, I think my mother said," the brown dog with the ridge on his back says and starts scratching his stomach.

"He's always doing that," Rex explains, "that's why we call him Ticks." The little dog with the long body wiggles forward. He stares at Ntate Matthews with bulging eyes and shakes his furry coat. "What's your name?" Ntate Matthews asks.

"Just because I'm little doesn't mean I don't bite," the small dog growls. "He's called Whiskers because he's got long whiskers like a catfish. Who knows, maybe he's half fish," Ticks teases him.

"Shut up, or I'll give you a flea bath," Whiskers yelps. "Chihuahua and dachshund, that's what I am!"

"Hey, you can't be a dog and not itch. Then you're just a pet." Ticks closes his eyes and gives himself a good, long scratch.

"Guys," Rex says, putting them in order. He's always in charge.

"Hold on," the last dog says. "What about me? Shorty, the ladies' man." Shorty, who is actually a little taller than Rex, is a good-looking dog with quite a thick long-haired coat. Compared to the others, he looks in good condition. He's a two-tone: black-backed with a tan stomach and legs. He has large pointed ears and a pink tongue curls from his long snout. In fact, except for his unimpressive tail, he looks very much like the dogs that ride around with the police in their vans.

"There always has to be a smarty-pants," Rex says irritated. "I suppose you get your name from your short tail," Ntate Matthew deduces.

"Spot on. Lost it in a dogfight," Shorty informs him.

"To one ugly dog called Beastie." Whiskers shivers at the thought.

"Beastie?" Ntate Matthews asks.

"You don't want to know him," Ticks says, giving himself an after-scratch shake. "If ever there was such a thing as the meanest dog in the world, Beastie would be that dog. They say he's half hyena. You would think it too if you saw him."

The conversation is cut short when MaMtonga, who lives next to Nolitye and her mother, opens her door and rinses out a bucket.

"Well, it was nice meeting you all," Ntate Matthews says, now more or less sober.

"Ja, and next time don't swear at us," Rex warns him.

"I won't do that again, believe me."

"What are you still doing here, Ntate? Talking to dogs?" The woman shakes her head. "You must be mad."

"Mind your own business, wena," Ntate Matthews answers back and clucks his tongue at her.

She goes back inside, clearly in no mood to argue with him.

Whiskers picks up a scent in the air and starts sniffing. "Do you guys smell what I smell?" he asks. They all sniff the air.

"Someone's having a braai," Shorty says, "and you know what that means."

"Bones!"

"See you later, Nolitye. And you - what do we call you?" he asks Ntate Matthews.

"Ntate Matthews," Nolitye quickly suggests.

Rex looks at Ntate Matthews with narrowed eyes.

Ntate Matthews clasps his forehead as if he is remembering something.

"Hey, do you know anything about the disappearing kids?" he asks the dog.

Rex's one ear moves slightly, but he does not answer.

Ntate Matthews mutters something about a Mean One, but Nolitye cannot catch the name he mentions.

"Rex, I'm starving!" Shorty growls.

"We have to go," Rex says, and the four dogs trot off, sniffing, snouts in the air.

"As for you, you didn't tell me your name." Ntate Matthews turns to Nolitye. "I've often seen you, but what is your name?"

"I'm Nolitye," she says and shakes his hand.

"Nice to meet you . . . This certainly has been a strange evening. Talking dogs, what next?"

Nolitye just smiles.

"I suppose I shouldn't tell anyone about this. Not that anyone would believe me . . ."

"It's getting late," Nolitye says. "I better go inside. My mother will be getting worried."

"Indeed. And I should be on my way too." Ntate Matthews shuffles up a narrow alley between the shanties.

But Nolitye does not go inside immediately. The sand is cool and soft under her bare feet. She sinks her toes into the soil, feeling for a stone. But she feels nothing but moist sand. High above the stars shimmer against a grey backdrop, the full moon watching over everything like a big eye in the sky. Nolitye shuffles her feet as she moves a little further. When she feels a small lump under her left foot, she smiles and bends down to pick up the stone. She turns it over in her hands, tracing its rough edges with her fingers; she can't see its shape and colour in the half-dark.

She kisses the stone and wishes that her father were there. Maybe if he were around they would also have a house built with bricks, with a small garden where she could keep a puppy. She'd call it Lucky and love it with all her heart. She closes her eyes and makes the wish. When she opens them, she feels better.

"Nolitye enough now!" her mother calls out. "I'm coming, Mama." Nolitye locks the door behind her.

"You and your silly stones. I have a good mind to throw them out one of these days."

"Please, Mama, don't. They're special."

"They're just silly stones."

"You don't understand, Mama."

For Nolitye each stone is like a memory. It helps her make sense of the big grown-up world. She crawls under the bed and drops her latest find among her collection of scores of stones which she keeps in an old enamel bucket.

"Who were you talking to anyway?"

"Ntate Matthews."

"I thought you were scared of him."

"I used to be, but he's actually a nice man."

"I don't understand you sometimes. Really," Thembi says in a strained voice. Nolitye can hear she is getting worked up. "Now come to bed!"

"But I still have to finish my homework, Mama."

"Then stop running around and finish it!" Thembi suddenly yells.

"Yes, Mama." Nolitye quietly sits down at the table. She doesn't understand her mother. Sometimes Thembi gets angry for no reason at all and shouts at her, a glint of meanness in her eyes. It confuses Nolitye. There are moments when Thembi is so hard on her that it feels as if they are total strangers. Nolitye tries to concentrate on her Maths, but she is bothered. Why does her mother become so unreasonably angry at times, shouting at her about the smallest thing? It is as if Thembi does it for no reason other than to make Nolitye feel bad.

"You better finish soon," Thembi adds angrily and turns her back on Nolitye.

There is only a little stump of candle left and Nolitye still has two sums to finish. She gives up and changes into her nightie, an old T-shirt that used to belong to her father. It's much too big and very old but it keeps her warm and she likes it. Her father died in a mining accident, but Thembi doesn't like talking about it, even though Nolitye never tires of hearing stories about her dad. She snuggles in next to Thembi and waits for the candle to burn out completely before she closes her eyes.

Nolitye is scared of the dark. She is afraid of the creatures that lurk in the night, like the Zim who they say is the one who's stealing the neighbourhood kids. Nolitye shudders. Why did Ntate Matthews ask Rex about the disappearing children? Does he know something about the Zim? And who is the Mean One he talked about?

"Lie still!" her mother grumbles.

Nolitye has never seen the great, hairy creature who they say eats children. His strength, they say, lies in the pinkie nail of his right hand, which apart from being as long as a man, is curved like a sickle blade and is even sharper. Anyone who crosses the Zim's path is mowed down by this weapon and gobbled up, they say, but the Zim is especially fond of eating children.

Nolitye doesn't like thinking about the Zim and tries to put him out of her mind. But there are other things too that make her fear the dark - strange noises like an owl hooting on a rooftop. Or gunshots that startle you from sleep, or people who suddenly start screaming, or a car screeching down the road as if speeding away from someone or something - maybe from MaMtonga next door.

Nolitye doesn't like the miserable old woman. She hasn't any teeth, except for one bad front tooth. A big pimple sits on her nose like a rotten pea and she's always in a bad mood. Just the other day, Nolitye was sweeping in front of the house when MaMtonga came out complaining that she was stirring up dust. She didn't stop shouting at Nolitye until she had put the broom away. And when the neighbourhood boys play football near her shack, MaMtonga chases them away. Once she was so angry that she grabbed the football and stabbed it with a knife, right in front of everyone's eyes. If Nolitye greets MaMtonga, the grumpy old woman doesn't ever bother to greet her back. Yet, when she doesn't greet her, MaMtonga complains to her mother, who always tells Nolitye that she must be nice to MaMtonga. But what's the use? MaMtonga is impossible to please. Her face is fixed in a permanent scowl.

Nolitye moves closer to her mother. The worst thing about MaMtonga is that people say she's a witch, an umthakathi. Everyone knows she's a traditional healer and that she has the power to use herbs to cure people, but not many sick people come to her for healing. No, people come to her to get potions with which to kill their enemies, they say. They come for muti that makes people go mad, or can put someone under a spell. And MaMtonga has a snake in her shack, they say. But Nolitye has never seen it. She is too scared of MaMtonga to go near enough to have a peep.

It takes a while before sleep comes, but when it does, Nolitye goes out like a candle.

Chapter Two

THE PRECIOUS FIND

WHEN Nolitye wakes up the next morning, Thembi has already washed and is dressed for work. The kettle is boiling on the Primus stove.

"Hurry up, Nolitye, or I'll be late for the taxi," Thembi says, busy making sandwiches for Nolitye to take to school. Their breakfast sandwiches are already done.

Nolitye hates mornings because they tear her away from her dreams in which all sorts of wonderful things happen: sometimes she flies around, other times she plays hopscotch all day with her best friend Bheki. She slowly slides out of bed, takes the orange plastic dish and pours some hot water into it. Thembi hands her a washing rag and a bar of green soap. Nolitye washes quickly, then sparingly squeezes a small blob of white toothpaste on her toothbrush.

Thembi has cut her peanut butter sandwiches for school into small triangles and wrapped them neatly in a plastic bag, but Nolitye has to iron her own gym dress and shirt for school herself. She carefully puts the solid metal iron on the Primus stove, and while it is heating up, she wets a square cut from a mealie meal bag. With this she presses her school uniform very carefully. When she is dressed, she joins her mother on the edge of the bed, and like every school day, they enjoy their breakfast of peanut butter sandwiches and tea together. Sometimes Nolitye drinks milk with the sandwiches, but today there's no milk.

Nolitye is careful not to get crumbs on the floor. She does not want to spoil her mother's good mood.

"Did you sleep well?" Thembi asks. "You were tossing and turning a lot last night."

"I had this strange dream," Nolitye begins. She still feels a little unsettled by it.

"What happened?"

"This man without a face was chasing me."

"What do you mean - this man without a face?"

"I mean just that, Mama. He was like a ghost." Thembi has stopped chewing. "Go on," she urges.

"He kept on asking me for a stone. In the end I gave him my bucket with stones, but he got angry and chucked them away. And then he told me that he was going to throw me down a hole. That's when I started running." Nolitye closes her eyes, trying to remember more. "Oh yes, Ntate Matthews was also in the dream, but he was just laughing his head off."

"It was only a dream," Thembi says. "Forget about it."

But her mother's advice doesn't make Nolitye feel better. The dream was too real to be pushed out of her thoughts so easily. She remains sitting on the bed, glancing nervously at her mother.

Thembi is a hawker. She has her own spot near the taxi rank in Noord Street in town where she sells her wares. It is hard sitting in the blazing sun all day, she always says, watching her goods all spread out in front of her. Most people walk past as if she doesn't exist; only sometimes someone needs a nail clipper, or a comb, snuff, or a small packet of earbuds. Thembi sells odd bits and pieces that most people only realise they do not have when they need them. The other hawkers all know Thembi as the woman who sells things people need but always forget to buy. Nolitye is not allowed to look in the box with the things she sells. Thembi has forbidden it because she says Nolitye will only mix them up.

Nolitye gathers her school bag and her mother takes her box of goods. They leave together, Nolitye's bag slung over her shoulder, Thembi carrying her box on her head. Nolitye always marvels at that. She once tried to balance a bucket of water on her head but it all splashed out. Her mother laughed. "Don't worry," she said, "in a few years' time, when you're a little older, you'll also be able to carry things on your head." Nolitye can't wait to grow old enough.

It is windy outside. Scraps of paper are flying about, dust and smog choke the air. Nolitye sneezes. It is a five-minute walk to the taxi rank where her mother catches a minibus into town. When it is nice and early, like today, Nolitye sometimes accompanies her there before she goes to school. Where they turn into the main road to town, they run into Ntate Matthews. He is wearing a suit and a tie, his face is clean-shaven and he looks nothing like the ranting and raving ruffian of the previous night.

"Good morning, MaDube," he greets cheerfully.

"Good morning, Ntate Matthews," Thembi says, doing her best not to look at him.

Ntate Matthews winks at Nolitye. She smiles shyly. "Isn't it a lovely morning?"

"A bit windy," Thembi says. "Just a little fresh air, I'd say."

Nolitye keeps quiet, her heart thumping in her chest. She hopes that Ntate Matthews doesn't remember talking to Rex and his pack last night. "These are strange days indeed," Ntate Matthews remarks. "What do you mean?"

Nolitye can hear from the way her mother asks the question that she isn't really keen to get into a conversation with him.

"Another child has disappeared."

"Oh, I didn't know that," Thembi replies, suddenly interested, and Nolitye listens intently.

"Yes, Sara, the Madi girl. The pretty one. Early this morning, her parents sent her to buy bread. The poor girl never came back."

Thembi shakes her head. "That is terrible."

Nolitye tries to recall what the girl looks like. She's only seen her once or twice because her family lives near the freeway and she went to another school.

"That's the second child in the last three months," Ntate Matthews says. "You better look after your daughter . . . It's Nolitye, isn't it?"

"Yes," Thembi says. "Say hello to Ntate Matthews, Nolitye. You told me you were talking to him last night."

But in daylight Nolitye is shy and keeps quiet.

With the box on her head, Thembi turns to Ntate Matthews. "I'm sorry, but you know kids. Their manners . . ."

"But this one isn't like the others." And looking at Nolitye, he says, "I once knew your father."

"My father. Really? What was he like?" Nolitye has completely forgotten to be shy.

"He was a man with special powers— "

"Nice talking to you, Ntate Matthews," Thembi interrupts him, and casting Nolitye a stern look, she says, "Come, Nolitye."

Nolitye doesn't move. "What do you mean, he had special powers?"

"I mean, he could do amazing things."

"It was nice talking to you, Ntate Matthews, but now we have to go." Thembi throws Nolitye another stern look and strides away.

"Wait, Mama. He's just telling me about Papa."

"Maybe another time, Nolitye," Thembi says over her shoulder.

"Sooner or later the girl has to know the truth about her father!" Ntate Matthews calls after Thembi.

"Goodbye, Ntate Matthews!" she shouts back and walks faster. Nolitye has to run to catch up with her mother.

They are quiet as they walk to the taxi stop. After a while Nolitye slows down and follows a few steps behind her mother. She hates it that her mother never wants to talk about her father.

At the taxi rank her mother joins the queue waiting for the taxi to Noord Street. Nolitye slips in next to her. "What did he mean when he said Papa had special powers?"

"Nothing, Nolitye. Ntate Matthews is just a confused man. You saw what he's like when he drinks. Listen, did you finish your homework last night?"

"But he said he knew Papa."

"They may have said hello to each other a couple of times, but I wouldn't say that means he knew your father. Now why don't you watch out for a taxi?"

Nolitye can see her mother doesn't want to talk about her father, and it hurts. She stands quietly, questions racing in her mind. A taxi arrives, kwaito music blaring from it. Two schoolgirls push their way to the front when they recognise the driver. The people in the queue begin to complain loudly, including Thembi.

"Eish, I decide who gets into my taxi. If you don't like it, then go," the taxi driver growls.

Nolitye waves goodbye to Thembi, not sure that her mother will notice, because she sits squeezed in between a man with a hat on and a woman wearing a big turban. As soon as the taxi is gone, she turns back. She spots Rex and his pack digging on the rubbish dump across the road. She walks right up to them because she doesn't want anyone to hear her talking to them. "Have you guys seen Ntate Matthews?"

"Good morning to you too," Shorty greets her with a wave of his half-a- tail.

"Sorry. Good morning, Shorty. It's just I'm in a rush to get to school, but I have to talk to Ntate Matthews first. Have you seen him?"

"You mean that silly drunk?"

"He's not that bad, Rex. It is just when it's full moon that he drinks too much."

"We saw him at MaMokoena's spaza shop a few minutes ago," Rex informs her. Ticks nods and carries on scratching behind his ear. Whiskers doesn't even lift his head to look at her, he is only interested in finding something to eat.

"Thanks, guys!" Nolitye runs in the direction of the spaza shop near the clinic in the middle of Phola. She jumps over a puddle of dirty water leaking from a burst pipe, careful not to soil her shoes. Children in school uniform pour from the alleys into the street, joining the men and women hurrying to work. Nolitye makes her way against the stream of people until she stands in front of MaMokoena's spaza shop. She doesn't see Ntate Matthews anywhere.

"Dumela, MaMokoena," she greets the woman behind the small counter.

"Dumela, my child."

"Have you seen Ntate Matthews?"

"He was here just a few minutes ago to buy some milk, but I don't know where he went."

"Do you know where he lives?" Nolitye asks urgently.

"No, sorry, my child," MaMokoena says.

A woman enters and asks for a loaf of bread. Nolitye steps aside, disappointed. "Bye, MaMokoena." She might as well go to school, she decides.

"I'm going to tear your ears off!" someone shouts outside. "Come back here, you little brats!"

Nolitye looks to see where the racket is coming from. She is almost knocked over by three boys sprinting down the narrow street, laughing. They're being chased by Ntate Matthews who is waving a sjambok in the air. But the boys are too quick. They have already disappeared among the shacks.

Ntate Matthews stops, huffing and puffing. He is only a few steps from Nolitye, but he doesn't see her. He is too busy trying to catch his breath. "Those little rats," he grumbles. "They were throwing stones on my roof again."

Nolitye keeps quiet, too scared to talk to him.

"I'll get them next time," he mumbles to himself and starts walking back in the direction of the clinic.

"Wait, Ntate Matthews! Please, I need to talk to you," Nolitye calls and rushes after him.

"Yes, my child," he says, still sounding irritated, but he stops walking. "Earlier, when you were talking to my mother . . ."

"Yes?"

"You said something about my father."

"I knew him."

"You said he could do amazing things. Please tell me, what kind of things?"

"Shouldn't you be on your way to school?"

"Please, Ntate. I need to know. I hardly knew my father. I was so young when he died."

Nolitye tries to remember how her father looked, but the harder she tries the less she can recall him. She looks up and sees Ntate Matthews looking hard at her, the expression on his face kind and friendly.

"Come back this afternoon after school and I will tell you."

"Really? Oh, thank you, Ntate!" Then she remembers: "But I don't know where you live."

"You know the taps next to the clinic?"

"Ja."

"And you know the big bluegum tree? Now if you stand under the tree and face the taps, turn left and count the dwellings in the front row. Mine is the seventh to your left. It's painted blue. You can't miss it."

"Thanks, Ntate!"

"Now off you go to school. I don't want to get into trouble with your mother."

"See you later," Nolitye shouts as she runs off.

It is still early enough for her to fetch Bheki. He lives in Mogale, across the main road, where the houses are built of bricks and people have their own small gardens. Bheki is her best friend. He's short, just like her, and has an impish face and small beady eyes. The other kids tease him because he's chubby. Bheki loves food. In fact, eating and reading are his favourite pastimes. That's why he's so clever, he always tells Nolitye with a happy twinkle in his eye. The other children think he's a cheese boy, but not Nolitye. She is proud that Bheki is clever and that the two of them always get good marks.

She gives a quick knock and pushes open the front door of the Zwanes' five-roomed house in Siswe Street. It is a quiet street, unlike the streets in Phola. All the neighbours have green patches of lawn and the kids don't play football in the street.

Bheki is sitting at the kitchen table slurping his porridge, while his baby brother is under the table pulling out his shoelaces. Bheki pulls his feet away. He hates it when his little brother does this.

"Ma, look what Khaya is doing," he complains. To Khaya he says, "You can be pleased Dad's gone already."

If ever there was a prize for the naughtiest toddler, Khaya would get it, Nolitye thinks, standing in the doorway. If he isn't pulling things off the table, he's putting them in his mouth. It's a full-time job just looking after him.

Bheki's mother walks in through the back door. She is also short and fat and when she walks, she waddles a bit. But Nolitye likes her.

"Dumela, MaZwane," Nolitye greets her. "Sawubona, my child."

She gives Nolitye a hug. She always squeezes Nolitye too tightly, but out of politeness Nolitye never complains, even though she sometimes feels she can't breathe and would pass out. Well, maybe not quite pass out, but she certainly always feels a little light-headed after one of MaZwane's hugs. Still, she loves being hugged by MaZwane. Her hugs are like gifts that make her feel special.

"Come on, Bheki," MaZwane says while she picks Khaya up. "You eat too much. Nolitye is already here and you're still eating."

"I'm almost done, Ma," Bheki says, scraping out the last mouthful of porridge.

His mother takes a red toy truck from the table and gives it to Khaya. The little guy is only too happy to be put back down on the floor with his truck, and MaZwane scoops up Bheki's school shoes and puts back the laces.

"Look at these shoes. Filthy," she fusses. "Give me the brush!" While she gives the shoes a quick shine, Khaya bangs his toy truck on the floor, trying to get her attention.

Nolitye excuses herself and slips into the bathroom. She does this whenever she visits Bheki, because Bheki not only lives in a brick house with two bedrooms, but the Zwanes also have a proper bathroom with a flush toilet. Back in Phola, Nolitye has to share five mobile toilets with the two hundred other people in her area. After using the flush toilet, she loves opening the hot water tap and letting the warm water flow over her hands.

Water should come out of a tap, she thinks, not leak through the roof every time it rains. In summer when there are heavy showers, she and her mother have to rush around and put empty buckets and pots all around the room, even on the bed.

Bheki is ready to go and his mother takes her wallet from her chest, gives him his lunch money and hides the wallet again. She hugs him and kisses him on the cheek. "Ma! I'm gonna be late," he complains and wipes his cheek.

"What's wrong, Mfana? Are you shy to be kissed in front of Nolitye?"

"We're going now," Bheki says, closing the door.

Outside the gate, Bheki gives his lunch money to Nolitye, who carefully hides it in her shoe. They do this because every day the class bully, Rotten Nellie, waylays them outside the school gates. Everyone knows that Nolitye's mother is too poor to give her pocket money to buy sweets, so nobody would suspect that she is carrying any money. Rotten Nellie only pushes her around and takes her peanut butter sandwiches, but then she searches Bheki for money because he doesn't take sandwiches to school. She has never found any money on him, and every time she grabs him by the back of his collar and demands, "What are you going to eat?" Bheki meekly replies, "I go home for lunch." But Rotten Nellie never gives up, the next day she again pushes her hand in Bheki's blazer and pants pockets, looking for money, and then shouts at him if there is nothing.

Nolitye and Bheki take the long route to school. They do not want to bump into Rotten Nellie before they get to the school gates where, if they are lucky, there will be school prefects on duty. They have to hurry because they have to walk around an open field and past the church where Nolitye sometimes goes with her mother on Sundays.

"Last night I had a strange dream," Nolitye says as they come in sight of the school.

"Don't tell me that you were being chased by frogs again!"

"Hey, that was quite scary. You should have seen how big they were."

"But who's scared of frogs? They can't even bite you, man."

"Anyway I was trying to tell you about last night's dream," Nolitye cuts him short.

But Bheki's mind is on something else. "I'm getting tired of this," he sighs.

Nolitye looks at where he is indicating with his eyes. Rotten Nellie and her gang, Thabo, S'bu and Four Eyes, are waiting for them at the school gates. Rotten Nellie and Thabo with folded arms and leaning against the wire fence.

The four call themselves the Spoilers. Thabo, the tallest of the boys, is good at football and always carries a football with him. His shirt is never tucked into his shorts and his socks are always down. S'bu is quite neatly dressed but doesn't say much and never smiles. He looks a bit dumb. Wherever Rotten Nellie and Thabo go, he goes too, walking very close to Thabo. Four Eyes, who wears big spectacles that cover half his face, with lenses that are so thick that they resemble magnifying glasses, looks out of place with the others. He doesn't seem tough enough. It is said that he has a rich father. As for Rotten Nellie, she is the only girl in school who refuses to wear a gym dress like the other girls. She insists on wearing a shirt and shorts like the boys. Even her school shoes are meant for boys. Bheki is scared of her because he once saw her punch a grade-seven boy in the face. When the boy started bleeding from the nose, Rotten Nellie bellowed with laughter as if it were the funniest thing she ever saw.

"Well, well, if it isn't Pumpkin Face and the Mop, my favourite idiots!" Rotten Nellie says, straightening up and swaggering towards Nolitye and Bheki.

Thabo, S'bu and Four Eyes laugh as if she had cracked a joke. They sound like cackling hyenas. S'bu is enjoying himself so much that he farts.

Rotten Nellie swings back and throws him a disgusted look. "Say sorry, you pig!" she scolds him.

"Sorry," he mumbles sheepishly.

Bheki looks around. There are no prefects patrolling the school gates, so Rotten Nellie is sure to get away with Nolitye's lunch. He feels like turning back, but he knows it will only make matters worse.

"I'm feeling a bit hungry this morning. I wonder if you can help me out," Rotten Nellie starts.

Nolitye casts a look at Bheki but says nothing.

"Hey, you Mop, I'm talking to you. Give me my food, I'm hungry!"

If only I was bigger than you, Nolitye thinks to herself. I'd shut you up with one smack. "My name is Nolitye," she says to Rotten Nellie.

"Nolitye, Mop - it's all the same to me. Just give me my food before I do something you won't like!"

Nolitye doesn't respond.

Rotten Nellie looks at her gang and nods. Thabo and S'bu leap forward, grab Nolitye by the arms and pull her school bag off her shoulder. Nolitye tries to swing her arms and free herself, but the boys are too big and strong. She glances at Bheki. Poor Bheki, he doesn't like fighting. There's nothing wrong with that, Nolitye knows, but sometimes she really wishes that Bheki was braver and would help her - she's not just going to hand over her sandwiches.

Rotten Nellie digs into Nolitye's school bag. "Aha," she says and takes out the sandwiches. Three of Nolitye and Bheki's classmates arrive at the school gates but they quickly walk past and pretend not to see what is happening.

Rotten Nellie takes the sandwiches out of the plastic bag and snarls, "Peanut butter! Again! What's wrong with you? Are you poor or something? You always have peanut butter sandwiches and I'm getting fed-up."

"Give back my school bag!" Nolitye demands and lunges forward.

"Hey! I asked you a question. Are you poor or what? Is that why you always have peanut butter sandwiches?"

Nolitye holds onto her school bag but Rotten Nellie doesn't let go. "Of course she's poor. Look at her clothes," Thabo says pointing at Nolitye's frayed shirt.

"You don't have to be so mean," Bheki finally says, his heart beating wildly.

"That's what we do, you stupid barie, you bumpkin," S'bu says. "We're mean."

Nolitye is still wrestling with Rotten Nellie to get her bag back, but with a violent shrug the much bigger girl shakes herself free." What is this Mop trying to do?" she asks her gang. They all giggle. S'bu looks especially silly with his two missing front teeth.

"Give me back my school bag," Nolitye demands again.

"Not until I have copied your homework first."

"You can't do that," Bheki protests, his voice going high.

"Says who, Pumpkin Face?"

Bheki straightens his shoulders and looks her in the face.

"Says me!" Rotten Nellie's face goes dark and her nostrils flare.

Bheki braces himself. Without warning Rotten Nellie suddenly storms towards him and pushes him so hard that he lands on his bum with a thud.

Nolitye knows how soft-hearted Bheki is and says, "You didn't have to do that." She helps him to his feet. He tries to hold back the tears but big drops start rolling down his cheeks.

"What's the matter? You want your mummy to wipe away your tears?" Thabo mocks.

The Spoilers laugh uproariously, except for Four Eyes. He grins but behind his thick glasses his eyes are serious.

Rotten Nellie fumbles in Nolitye's school bag and takes out her

Maths book. She taps Thabo on his shoulder and makes him bend his back so that she can use it as a table. With eyes darting from Nolitye's book to her scribbler, she quickly copies Nolitye's answers. She slams Nolitye's book shut. "Hey, you didn't finish the last two sums!" she accuses her.

Nolitye is saved by the arrival of the headmistress in her car. Rotten Nellie moves out of the way and as soon as the teacher has driven through the gates throws the book and the bag at Nolitye. "If you tell anyone, I'll knock your teeth out," she threatens.

Nolitye manages to catch the bag, but the book falls on the ground. She dusts it off and puts it back in her bag. "Don't listen to her," she tries to comfort Bheki. He is sniffling.

"If you want to tell on them, go ahead, but count me out. I don't want to lose my teeth, thank you very much," Bheki stutters.

At moments like these Nolitye wishes that her friend had a bit more courage and a little less fear. He gets bullied so easily.

"Come, let's go to class," she says. She slips the three rand out of her shoe and gives it to him. Together they will buy something and share it at lunchtime. They always do that when Rotten Nellie has pinched Nolitye's sandwiches. On their way to class Nolitye suddenly bends down and picks up a stone. A smooth, grey stone that she slips into a side-pocket of her school bag.

"What do you do with these stones that you're always collecting?" Bheki asks, a perplexed look on his round face.

"I just collect them," Nolitye says, impatient to get to class. She doesn't want them to get detention during lunch because they were late.

Nolitye and Bheki share a desk in the front row from where they can't see Rotten Nellie, who always sits at the back by herself. Rotten Nellie doesn't share a desk because she is so big that no one can fit on the seat next to her.

No one in the class knows for sure how old Rotten Nellie is, but everyone knows that she's repeating Grade Five and that she must be older than them. No one ever mentions this, because Rotten Nellie would go wild. It is only Moeder, their class teacher, who, when she sees that Rotten Nellie hasn't done her homework, dares to remind her that it is her second year in Grade Five.

As soon as everyone is seated, Moeder goes from desk to desk, checking everyone's homework. When she gets to Nolitye, she stops. Before she can even ask, Noltiye explains that she couldn't finish the last two sums because the candle burnt out.

"Don't worry, my child. I know you're a good student," Moeder says. She is happy to see that Bheki finished all his sums and that, as always, his work is neat. Bheki has the best handwriting in the class. Moeder likes to show it as an example to the others. Bheki doesn't like her doing this, because it makes him look like he wants to be teacher's pet. It is not the case; all he wants is to do well at school. He and Nolitye usually get top marks and if he does better than Nolitye in a spelling test, she congratulates him, and if she does better than him in a Maths test, he congratulates her. That's how it is. They are friends, and friends don't compete.

At lunch break Bheki and Nolitye are careful not to buy anything to eat while Rotten Nellie may be watching them. Some children go home for lunch, while others hang about the school, playing soccer or hopscotch, so no one looks twice at them when they slip out the school gates. They hurry down the road where they noticed Mamani selling her delicious roasted mealies, fatcakes, dried fish and guava juice. She is called Mamani because on her rounds in the neighbourhood selling her foodstuffs, she wears a traditional Shangaan blue-and-red striped skirt with flounces, and wire bracelets and anklets. Today she sits under a large umbrella near the crossroads without her baby who usually plays or sleeps on a blanket at her side.

Bheki and Nolitye buy two fatcakes, a little bag of dried fish and one guava juice to share. While Bheki is paying, a strange-looking stone near the cardboard box in which Mamani carries the foodstuffs catches Nolitye's eye. Even though it is not in the sun, it seems to shine with a purplish light. She picks it up and shows it to Bheki.

"Nice stone," is all he says.

Nolitye brushes the sparkling stone against her shirt sleeve. She is delighted with her find.

"What've you got there?" Mamani asks.

Nolitye holds out her hand. Mamani takes the stone and studies it very closely. "Hmm, lovely."

"It's a lucky find," Mamani says, handing the stone back.

The two take the food and head down the road to the park at the crossroads. But something makes Nolitye turn and look back. She blinks her eyes - a white dove is hovering above Mamani's head. "Bheki, look!" she gasps.

"Where? What?"

"There, above Mamani's head. The dove!" Bheki swings round but he doesn't see anything out of the ordinary. All he sees are school children gathered around Mamani to buy eats.

"Can't you see anything? There's a dove above Mamani's head!" Nolitye almost shouts and points. "Look there!"

"Is this a joke? 'Cause if it is, I'm not getting it." Bheki feels hurt. Nolitye never makes fun of him.

"Forget it," Nolitye says and sighs.

In the park they flop down on the grass to finish their lunch. Nolitye puts the stone in her lap and watches it shimmer and catch the sunlight. A weird tingling feeling comes over her. She starts giggling to herself.

"What are you laughing at?" Bheki asks. "Nothing." But she carries on giggling.

"It can't be nothing. You're giggling. No, you're laughing!"

Bheki hates being left out of a joke. "Please," he pleads with Nolitye, "tell me what is so funny."

"Okay, but you are going to think it is strange."

"What is so strange?" Bheki asks anxiously.

"It's the stone, it makes me laugh."

Bheki looks sideways at her as if she has suddenly gone crazy or something.

"Here, you try." She hands him the stone.

Soon Bheki says he has a tingling feeling, as if he's being tickled with a feather. He also starts giggling, and then laughing out loud, rolling on the ground until the stone drops from his hand. Nolitye quickly picks it up and puts it in her shirt pocket.

"Maybe it's a magical stone," Bheki says, tears of laughter still shining in his eyes.

"Eish, wouldn't that be cool?"

"It would really be great."

They sit in silence for a while, a silly grin on their faces.

"We better get to class," Nolitye says and gets up, her right hand protectively over her shirt pocket.

During lessons they pass the stone back and forth between them, giggling. The stone truly has the strangest effect on them. Moeder, who has never before had to tell them to behave in class, has to order them to be quiet. After school she asks both of them to stay behind.

Nolitye knows it can only mean one thing: a scolding. And no one scolds like Moeder, not even her mother when she is in a bad mood. She cringes when Moeder folds her arms and sternly says, "So come out with it. What was so funny that you two had to disrupt my lesson?"

"Sorry, Ma'am," they both reply.

"'Sorry, Ma'am' isn't good enough. Tell me what was so funny."

"It was nothing, really . . ." Nolitye begins.

"Don't be silly. Only fools laugh at nothing. Now, what was it?"

"Uhm . . . it was just a silly joke that Bheki told me," Nolitye says, poking Bheki in the ribs. She looks at Bheki to agree with her, but he stares at her blankly.

"And how does the joke go?"

"Uhm . . ." Nolitye fumbles. She has to think quickly. She doesn't know any jokes. If only they had put away the silly stone instead of passing it between them.

"Well, I'm waiting!"

"Uhm, Ma'am, it was really a stupid joke," Nolitye says desperately.

"I said I'd like to hear it," Moeder insists.

Nolitye says the first thing that comes into her head. "Uhm . . . it's about a chicken . . . that uh . . . crosses the road without looking and gets run over."

"What is so funny about that? You two think that's funny?" Moeder asks.

Bheki shakes his head. He looks lost and anxious. Nolitye glares at him. "Do you know how many people die on our streets every day because they didn't look left and right before crossing the road? And you think it is funny?"

Outside the door Rotten Nellie is listening very intently. She has never seen Nolitye and Bheki get in trouble for anything, so she sent the gang to the school gates, supposedly to keep watch. With her eyes closed and her one ear pressed to the keyhole, she is listening so hard that she doesn't notice the headmistress behind her. Mrs Lesufi taps her on the shoulder.

"What do you want?" Rotten Nellie explodes, thinking it is one of her gang. "Didn't I tell you to wait at the gates?"

When no answer comes, she turns around. "Bu ...I mean Ma'am," Rotten Nellie stumbles. "What I meant to say was -"

"Is that a way to greet me, young lady?" The headmistress is annoyed, peering through the spectacles perched on the end of her nose.

"I . . . sorry, Ma'am, I didn't realise it was you."

"Of course you didn't. You were too busy eavesdropping."

"Me? No, Ma'am." Rotten Nellie shakes her head. "I was just waiting for my friends."

"I'm sure your friends will be along any minute now. You best be on your way instead of looking like you're eavesdropping."

"No, Ma'am, I mean, yes, Ma'am."

The headmistress knocks, then opens the door and walks into the classroom. She greets Moeder and nods at Nolitye and Bheki and says, "Mrs Mofokeng, I just came to check if you remember about the staff meeting that's starting in ten minutes' time."

"Thank you, Mrs Lesufi, I do. But I had to deal with these two smart alecks who think it's funny to be run over by a car."

Nolitye wishes a big hole would open up in the polished cement floor and swallow her. She has never been scolded by Moeder, nor has Bheki, and for the headmistress to catch them like this!

"Doesn't sound terribly funny to me," says Mrs Lesufi, taking a step back.

"Hayi, these kids nowadays," adds Moeder.

If only I could explain, surely they will understand, Bheki thinks and opens his mouth. "Actually, Ma'am—"

But Nolitye jumps in before Bheki can say anything. "Yes, actually we see that it was a very stupid thing to laugh at and we promise not to do it again, Ma'am."

"Good. Your behaviour was very insensitive."

"Yes, Ma'am, you're right."

"Of course she's right," the headmistress puts in her two cents' worth. "Now go home and do your homework before I give you more work to do."

"Yes, Ma'am," they both nod at Moeder and with a quick glance at the headmistress scurry out of the room. They run down the passage and round the corner, slap bang into Rotten Nellie and her gang who have been waiting for them there.

"So now you think you're me, neh?" Rotten Nellie says, giving a filthy look. "Suka!"

Nolitye and Bheki stare at her. They don't know what she is talking about. "Don't look at me like the mouse that's just eaten the cat, you know what I'm talking about!" she yells. "It's my job to get in trouble with Moeder, not yours!"

"What?" Nolitye can't believe her ears.

"You're spoiling my reputation. Teachers' pets like you don't get into trouble. So stop it!"

"Ja," S'bu adds. "We're the ones that cause trouble. Trouble is us!"

"That's the silliest thing I've ever heard," Nolitye says, ready to go.

"Hold on. You won't think it's silly when I smash in your face!"

Bheki knows that Nolitye can't be scared that easily, but then Rotten Nellie turns to him. He gives Nolitye a pleading look and puts his hands in his pockets to keep them from shaking.

Nolitye gets a clever idea. She secretly slips her hand into her shirt pocket and holds the stone. Soon she begins to giggle. Rotten Nellie watches her with a frown on her forehead, her mouth half open. Nolitye starts to laugh. She laughs and laughs.

Bheki is getting more and more nervous. He pulls at Nolitye's sleeve and indicates with his eyes that he too needs the stone. Surreptitiously Nolitye passes him the stone. Bheki immediately feels relaxed. Now it is his turn to laugh.

Rotten Nellie is so confused and so furious that she can't think of anything to say or do. She detests being laughed at and she especially doesn't like being made to look like an idiot in front of her gang. For once Thabo and S'bu are also quiet. Four Eyes is biting his bottom lip and looking at his feet.

Nolitye is pleased with the success of her clever strategy. She knew it would work because it's very difficult to fight with someone who is laughing at you.

Suddenly Rotten Nellie leaps into action and gives Bheki such a hard shove that he falls on his backside. Bheki, who is clutching the stone in his hand, collapses with laughter, screeching at the top of his voice. This makes Rotten Nellie even angrier, but Bheki's laugh is so infectious that her gang starts sniggering. Four Eyes is laughing so much that his spectacles almost shake off his face.

"What are you idiots laughing at?" Rotten Nellie demands frantically. "At you!" Nolitye says boldly.

Rotten Nellie's face turns purple. Without a word, she storms off, her gang slinking behind her like a pack of hyenas. They know she's going to give them a hard time.

Bheki hands the stone back to Nolitye. "I told you it's a magic stone," she says.

"I didn't even feel it when she pushed me," Bheki sniggers. "What else do you think this stone can do?"

"I don't know, but shush," Nolitye says softly, "remember, the stone is our secret."

Chapter Three

STRANGE POWERS

NOLITYE and Bheki walk home with a hop and a skip, happy with their secret.

"So are you coming home for biscuits?" Bheki asks. "It's Saturday tomorrow, so you don't have to do homework this evening."

"Is food the only thing you ever think about?" Nolitye teases him.

"No . . . I think about other things too."

"Like what?"

"Like . . . like the delicious ginger beer my mother makes."

Nolitye bursts out laughing. "I can't come today, Bheki, sorry. I have to see Ntate Matthews."

"Who's he?"

"He's this man in Phola who knew my father. I've seen him often before, but I spoke to him for the first time last night. He says my father had amazing powers."

"Like?"

"I don't know. That's why I have to see him. He said I must come after school. You can come along if you want to." Bheki licks his lips. It is hard to choose between Nolitye and a snack at home.

"It's okay, I'll see you tomorrow," Nolitye says and starts to go.

"No, I'll come!" he quickly makes up his mind. "My mom says I'm getting too fat. Maybe I'll lose some weight if I go with you."

"You think skipping one meal is going to make you lose weight?"

"For sure. I get dizzy if I don't eat, you know. And I feel light." Nolitye chuckles.

They make their way across the busy main road to Phola. From a distance Nolitye spots some dogs on the rubbish dump near the row of public toilets. It looks like Rex and his pack. She also notices Rotten Nellie and the Spoilers approaching from a side street, snacking from a brown paper bag. They must have walked fast and come here directly from school.

Nolitye nudges Bheki in the ribs. They stop to watch. Rex, his legs stiff and his fangs bare, is growling at a big grey dog that has the mean look of a hyena. Shorty and Ticks are right behind Rex. Whiskers keeps rushing forward and then quickly retreats.

The huge shaggy grey dog has red eyes and fangs like daggers. With his head pulled back, he is inching closer to Rex, drooling and snarling.

"Take him, Beastie. Take him, boy!" Rotten Nellie encourages the ugly dog, throwing glances at Nolitye and Bheki.

"Rex, what's going on?" Nolitye asks.

"Stay out of this, Mop!" Rotten Nellie shouts. "I've been waiting for this dog fight for a long time."

"Don't do it, Rex," Nolitye says. "It's not worth it."

"This is my turf," Rex replies without taking his eyes off the intruder.

"Ja, so get out of here," Whiskers yelps and rushes a few steps forward.

"Oh look, the sausage can speak," Beastie sneers. Nolitye can hardly make out what he says, but Rotten Nellie and the Spoilers laugh so loud that Whiskers retreats nearer Nolitye and Bheki.

"Shut up, Mongrel Face," Shorty quickly adds his own insult.

"You're a fine one to speak," Beastie growls. "I'm hungry, let's get this done and over with."

"Stay out of this, guys. I've got this covered." And Rex, keeping his eyes fixed on Beastie, takes an unexpected leap forward.

Beastie pounces on Rex and grabs his left flank in his teeth. Rex shuts his jaws on Beastie's right paw. While Rotten Nellie and the

Spoilers cheer them on, the two dogs snap and tear at each other, occasionally getting in a really nasty bite. Bheki can see how Four Eyes winces every time one of the dogs sinks his fangs into the flesh of the other.

Soon Rex is bleeding badly from his side, but he won't give up the fight. Beastie seems to be winning. "Stop it! Stop it!" Nolitye shouts at the grey monster. "You're hurting him."

From somewhere a woman hurries towards the dogs with a bucket of water. "Get out of here, you beasts!" she screams and pours the water over them. The dogs calm down a bit but still won't let go of each other. The woman rushes over with a second bucket of water. This time Rex and Beastie separate.

"I'm not done with you, doggy bag," Beastie says before scurrying off. Rex limps away, a big red gash visible on his left side, Shorty and Whiskers at his heels.

"Rex! Rex!" Nolitye shouts after him. But Rex doesn't turn back.

"He'll be alright," Ticks says, happy to have a chance for a quick scratch. "All I can say is, it's a dog's life."

The pack disappears down a path that leads into thick grass where Rex can lick his wounds.

"What are you brats still doing here?" the woman scolds the Spoilers. "Do you also want a bucket of water?"

Rotten Nellie throws the woman a dirty look and stomps off with her gang. The woman glances over to where Nolitye and Bheki stand. Nolitye takes Bheki's arm. He looks paralysed with fear. "Come on, Bheki, let's go," she says. She pretends not to see how scared he is. "I hope Rex is okay," she says after a while.

"He didn't look okay to me."

"I know. Did you see that wound?"

"Maybe just as well that that woman came."

Nolitye falls silent. Bheki looks at two girls washing socks and hanging them on a sagging wire washing line. Phola is so different from Mogale, he thinks.

Some boys wheeling tyres between two sticks brush past Nolitye. "Hey, watch it!" she shouts after them.

"You're worried about Rex, aren't you?" Bheki asks. "He'll be fine. He looks like a real street dog."

"Sure, but that doesn't mean he doesn't feel pain when he's hurt."

They pass MaMokoena's spaza shop. A queue of children and some grown-ups are lined up outside. Nolitye waves to MaMokoena.

First she and then Bheki jumps over the trickle of water coming from the taps where a group of women are doing their washing. They work rhythmically as they wash and rinse. Nolitye walks to the bluegum tree Ntate Matthews mentioned and starts counting the shacks.

It is easy to find his shack. It is painted a cool blue colour. Ntate Matthews, still dressed in his suit, is sitting in an easy chair outside, smoking a pipe and enjoying the afternoon sun.

"Dumela, Ntate Matthews," Nolitye greets him. "This is my friend Bheki."

"Pleased to meet you." Ntate Matthews nods at Bheki.

"Sawubona, Baba."

"Well, don't just stand there. Go inside and get the bench," Ntate Matthews tells them.

It is dark inside Ntate Matthews's shack; there are no windows and it smells odd, but otherwise the place appears neat. Nolitye and Bheki quickly carry the bench outside and put it down next to Ntate Matthews's chair.

Questions are buzzing in Nolitye's head but she doesn't know how to ask them or where to begin.

"So how was school today?" Ntate Matthews asks after a while. He blows out a cloud of smoke, cradling the pipe in his hand.

"We got into trouble," Bheki says absentmindedly. Nolitye kicks his foot to remind him of their secret.

"I mean . . . there was some trouble after school. These dogs were fighting," Bheki hurriedly explains, peering at Nolitye out the corner of his eye.

"You mean Rex and his pack?" Ntate Matthews asks.

"Yes," Bheki says uneasily. He looks at Nolitye for a response. "It's okay, he knows," she nods. "He can hear them too."

"Well, it was the most amazing thing. There I was . . . I had a little too much to drink."

"A little, Ntate?" Nolitye says, smiling.

"Fine, I was very drunk. It happens now and then. Anyway, my point is . . . all of a sudden I could hear these dogs speak. I thought I was going mad."

"As I said, you weren't supposed to hear them . . . I mean, grown-ups are not supposed to hear animals talk. Only kids."

"It doesn't surprise me at all that we shouldn't be able to hear them. It's too crazy. One can't believe one's ears and you can't tell anyone because they'll think you have gone mad. Anyway, it hasn't stopped. Since last night, I've heard the cats next door cursing each other, the pigeons squabbling over scraps of food. But the weirdest was hearing a donkey speak this morning. Well, that just took the cake."

"You mean Mandla, the donkey that pulls the coal cart?"

"Yes, that one. Very stubborn you know. He stopped the cart in the middle of the road and wouldn't budge. The coal man kept whipping him to move but the animal just stayed where he was and complained that he didn't have enough to eat for— "

"Ntate Matthews," Nolitye cuts in. She can see that Ntate Matthews is the kind of person who never tires of talking, whether sober or intoxicated. "We've got some chores to do at home . . . so I was just wondering if . . . you know . . ."

"Oh yes . . . about your father."

"Yes, please tell me about him," Nolitye asks eagerly.

Ntate Matthews thinks deeply before he says, "He was a very quiet man. Kept to himself when he wasn't working."

"But you said he had amazing powers!"

"Nolitye," Bheki reprimands her, "he's getting to that!"

"He had the strange ability to disappear every now and then," Ntate Matthews says quietly.

"What do you mean - he could disappear?"

"A few times when I was with him he would just vanish from sight."

"Did he do this in front of other people?"

"No, he was quite careful, I must say. He only did it in front of me."

"And where would he go?" Nolitye, her eyes big and round, looks at Bheki who seems enthralled.

"I'm afraid I don't know. What I do know is that your father had the makings of a healer. He definitely had the calling; he just refused to become a sangoma. I suspect he knew that he was blessed with immense powers, and maybe he feared using them."

Nolitye moves closer to Ntate Matthews. "But what was there to fear?"

"Answering the calling to be a healer is not that simple, my child. There are a lot of evil forces - witches and wizards - out there that try to harm those who want to help people. The evil forces would like sangomas to harm people, not heal them."

"So Papa knew this?"

"I'm sure he did. That's probably why he didn't answer the calling."

Such a long silence follows that a frown appears on Bheki's forehead. He is about to tap Nolitye on the arm when she says, "What else can you tell me about him, Ntate? Did he also smoke? Mama says it's not good for your health."

"No, he didn't smoke, my child," Ntate Matthews says with a laugh. "But I think you have a lot of him in you."

Nolitye's eyes light up. "You do?"

"Something in your eyes tells me that you also know things."

"I'd better get going or my mother will start worrying," Bheki says out of the blue and gets up from the bench.

"Yes, me too," says Nolitye, "I've still got to do some washing," but she remains seated, a happy smile on her face, until Bheki grabs her by the hand.

"Well, it was nice seeing you, children," Ntate Matthews says.

"Don't worry about the bench. I'll put it back."

Nolitye walks away shaking her head. She can't believe that her father could vanish. "Where do you think he used to go to when he vanished?" she asks Bheki.

"I don't know . . . the moon?"

"No, man. Don't be silly. What if he went to the underworld?"

"What do you know about the underworld?"

"That's where they say the Zim lives. And he would only be too happy to eat someone as chubby as you." And Nolitye pinches Bheki in the waist to feel how plump he is. "Yes, he would be very happy to eat you," she concludes.

"Very funny!"

Before Nolitye takes a short cut to her house, they decide that Bheki will come to her house at ten o'clock the next day. "On the condition that I may hold the stone again," he says with twinkling eyes.

When Nolitye gets home, her mother is not there yet, so she sits down on the bed and takes the magic stone out of her shirt pocket. Holding it in her right hand, she strokes it with the left. The bluish stone glimmers with the same faint purple glow of before. She has never before seen such a strange stone. She loves looking at it. It makes her feel calm and happy. Then she remembers the washing, leaps to her feet, and in the cooking corner she tears a piece from one of the old newspapers her mother keeps at the bottom of the cupboard. She smiles with delight when she reads the name: The Star. She wraps the stone carefully in the paper, crawls in under the bed and puts it in the enamel bucket with her other stones.

Chapter Four
FATCAKES AND FUN

WHEN Thembi returns, the washing is done and Nolitye has already cooked supper. Thembi is tired. She has had hard day at work. Early on it was windy, so she had to close her stall for a while because everything kept blowing over, she tells Nolitye. And when the wind dropped, it became so hot that she got a headache.

"So what did you learn at school today?" she asks, stacking her goods in the usual place in one corner of the room.

Nolitye smiles where she is sitting at the table. "I learned to stand up for myself . . . and Bheki too."

"Oh, that's good. What happened?"

Nolitye puts her elbows on the table and takes a deep breath. Grown-ups always want to know everything; they like lots of details. How will she be able to explain about the giggling if she cannot talk about the new stone, her and Bheki's secret? A secret is not a secret if it is shared with anyone else, even one's mother.

Nolitye chooses her words carefully. "You remember this big girl Rotten Nellie, Mama?"

"I remember you talking about a Nellie . . ."

"It is actually Nellie, but she's so nasty that everyone calls her Rotten Nellie."

"And she knows this?"

"I'm sure she does."

"But what a terrible name!"

"Mama, I'm trying to tell you what happened!"

"I'm sorry. Please carry on." Thembi takes off her shoes, slips her feet into her push-ins and sits down opposite Nolitye and helps herself to some beans and rice.

"You see, Mama, this Rotten Nellie is always bullying the other kids, me and Bheki too."

"Really? You never told me about being bullied."

"That's because I didn't want you to worry about me, Mama."

"But that's my job, Nolitye. I'm your—"

"Anyway, so today after school Rotten Nellie wanted to push me and Bheki around again."

"And?"

"We laughed at her!" Nolitye can't suppress a happy smile.

"You *laughed* at her?"

"Yes, we laughed at her. And you should have seen the look on her face. She was like a tomato that was about to burst. She was so angry that she walked off. Even her gang was laughing at her."

"Are you sure it's a good thing to laugh at a bully?"

"Yes, because then she can see that we're not scared of her."

Thembi sighs. "You see, this is why I never tell you anything, Mama. You worry too much. And I'm a big girl. I can look after myself."

"You're my only child, Nolitye. Before your father died I promised him that I would look after you with my life."

"I know, Mama," Nolitye says, with a sudden pang of sadness. It has been five years since her father died when one of the underground tunnels in the mine collapsed. It happened just after she went to school for the first time. Nolitye is tempted to tell her mother what Ntate Matthews told her about her father, but then decides not to.

They eat in sombre silence.

"So what are we doing tomorrow?" Nolitye asks when they have both finished their food, trying to cheer up her mother.

"I thought maybe we could make fatcakes in the morning and you could sell them at the train station while I sell my wares in town. I know it is quite a long way to walk, but on a Saturday morning people have money in their pockets."

"That sounds great! I'll ask Bheki to help me."

"Do you always have to do everything with that little friend of yours?" Thembi sounds irritable.

"But he's my best friend and we— "

"You must learn to do things on your own!"

"But Mama— "

Thembi pushes her chair back with a scraping sound, and with her hands pushed down on the table, she leans forward. "I won't take backchat from you, Nolitye. You hear me?"

"Yes, Mama." Nolitye is bewildered. Just moments ago her mother seemed so happy and now she is angry and her eyes and voice are hard.

"You can't rely on friends. They just twist your mind," her mother continues. "And that little fat guy looks lazy, if you ask me."

Nolitye stares at her empty plate. How can her mother say such a terrible thing about Bheki? Sure, he likes food, but he's not lazy. She can't think of anything to say. She really can't understand why her mother would suddenly turn mean like this. It was never this bad before. Quietly Nolitye gets up and starts washing the dishes.

The next morning Nolitye and her mother are up early. While Nolitye runs to the spaza shop to buy some extra yeast from MaMokoena, Thembi lights the Primus stove. Near the taps Nolitye sees Rex limping away between the shanties. He is on his own. Before she can greet him, he makes a quick left turn and disappears from sight. Poor Rex, she thinks, he is not well.

The first batch of fatcakes is already cooking when Nolitye gets back. In no time Thembi has mixed another bowl of batter. With Nolitye's help it goes quickly and soon they have baked a small mountain of fatcakes. Thembi lines their green plastic bucket with clear newsprint that she gets from the kind butcher near MaMokoena, and starts packing the fatcakes inside as soon as a batch has cooled down. Just after ten Bheki shows up.

"Sawubona, MaDube," he greets Nolitye's mother. "Morning, Bheki," Thembi says coldly.

The unfriendly greeting and the strange way in which Thembi looks at Nolitye make Bheki feel uncomfortable. "Is something wrong?" he asks, looking from the one to the other.

"No . . . nothing," Thembi says. "I'll talk to Nolitye later." Nolitye smiles as if nothing is amiss.

"So I hear that you and Nolitye have been fighting with bullies by laughing at them," Thembi says, a bit more friendly.

A confused look settles on Bheki's face, but Nolitye quickly reassures him by silently shaping the words "I didn't tell her about the stone" with her mouth.

He relaxes visibly. "Yes, MaDube, and it was the first time they left us alone."

"Here, Nolitye." Thembi has put the last fatcakes in the bucket and pushes the lid down tightly. "Please be alert, there are always people trying their luck out there. Don't be fooled when someone insists that he or she has been short-changed."

She collects her goods and explains to Bheki, "I'm going back into town to see if I can sell a few things there this morning. Yesterday was really bad for business."

Bheki promises that he will keep an extra eye on the money and on the change they have to give. Then he and Nolitye head for the train station, carrying the bucket between them. Nolitye clutches some extra pieces of newsprint under her arm, and it is Bheki's duty to carry a few new plastic bags. Thembi walks to the main road to catch a taxi to town.

"So where's the magic stone?" Bheki asks as soon as they are alone.

They put the bucket down and Nolitye pulls a small patchwork bag on a string from under her blouse. She takes out a crumpled cotton hanky and opens it. The stone shimmers against the pale blue cotton. It sends a bolt of giggles through Nolitye as soon as she takes the stone in her hand.

"Let me hold it for a while," Bheki begs, impatiently holding out his hand. Soon he too is giggling. Nolitye quickly takes back the stone, returns it to the small patchwork bag and says, "We don't want people thinking we're strange."

They pick up the bucket and continue on their way.

"For a minute back there in your house I was worried you'd told your mother about the magic stone," Bheki says, "when she was talking about us laughing at Rotten Nellie."

"Never. It's our secret only. And you know what?"

"What?"

"I don't think I'm ever going to pick up another stone again. This is the stone I have been waiting for all this time. I just feel it."

"So you knew all along it was out there?"

"No, I didn't, but something tells me that this stone knew about me." Bheki doesn't quite understand, but he doesn't say anything, he just saunters along, holding onto the handle of the bucket.

"All this time I've been picking up stones whenever I felt like it." Bheki shakes his head. "I don't understand it."

"Gogo used to say, you mess with a woman, you mess with a stone. So I figured since I'm so small I might as well have some stones around, because you mess with me, you mess with a stone."

"You better not tell Rotten Nellie this," Bheki says with a little laugh.

The entrance to Mogale train station is beyond the soccer field on top of a small rise. This is where they decide to sell their fatcakes. Nolitye is happy to see that Mamani has set herself up on the other side of the entrance. Today she is selling roasted mealies which she cooks over a mbawula. Her baby is strapped to her back. Through the holes in the metal drum Nolitye and Bheki can see the coals glowing pink and red.

People are streaming in and out of the entrance. Some are catching a train to go and do their shopping in the city; others are arriving to visit friends or family. Across the road, at MaQueen's Shebeen, a group of men are sitting on white plastic garden chairs sipping beer and watching a soccer match on a big television set mounted on the wall. Every time a goal is scored half of them cheer wildly while the other half groan. A travelling barber has set up shop on the pavement next to the shebeen. He's busy cutting a small boy's hair. The little guy is crying bitterly but his mother won't relent.

"I can't wait for my mother to take Khaya to the barber for the first time," Bheki says. "I hope the man won't be wearing lace-up shoes, because—"

"Look, Bheki, here comes the coal man with Mandla, the donkey Ntate Matthews talked about."

The coal man cracks his whip, just missing Mandla's ears, and Mandla brays while he struggles uphill with the heavy cart. Nolitye and Bheki wave at him as he passes by.

"This fool thinks I run on water. Where did you ever hear anything so ridiculous?" Mandla grumbles.

Nolitye and Bheki laugh.

"Sounds to me that one is always complaining," Bheki says under his breath.

"You would too if you had all that load to carry," Nolitye points out and in the same breath calls out, "Fatcakes for fifty cents!" Bheki is impressed. It sounds as if Nolitye is singing out the words. A granny and her two grandchildren have just exited the station. The old lady slows down and walks over to them. She buys two cakes.

After their first sale business is slow. It must be close to midday because Bheki is getting hungry and still they have sold only eight fatcakes. They pass the time by chatting to Mamani and by watching a boy herding a few cows and a young calf on the banks of the river across the freeway that cuts across the bottom of the rise. The reeds and grass are so tall that the calf sometimes disappears from sight. Occasionally, Nolitye glances across at Mamani to see if the white dove has not returned, but there is no sign of the mysterious bird that Bheki couldn't see yesterday.

"Fatcakes for fifty cents!" Nolitye announces again. It is getting hot and she is worried that the fatcakes in the bucket will spoil in the sun.

Then Bheki gets a bright idea. "Hey, maybe we can use the magic stone to help us sell more fatcakes!"

Until now they did not want to take out the magic stone. Nolitye looks over to where Mamani is chatting to a customer. "But how?" she whispers to Bheki.

"I don't know. Let's just put the stone at the bottom of the bucket and see what happens."

"Maybe we should also make a wish to sell more fatcakes?" Nolitye is getting excited.

Bheki breaks into a smile and rubs his hands together. "Ja!"

With her back to Mamani, Nolitye rubs the magic stone. She bends down and holds it in the light to make sure it is clean. The stone catches a ray of light and glints. Nolitye drops the stone.

"What's wrong?"

"Nothing. I just had something in my eye," Nolitye says, picking up the stone. She doesn't tell Bheki about the strange feeling that came over her the split second the light blinded her. It was like being pulled somewhere, and a picture flashed into her mind. She was standing at the bottom of a valley and could hear a river babbling nearby. She clearly saw a large egg, much, much bigger than an ostrich egg, even bigger than Mamani's mbawula. At the same time she saw a tall baobab tree with strange root-like branches reaching into the sky.

"Wait," she says and walks across to Mamani and asks for some water. She returns with half a cool drink bottle of water. Nolitye wets the hanky and carefully rubs the stone clean before she lets it slide to the bottom of the bucket. Then, to make Mamani think she was thirsty, she drinks the rest of the water and wipes her mouth.

"Okay, Bheki, let's make our wish," she says.

"I suppose we should hold hands." And Bheki takes Nolitye's hands.

"I wish we sell all the fatcakes," Nolitye mutters with closed eyes, the image of the large egg and the baobab tree in a quiet valley lingering on her mind.

"Are you okay?" Bheki asks when Nolitye keeps holding his hands and doesn't open her eyes.

"Oh yes. I'm fine," Nolitye says, blinking her eyes like someone waking from a dream and letting go of his hands. She puts the bucket with fatcakes between them.

It is not long before an elegantly dressed lady in high heels comes up to them. "Your fatcakes smell simply delicious," she says, peering into the bucket.

"Really?" Nolitye didn't expect the stone to work that fast.

"Yes. I was actually going to catch the next train but I couldn't resist the smell."

"Well, they are only fifty cents each, Ma'am," Bheki says. "I'll take eight."

"Eight?" Nolitye gasps.

"No, you're right. All the visitors will want to taste one. Make it fourteen."

Nolitye pretends that buying fourteen fatcakes is the most normal thing on earth and puts her hand inside a new plastic bag which Thembi insisted they bring along. Then she starts to count off fourteen cakes. Bheki holds out a sheet of clear newsprint and wraps the cakes. In return for the wrapped parcel, the lady gives them eight rand.

"Ma'am, excuse me," Bheki says. "You've given us a rand too much."

"That's a tip," the lady says and waves a hand with long red nails, "for a job well done."

"Thanks a lot!"

"Have a nice day," Bheki murmurs as the woman struts away on her high heels. He gives Nolitye a playful punch on the arm. "See, the magic is working again."

"Shush," Nolitye warns him, because a striking gentleman and his family are heading their way. The two sons are complaining that they left the house in such a rush they didn't have a chance to eat their breakfast porridge. "And who's to blame?" the mother reminds them.

"Okay, boys, I'll get you something to eat," their father promises and takes out his wallet.

"Dumela, Ntate," Nolitye greets him.

"Dumelang, bana," he says stiffly. "May I please have six fatcakes?"

"Make that eight, please, Papa," the elder son pleads.

"Okay, eight. And you, my dear?" he asks, looking at his wife. The mother's hair is braided into intricate corn-rows and Nolitye envies her elegant African-print dress. It is not often that she sees such a beautifully dressed woman.

"I'm fine, love," the woman says politely. "Let the boys eat." Nolitye guesses that with her stunning figure she probably watches her diet.

It is Bheki's turn to slip his hand into a clean plastic bag and take out the fatcakes. He carefully counts out eight, wraps them in newsprint and hands the parcel to the man.

"How much will that be?" he asks. "Four rand, please, Ntate."

"Thanks. You saved us," the older boy smiles at Bheki. "Sure, M'fethu."

"Such polite children," the father says, and to Bheki: "I hope you'll sell all your fatcakes."

"Hmm, they are delicious," the younger boy says after swallowing the last morsel of his fatcake.

"Hambani kahle," Bheki calls after them as the family disappears into the station.

"Sure M'fethu?" Nolitye laughs. "Since when do you talk like a thug?"

"Hey, don't forget that I'm a jita," Bheki says.

"A jita excuse me!"

"Ja, a jita - a guy - and don't you forget it, Sista," Bheki teases her back. More people come to buy their fatcakes. Nolitye doesn't even have to sing "fatcakes for fifty cents" any longer. It is as though the magic stone draws the customers straight to the bucket, which is only quarter full now. A small queue is forming.

"Bheki, we've only got ten fatcakes left," Nolitye whispers, looking at the people lining up to buy from them.

"I know."

"Can I have four fatcakes?" a girl asks. She's barefoot and wears a skimpy dress, but her hair is neatly combed and her eyes are bright. She takes out a small pouch and carefully counts off a handful of small coins until the amount comes to two rand.

"You also go to Nka Thutho, don't you?" Nolitye says, recognising her from school.

"Yes, I'm in grade four," the girl says proudly. "And we don't live very far from you. We moved there just last week."

"I haven't seen you there yet, but I'll watch out for you!" Nolitye wraps five fatcakes in newsprint.

"I've only got two rand," the girl says. Nolitye winks at her.

"Thanks," the girl says, her face lighting up with a smile. "By the way, what's your name?" Nolitye asks.

"Hey, I have a train to catch," a man behind the girl grumbles.

"Mbali," the girl quickly says. "See you at school. Or in our street."

The man pushes past her. "Eight fatcakes," he says in a rush. "And hurry up."

"I'm sorry, but we've only got five left," Nolitye informs him.

"You've only got five left!"

"That's all."

"I'll pay sixty cents for each fatcake," a woman behind the man says.

"I'll pay seventy cents!" the man offers.

"Ninety cents!" someone else says.

"One rand!" A boy pushes to the front, already counting out his money. "Okay, one rand fifty, that's my final offer," the man desperate to catch his train says. He quickly takes out the money and pays before anyone can counter his offer. Nolitye stands there with the seven rand fifty in her hands. She can't believe that someone has paid seven rand fifty for five fatcakes. Bheki quickly takes the money from her and puts it in his back pocket.

"Are you sure you've got nothing left?" the woman asks. "Sorry," Nolitye says.

The other customers too are disappointed and walk away. Nolitye and Bheki look at each other, amazed by what has just happened. "Yeah!" they shout in unison and smack their hands together, do a little jig, skipping and laughing.

"Eish! That was great." Bheki's face shines with delight as he takes the money from his pocket. He counts. Aloud he says, "Twenty-eight rand . . . We've made twenty-eight rand fifty!"

"That calls for another dance," Nolitye says. They link arms and swing about, celebrating selling all their fatcakes and making such a handsome profit. Hearts beating fast, they sit down next to the bucket.

"I'm sure we can do more than that with the stone," Bheki says after a while.

"Let's not get greedy," Nolitye warns him.

"I know. I just thought your mother would be so pleased . . . and the money could . . . Sorry, it was a stupid idea."

With Bheki, Nolitye doesn't have to pretend that they don't need money, so she says, "It's not a stupid idea. I just want to be careful with the stone . . . it's precious."

"I know. I agree. But you know what . . . I think you found it so that it can help you out."

Nolitye draws circles on the ground with her finger. "Maybe you're right," she says. "I also think I found the stone because it can help me out of all sorts of problems."

"And there's no harm in that. Right?"

"Right. But what else can we do with it?"

"What if we wish for the bucket to be filled up with fatcakes again?" Bheki suggests boldly.

"Do you think the stone can do that?"

"It's worth a try."

"I suppose there's only one way to find out."

Nolitye covers the bucket with the lid. Then she takes Bheki's hands and holds them tightly while she mumbles respectfully, "I wish for the bucket to be full of fatcakes again."

No sooner have the words left her mouth than the bucket starts shaking all on its own. The shaking lasts only a few seconds. Nolitye looks at Bheki and then she looks at the bucket. She is suddenly scared to lift the lid. What if the wish went wrong and instead of fatcakes the bucket was filled with frogs, or worse - bats?

"Go ahead, open it," Bheki eggs her on.

Nolitye closes her eyes and slowly lifts the lid. The enticing smell of fresh fatcakes fills her nose. She gasps with shock and delight when she opens her eyes. The bucket is full to the brim with delicious fatcakes again, smelling and looking just like the ones her mother made.

At once, customers start coming over. And now they do not buy just one or two fatcakes at a time, they want between four and ten! Bheki is alert and makes sure that in their excitement they don't become careless when money is exchanged.

When almost half the fatcakes have gone, Bheki looks up. His smile vanishes. Four figures are sluggishly walking towards them. "Get out of my way, wena!" a familiar gruff voice says, and a small boy munching on a fatcake is pushed aside roughly, causing him to choke.

Nolitye looks up nervously. Rotten Nellie walks in front, flanked by Thabo and S'bu, while Four Eyes with his smudgy spectacles brings up the rear.

"Well, well, what have we got here, boys?" swaggers Rotten Nellie. Sometimes Rotten Nellie forgets that she's a girl, Nolitye thinks.

"If it isn't Pumpkin Face and the Mop, my two favourite midgets!"

The other Spoilers give an ugly laugh. Rotten Nellie seems to have chased the customers away. No one is buying the delicious-smelling fatcakes any more! Nolitye's spirit sinks.

Rotten Nellie sniffs the air. "Hey, that looks good," she says, eyeing the fatcakes.

Without permission, she reaches into the bucket, grabs four fatcakes and shares them out among her gang.

"They are fifty cents each," Nolitye informs her.

"Sorry, but I've got no money," says Rotten Nellie, who is beginning to look more and more like a large fatcake to Nolitye. The Spoilers bite greedily into the fatcakes. "These are excellent fatcakes," Thabo says, smacking his lips. S'bu and Four Eyes nod, their eyes glued to the bucket.

"These fatcakes taste like cardboard!" Rotten Nellie shouts with a sour face.

S'bu jumps to attention. "Yes, they do," he agrees and passes wind.

"S'bu, you pig, what did I say to you?"

"That I must stop farting."

"So?"

"I can't help it," he says with a hangdog look.

"I'm warning you, S'bu," Rotten Nellie threatens, her eyes narrowed to slits.

What kind of a person threatens her friends? Nolitye thinks.

"Now back to you, Mop. These fatcakes are awful. They could use a little salt. But don't worry, I've got an idea." And Rotten Nellie throws her half-eaten fatcake to the ground and grinds it into the soil with her shoe. Then she takes the sandy pulp and chucks it back into the bucket. "What are you going to do now, laugh like a silly fool?" she sneers.

Nolitye and Bheki look at each other. There's nothing they can do because the magic stone is at the bottom of the bucket and they intend keeping it a secret from everyone. So they just sit there and wait for Rotten Nellie and the Spoilers to go away.

"I hope you've learned your lesson, Pumpkin Face and the Mop. Don't ever laugh at me again. You won't like what I'll do to you. You're lucky I didn't hit you." She turns around and marches off, followed by the other three - but not before they cackle "Pumpkin Face and the Mop!" at the top of their lungs.

For a while Nolitye and Bheki say nothing to each other. They stare glumly at the ruined fatcakes. No one is interested any more. The worst is that people just stood by and watched the Spoilers ruin their fatcakes. Nobody did or said anything, not even Mamani across the way, or the travelling barber. They just carried on as if nothing was happening.

"Bheki, we can't take these cakes home and we can't sell them. What shall we do?"

"Give me two, and I'll go and empty the bucket into the vegetable crates over there."

Nolitye carefully removes the squashed fatcake from the bucket and reaches into the bottom for two fairly clean ones and the magic stone. Hastily she slips the stone into the small bag and hides it in her clothes, after checking that no one is looking on, and then hands Bheki the bucket.

"I have a feeling the stone will help us sort out the Spoilers," Bheki says, taking the fatcakes from her on his return.

"I think we must be careful with that stone though."

"Why?"

"We still don't know what it's capable of doing."

Just then an irresistible urge to hold the stone in her hand overcomes Nolitye. She pulls the small bag from her blouse. Making sure that no one but Bheki is looking, she takes it out and watches it glimmer in the midday light. It is not as bright as earlier.

"Nolitye," someone whispers.

"Bheki?"

Bheki peers at her. "I didn't say anything."

"Nolitye."

"What is it, Bheki?"

"Hey, Nolitye, stop fooling around. I didn't talk to you." He looks at her as if she's not all there.

"Nolitye," someone whispers a third time. And now Nolitye can hear it isn't Bheki's voice.

"Who is it?" she asks, holding her breath. She looks around nervously but sees no one. Then she hears the voice again: "It's me, the Spirit of the Stone."

Nolitye becomes so frightened that she drops the stone. She and Bheki bend down at the same time and in their eagerness to pick up the stone they knock their heads together. They laugh at their own clumsiness, but only briefly.

With the stone once more safely in her hand, Nolitye says, "I'm listening, Spirit of the Stone." She speaks softly so that no one will think her mad to be speaking to a stone. Bheki looks at her, his face puckered with concentration. He can only hear what Nolitye says.

"There are a few things you should know about me."

"Yes?"

"Firstly, you can't keep me forever. And even if you tried I would vanish."

"I'll remember that," says Nolitye, solemnly nodding her head.

"But for now I'm here because you need my help."

Nolitye picks up the bucket, takes Bheki by the arm and drags him around the corner of the entrance where no one can see her talking to a stone.

"I like lots of sunshine," the Spirit of the Stone says. "Every day you must put me in the sun for at least one hour."

Bheki tugs at Nolitye's arm, but she puts her finger on her mouth before he can say anything. "But when will you want us to let you go?" she asks the stone.

"That is for me to decide still. But I promise I will leave only when things have been sorted out."

"So you're a talking magic stone?" Nolitye asks.

"I'm more than that. Like your grandmother said, you strike a woman, you strike a rock. I'm the child of a rock just like you are the child of a woman. I've been silent all these years, waiting for someone to awaken my spirit. My spirit could only be awakened by someone who truly wants to see, like you. I know how hard things are for you."

"And what about Bheki?" Nolitye asks. She can see he feels left out.

"Boys and men are like water. They go everywhere and anywhere because that is their spirit." It sounds like a riddle to her, but Nolitye nods her head as if she understands.

"Like human beings, I also get lonely," the magic stone continues. "At night I want to sleep with your other stones in the enamel bucket."

"I hear you, Spirit of the Stone," Nolitye says and bows to show her respect. But then she remembers. "What will we do about the Spoilers?" she asks.

"Depends on what you want to do to them."

"I just don't want them to bully us all the time," Nolitye says. "We are tired of it." Although he still can't hear what Nolitye hears, Bheki doesn't interrupt.

"Then think of a way of doing something to the Spoilers."

"Like what? You can't do anything to the Spoilers, but they do stuff to everyone else all the time. Horrible stuff," Nolitye says bitterly.

"What to do is for you to figure out. For now, I must be in the sun."

After this, the voice falls silent. Nolitye turns to Bheki. "I know you will find this hard to believe, but the stone has just told me that it needs to be put in the sun."

For a moment Bheki looks dumbfounded. "Are you playing the fool?" he asks anxiously.

"No, I'm dead serious. I'll never joke about the magic stone."

Reassured, Bheki immediately says, "I know where we can put the stone in the sun where no one will see. You know our garden. At the bottom these prickly things grow, I forget what they are called, but I know that if we leave the stone there, it will be safe."

Chapter Five

THE CHALLENGE

O N the outskirts of Phola some waste disposal men are loading four mobile toilets on a big municipal truck and replacing them with new ones. Nolitye and Bheki are on their way to Bheki's house with the magic stone after having put away the fatcake money in Nolitye's home. She stashed it in an old condensed milk tin on top of the cupboard. This is where her mother keeps all their household money, she confided in Bheki before closing the door and opening the curtain of the little window ever so slightly to let in some light. No one must see where they hide their money.

"Dumelang, Banna," they greet the men. "Dumelang, Bana," the men return the greeting.

"I don't think I would be so friendly if I had to work on a Saturday afternoon," Bheki says, and in the same breath: "Isn't that Rex's pack over there?"

It is indeed Whiskers, Ticks and Shorty. But Rex isn't with them. "Where's Rex?" Nolitye asks.

"Good afternoon to you too, Nolitye."

Nolitye slaps her hand over her mouth. How is it possible that she always forgets to be polite if she is worried? Hanging her head, she says, "Sorry, Shorty. Hello."

"Never mind," Shorty says. "Thing is, we don't know." Shorty seems to have taken over the leadership of the pack, and says, "I'm as worried as you are!"

"He just disappeared. We haven't seen him since the big fight with Beastie," Ticks says, for once not scratching his stomach.

"I hope he's alright," Nolitye says. "The last time I saw him he was still limping."

"Listen." Shorty trots closer and drops his voice, "It is a good thing we saw you two. If you want some free advice, stay in after dark tonight."

"Why? What's going on?"

"There are some things that even dogs can't tell human children. Just take my advice."

With a wiggle of his short tail and nose to the ground, Shorty trots off toward the centre of Phola. The other two dogs follow suit.

Nolitye and Bheki feel unsettled. What could possibly make Shorty say that they must stay indoors after sunset? "Let's worry about that later," Nolitye says. "First we must get the stone in the sun."

Out of breath from walking unusually fast, Bheki opens the gate of his house. He is happy to see his father's bakkie parked in the shade of the fig tree. Before they walk up the short driveway, Bheki takes a quick look around to see if anyone is watching them. Shorty's warning has made him very worried for the safety of the stone.

MaZwane is in the kitchen doing some ironing. A heap of damp clothes is waiting their turn in a big wicker basket. "Bheki, where have you been? You didn't even come home for lunch," she bursts out when she sees him. "Look, it is almost two."

"Ma, I was with Nolitye."

"How are you, Sisi?" MaZwane asks and gives Nolitye one of her dizzying hugs. Before Nolitye can answer MaZwane says, "Your food is in the oven, Bheki."

But Bheki has the magic stone on his mind. "Where's Khaya?" he asks. "Sleeping."

"And Dad?"

"Watching football in the lounge. Go in and say hello to him."

"Come," Bheki gestures to Nolitye.

"Yes, my child, how are you?" Bheki's father says without looking at her. He simply can't tear his eyes from the TV.

"I'm fine thanks, Ntate," she says shyly. She is a little nervous around other people's fathers, because she's no longer used to having a father in the house.

"Hi, Dad."

"Son . . .You mustn't stay out during mealtimes. You know how your mother worries," Bheki's father says, his eyes still glued to the screen. Someone scores a goal and half the stadium erupts into joyous cheering. For a moment it is impossible to talk.

"No, man!" Bheki's father shouts, disappointed that the wrong side scored, and sinks back into the sofa.

"I know. I just lost track of time. I'm sorry, Dad."

"It's your mother you must think about."

"Yes, Dad."

"You must both be hungry," Bheki's mother says when they pass through the kitchen. "Here's plenty of food." She is ready to dish up a second plate for Nolitye.

Nolitye looks at Bheki. "Not now, Ma. Thanks. We'll be at the bottom of the garden." With a sigh his mother turns back to her ironing.

The back garden is well kept. A patch of lawn runs from the back door to the bottom of the yard where a row of prickly-pear bushes marks the boundary. Two huge peach trees stand on either side of the prickly pears.

Bheki and Nolitye squat down near the cacti. Nolitye takes out the stone. "Do you remember the instructions?" Bheki asks.

"The Spirit of the Stone said to leave it in the sun for at least an hour every day."

Nolitye puts the stone on the grass, her fingers tingling. The last time she was so excited was at the beginning of the year when she got a new pair of school shoes. But the excitement she feels now is different. For a reason she cannot understand or explain, she has been chosen to look after the stone. A magic stone. She feels shaky if she thinks what powers the stone might have besides making them giggle in the face of danger and producing fatcakes.

Bheki too can't keep his eyes off the stone. Together they watch its faint colour grow stronger in the sun, twinkling and sparkling with a soft purplish- blue light.

"I wonder what kind of a stone it is," Nolitye muses.

"What do you mean? It's a stone like any other stone."

"No, man. Stones have names. Like rose quartz or amethyst or tiger's eye. Quartz looks a bit like cracked glass. And then there's slate, which is solid grey and smooth. My mother says when she was a little girl they used to write on slate slabs at school."

"How do you know all this stuff about stones?"

"From school."

"But we read the same books and I never saw anything about stones."

"From the library, man. From the encyclopedia. It tells you everything about everything. Sometimes I go there when your father picks you up after school to go to town."

"Oh," Bheki says, feeling that he has missed out on a good book. He rolls over on his back, and with his head resting in his hands he looks at two swallows swerving and diving in the sky. After a while he says, "Maybe we can challenge them to a game."

"Who?" Nolitye asks, her eyes still fixed on the stone. "The Spoilers."

"The Spoilers? What good will that do? And why would they want to play with us?"

"We'll challenge them, and if we win, then they must agree never to bother us again."

"But what happens if we lose?"

"We won't lose if we have the magic stone," Bheki says confidently. Nolitye nods, a smile on her face. She is pleased with Bheki. He may not be the bravest friend, but he certainly can think up clever plans.

"What game shall we challenge them to?" she asks.

"Something they think they will win . . ."

"I know! I have an idea!" Nolitye jumps up excitedly. "Rotten Nellie is supposed to be the best ngeto player in the neighbourhood, right? She's always beating the other girls. Maybe I can challenge her to that." As far as Nolitye knows, ngeto is the only girlish activity Rotten Nellie tolerates. Probably because she is so good at it.

"That's a great idea," Bheki says. He has often watched Rotten Nellie play this traditional game. She can throw a pebble in the air while moving other pebbles in and out of a hollow faster than any other girl in the school, never making a mistake by moving the wrong number of stones.

"And what should I do?"

What can Bheki possibly do to challenge the boys? Nolitye thinks. "What about showing off some soccer skill?" she suggests.

"But you know I've got two left feet when it comes to soccer. I'm a lousy soccer player."

"Not if you have the stone on you," Nolitye reminds him. Bheki's face lights up. With the stone anything is possible.

"You better have something to eat now. Your mother was looking worried," Nolitye reminds him.

"You're right."

While Bheki makes sure no one is watching, Nolitye hides the stone under a dried-out prickly-pear leaf.

MaZwane is only too happy to dish out a plate of mnqusho and beef stew for Nolitye. Bheki takes his plate from the oven. Suddenly ravenous with hunger, the two wolf down the food, their spoons flying between their plates and mouths. MaZwane hums while they eat, pretending not to see what big mouthfuls they take. When they have finished, Bheki clears the plates and puts them in the sink. He opens the cupboard to take out some dishwashing liquid.

"Don't worry, Mfana. I'll do that later," MaZwane says. "Thanks, Ma."

"Thanks, MaZwane. That was very delicious," Nolitye says.

Bheki looks at Nolitye. "Ma," he says, "I'm going out with Nolitye again, but this time I won't come home late."

"Please, Mfana," MaZwane says. "It is just after three now. I want you back here before it gets dark. I don't want any of you out then." She gives Bheki and Nolitye a stern look. "You know what has been happening."

Bheki steals a nervous look at Nolitye. Shorty also warned them this morning. Very earnestly, Nolitye says, "MaZwane, we promise to be back long before dark." It seems to satisfy Bheki's mother and they go to the bottom of the garden to fetch the stone. Nolitye heads for the prickly-pear bush. "Bheki!" she shouts.

"What! What is it?"

"The stone isn't here!"

"Ag no! Are you sure?" Bheki is down on his knees, frantically searching with his hands over the grass and soil beneath the cactus bush.

"Only joking," Nolitye laughs, holding up the stone. She puts it back into the little bag.

"I'm going to kill you!" Bheki says annoyed. "I thought we were done for."

"Relax, man."

"This stone is serious business, Nolitye, and you're fooling around."

"I know it's serious . . . but come on, let's not forget to have some fun as well."

They set off looking for the Spoilers. Rotten Nellie lives in the same neighbourhood as Bheki, but the gang could be anywhere because they like roaming. There are hundreds of look-alike houses, streets and small alleys, shops and spaza shops where they could be hanging out, not to mention the train station and the soccer field.

Bheki and Nolitye start at the nearest clothes shops. Rotten Nellie and the Spoilers often play spin there. Moeder has repeatedly warned them that no good will come to anyone who spends their time gambling, but Rotten Nellie and her gang never pay any attention to Moeder's advice. In fact, once Moeder caught Rotten Nellie playing spin at school. So she called in Rotten Nellie's mother, a big woman with a pudgy face just like Rotten Nellie's, except that she never smiled and carried a permanent scowl on her face. She became so angry when she found out that Rotten Nellie had been given detention that she started yelling at her while Moeder was still trying to talk calmly to her. She completely drowned out Moeder's voice. It was the only time that anyone at school ever saw Rotten Nellie looking embarrassed.

The Spoilers are not at the big grocery shop either. Instead, some elderly men are sitting on the stoep sipping umqombothi which they've bought from the take-away shop next door. But they're not drinking the real stuff, traditionally brewed sorghum beer. The umqombothi they're drinking is brewed in a factory and sold in cartons. The older neighbourhood boys say that anyone who drinks it and isn't used to it will be drunk for days. The men don't seem drunk, Bheki thinks, just very pleased with themselves.

They leave the men to their beer and walk across to Mogale station. Sometimes the Spoilers sit on the low wall up near the entrance from where they have a good view of anyone coming up the road. If they don't like the person, they'll taunt him or her.

But the Spoilers aren't there. Instead, Nolitye and Bheki notice that Mamani is back, selling roasted mealies. The travelling barber is still cutting hair. He is trimming a young man's hair. On a small clearing nearby some boys are playing marbles. Bheki watches, fascinated. The point of the game is to shoot a marble from the ground and get it to pass through a narrow gap between two stones.

"They are not here, Bheki. Let's go," Nolitye says.

They cross the bridge to the other side of the railway line where there is another small complex of shops. They only find some older boys washing cars to make extra pocket money. Three minibus taxis are lined up, all vigorously being washed from their wheel caps to their rooftops. Bheki asks one of the boys if they have seen a big girl and three boys, one wearing thick glasses, but a shake of the head is the only answer.

Nolitye and Bheki retrace their steps over the bridge and decide to try Uncle Tom's, the community hall on the opposite side of the township. After school young children can go there to play games like snakes-and-ladders and ludo; older children play ping-pong and do karate. Or boys can learn woodwork, while girls are taught how to sew and do beading and needlework. Not that the Spoilers would be interested in any of these activities. If they are there, it would be to cause trouble.

It is a fair distance to walk. Along the way, Nolitye and Bheki overtake a group of Zionists dressed in their flowing white and blue religious robes, the men looking like nomads with their walking sticks. At a corner house where some elders sit in a tight circle holding a kgotla, they turn down a quiet side street.

A tourist bus has just arrived at Uncle Tom's hall, and while a few people have remained in the bus the rest of the tourists walk around the small stalls beside the hall buying beadwork and clay pots and sculptures. They point and prod and ask many questions. Bheki and Nolitye mingle with the tourists, looking for Rotten Nellie and the Spoilers. Not finding them outside, Bheki and Nolitye look inside the hall, but there is no sign of them there either. "When you don't want to see her, she's in your face, but try to find her and it's like looking for a monkey in a forest," Bheki says, bored with the search.

"You know what, we haven't tried the soccer field yet," Nolitye remembers.

"Oh no, and we were right there. Now we have to walk all the way back to Mogale station," Bheki complains.

"Hey, do you want Rotten Nellie bothering us for the rest of our lives?"

"No!"

"Then, let's go."

They take a short cut down a small street where some children are cooling off by spraying themselves with a hosepipe. "Oh look, Bheki!"

On a piece of old carpet at the foot of one of the tall street lamps, Rex is lying huddled up. Bheki can hardly recognise him he is so thin.

"Rex!" Nolitye calls as they rush over to him. The wound on Rex's flank is festering. His breathing is shallow but his eyes are half open. The dog just looks at them, not making a sound, a faraway look in his eyes.

"He doesn't look so good," Bheki says.

"Yes, we can't leave him here."

"But there's no animal clinic around here, you know."

"I know that, Bheki."

"Sorry, I'm just trying to help."

Rex lifts his head and listlessly licks his wound. But it's no use. The wound is infected.

Two boys walk by. "Hey, what are you doing with this animal?" one of them asks. "Leave it to die in peace."

"Ja, just get out of here," the other one says. Nolitye squats down next to Rex. "But it is hurt."

"And who are you? The Minister of Health?" The boys roar with laughter and carry on walking.

"There's only one thing to do," Nolitye says. She takes out the stone. "What are you going to do with it?"

Nolitye looks at Rex. He looks back with pleading eyes. "Spirit of the Stone, please cure Rex," she whispers, and kisses the stone. A little shock wave runs up her arm. She bends down and holds the stone over Rex's head. He is too weak to be bothered by what she is doing; he just lies there, eyes clouded with sickness. "Heal, Rex, heal," she says as she moves the stone in little circles above his skull. After a while she gets up and looks at him.

"Nothing's happening," Bheki says. "Be patient!"

They stand back and watch. After some time Rex blinks a few times, then he opens his jaws and yawns. From nowhere a small wind comes and stirs dust and rubbish into the air. Bheki and Nolitye close their eyes to prevent the grit being blown into their eyes. They open them when the wind has died down.

"Look!" Nolitye says, excitedly pointing at the wound.

Before their very eyes the wound starts closing up. A small trail of smoke floats up into the air. Bheki clutches at Nolitye's arm. The wound keeps shrinking till there is only a scar left. But even the scar soon disappears as the fur grows back. Rex shakes his head and slowly gets up. He wags his tail, wobbly on his feet at first, but he stretches and soon regains his balance. Then he gives a hearty sneeze. Nolitye and Bheki laugh nervously.

"Rex, you're back!" Bheki shouts.

Rex answers with a loud bark. "Thanks, guys. I thought I was a goner." Nolitye looks at the stone with wonderment before she puts it back in the little bag round her neck.

"Man, I'm starving," Rex says. Bheki tells him about the braai they saw a few streets back. "Thanks again," he growls, and trots off.

Bheki shakes his head from side to side. Nolitye is deep in thought. Neither of them say anything until they reach the soccer field, where, to their relief, they notice four familiar figures fooling around with Thabo's football. Rotten Nellie's unshapely figure is unmistakable.

But the Spoilers have also spotted them. "Oh rats!" Rotten Nellie shouts. "It's Pumpkin Face and the Mop. The two people I just love!" She beckons the other three to come and stand close to her.

Nolitye and Bheki stop in their tracks. Bheki sighs. "Courage," Nolitye whispers and takes a deep breath. This isn't going to be easy; they will have to put up with Rotten Nellie's insults. She gives Bheki a little nudge and they resume walking - right up to the gang.

"So what do you pipsqueaks want?" Rotten Nellie asks, nose in the air. "We want to challenge you guys," Nolitye replies, trying to make it sound like a very normal suggestion.

"Ha ha ha!" Rotten Nellie hoots in her deep voice.

Nolitye and Bheki don't budge. They ignore Rotten Nellie's rudeness. "We want to challenge you guys to a game of ngeto and a show of soccer skills," Nolitye repeats.

"What for?"

"If we win, you guys must promise to leave us alone. If you win then . . . then . . ."

"Then I'll tell you what: you'll have to let us copy your homework every day."

"But that's not fair. If we win you only have to leave us alone."

"That's the deal, take it or leave it!" Rotten Nellie says, hands on her hips. Nolitye and Bheki look at each other. This is probably their only chance ever to get Rotten Nellie and the Spoilers off their backs with the help of the stone.

"Okay?" Rotten Nellie sneers. "Okay," Nolitye agrees.

"First things first," Rotten Nellie begins, trying hard to sound like Mrs Lesufi, the headmistress. "I think the boys should start off with a show of soccer skills."

"But I thought ladies went first," Nolitye says, a twinkle in her eyes. She knows her comment will drive Rotten Nellie mad.

"Oh shut up with the lady stuff!" Rotten Nellie explodes. "Do I in any case look like a lady?"

"Maybe if you— "

But Rotten Nellie cuts her short: "Let's just get on with the game so that you two idiots can do my homework for me."

"How about a show of tapping the ball?" S'bu suggests. "The one that taps the highest number of times without a break wins."

"Fine," Bheki agrees.

"This is going to be so easy it'll be like stealing sweets from a baby," Rotten Nellie boasts.

First Thabo goes, because they're using his football. He is quick with his feet and manages to get thirty-five taps. Thabo is confident that nobody will be able to beat him, for he is known as an ace football player throughout the township. Now it is S'bu's turn. He gets a steady twenty-nine taps and even manages not to let go of a fart.

Next it is Four Eyes's turn. Thabo and S'bu look uncomfortable. Bheki and Nolitye have often wondered why they allow him to be a Spoiler and decided that he probably bought his way into the gang with money or favours. Everything he does with them looks fake, as if he is desperately trying to impress the others. Afterwards, he often hangs his head as if he feels guilty.

Four Eyes fumbles with the ball. Rotten Nellie looks irritated. "Eish! Just get on with it, Four Eyes!" she finally yells.

"Okay, okay," he says, looking even more nervous. He adjusts his glasses so that they sit properly on his nose. S'bu and Thabo look on impatiently.

Four Eyes starts tapping the ball, but, alas, after only three bounces the ball veers off.

"Three," Four Eyes says, pushing back his spectacles into place.

"Okay, okay," Rotten Nellie says. "Just get out of the way." Turning to Bheki with a nasty grimace, she announces: "Now it's your turn, Pumpkin Face."

Nolitye gives Bheki a quick hug, secretly slipping the magic stone into his left breast pocket, and Bheki softly whispers, "Let me win."

"Hey, what is this? Stop acting like girls!" Rotten Nellie protests.

Bheki takes the ball. He seems a bit uneasy at first, glancing furtively at the Spoilers. They look pleased as can be because they're probably thinking they'll never have to do homework again. Bheki takes a deep breath, then releases the ball into the air.

And then something strange happens. An invisible magnet seems to draw the ball to his feet. He starts tapping, clumsily at first. Once he almost falls over, but the ball remains close to his feet. After twenty taps, the smug look on the Spoilers' faces disappears. It is clear Bheki is going to make thirty.

Rotten Nellie tries to distract Bheki by pretending to sneeze, but Nolitye sees her plan and quickly shouts, "Go, Bheki! Go!"

Bheki dare not look at her but a smile flits across his face. Rotten Nellie releases another fake sneeze, but it doesn't bother Bheki, because it's too late. He's going for forty-five taps! At fifty he stops. He rushes to Nolitye and they jump up and down with excitement. They've beaten the Spoilers.

The Spoilers are speechless. Rotten Nellie is the first to get her voice back. "It's not over yet," she says sourly. "We still have to play ngeto."

"Piece of cake," says Nolitye.

This makes Rotten Nellie fume with anger. She glares tight-lipped at Nolitye. "Piece of cake, huh? We'll see about that," she hisses back.

"Where are we going to play?" Nolitye wants to know.

"Right here." Rotten Nellie stamps her foot on the baked red earth. "Fine."

Rotten Nellie flexes her fingers and stretches them. Most people stop ngeto at the tenth round, but Rotten Nellie decides the game should stop at round fifteen, which means the winner must remove fifteen stones at once.

Nolitye tries to stay calm. It is going to be a very hard game.

Rotten Nellie gathers her gang into a tight circle. She whispers something to the three boys. With his eyes Bheki asks Nolitye what is going on. Nolitye shrugs her shoulders. There is a slight tremor in her fingers, but she keeps telling herself that she can do this.

Rotten Nellie returns and smashes her right fist into her left hand. "Let's go, missy," she says to Nolitye. "We need to find ourselves fifteen pebbles, and the only place we'll find the right kind of stone is across the freeway at the river. They boys can wait here for us." Before Nolitye can say anything she grunts, "Don't argue with me, I know what I am talking about."

I know more about stones than you do, Nolitye thinks to herself, but she follows Rotten Nellie to the side of the soccer field and down the slope. Even Rotten Nellie looks left, right and left again before she dashes across the road, Nolitye close behind her. Fortunately the road is not so busy on a Saturday afternoon.

Nolitye has never been to the Amanzi Mnyama river, because she is not allowed to cross the freeway. She can see why the river is called Black Waters; the water has a muddy, dark colour. On the other side of the river she notices some mottled cattle grazing lazily near a kraal.

"Stop dreaming!" Rotten Nellie shouts, and walks towards some tall reeds growing along the water's edge. She starts picking up pebbles. Nolitye keeps quiet as she watches Rotten Nellie choosing big pebbles instead of small ones. Rotten Nellie clearly thinks that because her hands are bigger than Nolitye's, she will be able to handle bigger pebbles better than her opponent. She selects fifteen pebbles that can hardly fit into Nolitye's hand.

Rotten Nellie puts the pebbles in the front of her T-shirt and holds it like a pouch. "Come on, pipsqueak, let's go," she says to Nolitye.

This time they have to wait at the roadside as some taxis and cars zoom past. When the road is clear, they run across and scamper up the slope. The boys are where they left them, and Nolitye is happy to see that the Spoilers have left Bheki alone. She notices that Four Eyes is standing a little apart from the others, closer to Bheki.

Now they have to decide whether they are going to play using a circle drawn on the ground, or whether they are going to play the old-fashioned way by making a hollow in the soil. Rotten Nellie doesn't even ask Nolitye, she decides that they should go for the traditional way. It is more difficult to play ngeto this way, because you need to scoop the pebbles from the hollow, plus pick them up in one movement. Rotten Nellie finds a flat peice of stone near the goalpost and digs a small, even hole. She puts the fifteen pebbles inside.

"Let the game begin!" Four Eyes says excitedly. Rotten Nellie gives him a dirty look that makes him shrivel up with embarrassment.

The two girls sit on the ground, the boys remain standing. Rotten Nellie is about to start when S'bu burps. She throws him a furious look.

"Sorry," S'bu mumbles.

"You big pig!" Rotten Nellie lashes out. "I told— "

"But I only burped," he says, confused.

"Just be quiet! Stop distracting me. I'm going to win if it's the last thing I do."

Rotten Nellie starts. She throws the main pebble into the air. Before she catches it, she must move all fifteen pebbles out of the hollow. It is sort of a juggling act which she performs successfully. Now she throws the main pebble back into the air and before she catches it again she puts one pebble back into the hole. To show that she has completed the first round, she pats the ground while throwing the main pebble into the air again. Up flies the pebble and Rotten Nellie removes the first stone from the hollow. Up flies the pebble and she puts two pebbles back into the hollow. She pats the ground; it is on to round three.

Rotten Nellie makes it look easy, grinning each time she adds a pebble to the number she must replace: four, five, six, seven, eight, nine, ten, eleven. After round twelve she gives Nolitye a dismissive look.

At round thirteen the game gets very tense. Instead of pushing all thirteen pebbles back in one go, Rotten Nellie uses a special trick: she picks up one pebble at a time until she has put the required thirteen pebbles in the hole. The Spoilers start smiling as if she has already won.

"Show her what we're made of, Nellie!" Four Eyes cries out.

"Shut up, wena. It's not over yet," Rotten Nellie says coldly, telling him off for the second time.

Nolitye watches Rotten Nellie throw the main pebble back into the air. She is biting her lower lip in sheer concentration and successfully removes all thirteen pebbles. Now she must put back fourteen pebbles without dropping the main pebble. This time Rotten Nellie decides to shovel in three or four pebbles at a time. Two more to get into the hole.

Nolitye's eyes dart between Rotten Nellie's hands and face. A smile spreads over Rotten Nellie's face because she is doing an even fancier trick: she grips one pebble between her index and middle fingers and throws the main pebble into the air with the same hand. Everything goes smoothly until she tries to shovel the remaining pebble into the hole. Just then the pebble slips from between her fingers and drops into the hollow.

Rotten Nellie didn't reach the final round!

Showing off doesn't help, Nolitye thinks as she gets to her feet. All eyes are on her. It is her turn. She hugs Bheki, who carefully slips the stone into her hand. Nolitye softly whispers "I will win" in his ear. "Good luck!" he says aloud.

"How come we don't ever wish each other good luck?" Four Eyes asks enviously.

"If you open your big mouth again, Four Eyes, that'll be it, you'll be out of the gang. You *and* your stupid beetroot-and-polony sandwiches!" Rotten Nellie yells.

"But I thought you liked them . . ."

"Liked them? Hell, the only reason we ate them was because we were hungry, you idiot." Rotten Nellie gives him a shrivelling look that makes him move closer to Bheki.

Nolitye sits on the ground. She has never been good at ngeto because of her small hands, but with the magic stone around her neck she hopes for the best. She takes a deep breath and throws the main pebble into the air, and to her relief manages to take all fifteen pebbles out of the hollow in one go. It is as though the pebbles are drawn to her hand. With a quick glance, she chooses one pebble before she throws the main pebble back into the air, then carefully pushes the chosen pebble back into the hollow. She catches the main pebble in time and pats the ground to indicate that she is moving on to round two.

When Nolitye gets to the sixth round, Rotten Nellie starts fidgeting agitatedly. Four Eyes moves closer to have a look. To Bheki's obvious surprise, Four Eyes winks at him from behind his thick spectacles. For some reason Four Eyes is happy to see Nolitye doing so well.

It becomes dead quiet. Everyone's eyes are on Nolitye. When she gets to round nine, Four Eyes edges even closer. Without any problem Nolitye manages to get nine pebbles back in the hollow. But as she throws the main pebble into the air to pat the ground, Four Eyes trips over his own feet and bumps into her. The main pebble tumbles to the ground.

"That's it, I win!" yells Rotten Nellie.

"Hey, but he bumped me," Nolitye protests.

Four Eyes, looking at his shoes, says, "I'm sorry."

"That's not my problem. I win," Rotten Nellie insists.

"But that's against the rules. You didn't win fair and square."

"Besides, I beat the boys," Bheki says, "so that makes us even."

Rotten Nellie hates to admit it, but she can't argue: they really are even. "Okay," she says unwillingly. "Let's call it quits." Even so, Rotten Nellie marches off with a triumphant swagger. "That'll teach you never to mess with me," she says and cackles loudly.

Thabo and S'bu follow her. "Hey, Four Eyes, are you coming or are you going to hang out with a bunch of losers?" Thabo shouts over his shoulder.

No answer from Four Eyes at first. Then, strangely confident, he announces, "I'm not coming." He is shaking his head from side to side, and even when Rotten Nellie stops in her tracks, turns back and glowers at him, he doesn't stop doing it.

"What?" she yells. "Did you say you're not coming?" Four Eyes looks straight at her. "You heard me."

"You know what this means, don't you?" She takes a step towards him. Now Four Eyes nods his head up and down.

Rotten Nellie turns round with a jerk of her shoulders and walks off in a huff, Thabo and S'bu traipsing silently after her once again.

"I'm sorry I made you lose the game," Four Eyes says to Nolitye. "Really. I so badly wanted to see you win. I don't know what happened. I tripped. I guess I'm just clumsy."

"You're not clumsy," Bheki says, putting his arm around his shoulder. "It was just an accident."

"Ja, accidents happen all the time," says Nolitye. On the one hand Nolitye is sad that she could not complete the game, on the other hand she is relieved that she had to stop. What if she could not finish it, even with the magic stone's help?

"So where are you going now, Four Eyes?" Bheki asks.

"Home, I guess. I don't think the Spoilers would ever want to be friends with me again."

"Well, you can come with us if you want to."

"Really?" Four Eyes immediately brightens up. He pushes back his glasses to see better, a happy smile on his face.

"Just remember, we don't do stupid things like bully other kids and steal their lunch money," Nolitye says.

"I know. I really hated doing that. It was just— "

"Don't worry. That's all in the past," Bheki changes the subject and proudly says, "With us you can be just who you are and we'll still like you."

"Wait, Bheki," Nolitye says. "If Four Eyes comes with us now, he can't go back to the Spoilers later."

"But I don't want to! I was never happy to be a Spoiler."

Four Eyes looks so anxious that Nolitye quickly says, "Okay, but don't you think we have to do something about your name? I'm sure your parents don't call you Four Eyes."

"No. My dad calls me Shaun." He waits a few moments before he adds, "My mother died when I was a baby."

"I'm sorry," says Nolitye.

"It's okay. I was too young to know her. So I grew up with only my father. But sometimes I think of her and wonder what she would have been like."

"I bet she would've been proud of you today," Bheki says.

"Why?"

"It took a lot of guts to stand up to the Spoilers the way you did."

"It wasn't that hard. Standing there, I just realised they never liked me anyway, so they can't be real friends."

"No, not the way Rotten Nellie talked to you," Nolitye agrees.

"At first, I really thought the Spoilers liked me. I tried very hard to fit in with them. I told myself that they liked me for myself and not because I shared my delicious beetroot-and-polony sandwiches with them. They don't know what's delicious anyway," he says angrily.

"We couldn't figure out what you were doing with them . . . I mean you're not like them," Bheki says.

"I was the smallest and they always made me feel that. Mostly they decided things without even asking me. I guess you're right, I didn't fit in. But I felt safer with them than on my own. You know, with all the stories about the Zim . . ." The words are just pouring from Four Eyes's mouth. "But they made me feel rotten. I'm not good at soccer like S'bu and Thabo and I can't be bossy like Rotten Nellie. The only thing I'm good at is schoolwork, but the Spoilers hate school, so I had to pretend I do too."

Nolitye feels sorry for Four Eyes. Maybe he became so clumsy because the others were always telling him off, she thinks. If he wasn't tripping over something, his spectacles were falling off or he said something stupid.

"Hey, how about a game of cards at my place? I'll ask my mom to mix us some Oros orange juice," Bheki suggests.

"Let's go!" Nolitye says. "It's getting late in any case."

"Yeah, why not?" And Four Eyes gets into step beside Bheki. "My father usually doesn't get home before dark."

"So we'll call you Shaun from now on?" Nolitye begins. "Well, I kind of like Four Eyes."

"Really? Well, whatever you say, buddy." And Nolitye gives him a bright smile.

Upon hearing Nolitye calling him "buddy", an equally bright smile lights up Four Eyes's face.

Bheki's father is out because his bakkie isn't there, but his mother has been baking biscuits. Khaya gives a shriek of joy when he sees Bheki, and MaZwane looks up from the table where she is sorting the biscuits into little stacks.

"Ma, this is our friend Four Eyes," Bheki introduces him.

"Four Eyes?" MaZwane says. "You must see really well with four eyes." Four Eyes smiles shyly. MaZwane gives him such a hearty hug that he has to push his spectacles back onto his nose afterwards, and Nolitye grins knowingly.

"Here, let me clean them for you," MaZwane fusses and gives his spectacles a quick wipe with a dishcloth. "You boys are all the same. Nolitye, I don't know how you tolerate them." Nolitye shrugs and giggles, happy to see how much Four Eyes is enjoying the attention.

Khaya crawls to Bheki's leg and starts playing with his shoelaces. "Ma, look what Khaya is up to again," Bheki complains.

MaZwane picks Khaya up, wipes his nose and at the same time asks, "Now how about something to nibble on?"

Armed with a plateful of star-shaped cookies and three tall glasses of cold Oros, Bheki and Nolitye and Four Eyes walk to the bottom of the garden, where they settle down to play cards. Just before the sun touches the ridge of the neighbour's roof, Nolitye jumps up and says, "Bheki, have you forgotten about Shorty's warning?"

"Who's Shorty?" Four Eyes wants to know.

"He's part of Rex's pack," Bheki explains. "You know the dog that Beastie attacked yesterday?"

"Ja, I could hardly look."

"Well, Shorty is the big dog that looks like an Alsatian but has only half a tail. And he said we should be indoors after sunset today. But he wouldn't say why."

"Then I better go too," Four Eyes says, getting up. "My father says the stories about the Zim are nonsense, but he still worries about my safety. And in any case, I don't want to walk home in the dark."

Nolitye and Four Eyes walk a little way together. In the distance, they hear Mandla braying. He hee-haws for a while before he calms down. Four Eyes explains to Nolitye where he and his father live, because she has promised that they will fetch him after church tomorrow to come and play.

Chapter Six

THE NIGHT PROWLERS

NOLITYE gets to MaMokoena's spaza shop just as the sun disappears below the horizon. The sky is awash with a deep red colour. A cloud of smoke hangs above Phola, but it is not thick enough to blot out the moon that is climbing up behind the shanties.

Music blares from MaMokoena's neighbour's house and children play games in the street. Nolitye is happy to be back where she knows the sights and sounds and smells. To her surprise, Ntate Matthews steps from MaMokoena's spaza shop.

"Ntate Matthews!" she calls and hurries to him.

"Yes, my girl?" he asks with a silly smile on his face. Nolitye notices that he sways a little.

"Please, I'd like to hear more about my father."

"Oh yes, your father. It is hardly the time to talk now, but I can tell you he was a fine man."

Nolitye can smell beer on Ntate Matthews's breath. She is disappointed, because he seems to become very difficult once he's had some umqombothi. But he is friendly enough and starts walking towards her house with her. On a fairly quiet stretch of the way, a ball comes flying out of a shack and hits Ntate Matthews on the shoulder. He grabs the ball.

"You little louse!" he shouts.

"Sorry, Baba, we didn't mean to hit you, Baba," one of the boys apologises.

"It was an accident. Really, Ntate Matthews," Nolitye pleads with him. Ntate Matthews looks at Nolitye. "Sorry, my girl," he says. "I should watch my temper." He hands the ball back to the boy. Without even thanking him, the little guy and his friends go tearing after the ball. Nolitye cannot suppress a smile.

"Now what was I saying about your father? Oh, yes, that he would be proud of you if he knew that you found the stone."

Nolitye freezes. She looks Ntate Matthews in the face and searches his expression. How can he know about the stone? They have been so careful always to keep it hidden.

Ntate Matthews carries on walking as if nothing unusual has happened. "How do I know about the stone? Is that what bothers you?" he asks when it is clear that Nolitye is at a loss for words. This time he has a mysterious grin on his face. "I know a lot of things about you," he says and pats her on the head.

"Then please tell me more."

An old man slowly walks towards them. When he sees Ntate Matthews he asks, "Matthews, have you forgotten about the meeting in Zone Three?"

"Almost, almost," Ntate Matthews says. "But not quite." And he turns to go with the man.

"Wait, what about me?" Nolitye asks anxiously. She has too many questions for Ntate Matthews. He can't leave now, she thinks.

"There'll be plenty of time to talk, my girl," Ntate Matthews says, and puts his hand on the other man's shoulder.

Disappointed, Nolitye watches them go. She wanted to hear more about her father, and she still can't figure out how Ntate Matthews found out about the stone. She glances around and, satisfied that nobody is looking, takes out the stone and holds it in her hand. Soon she gets the giggles and quickly slips it back into the little bag.

When she opens the door to their house, she is greeted by the smell of fried chicken, pap and butter beans. Her mother is sitting at the table doing some sewing, a big smile on her face. Before Nolitye can even greet her, Thembi gets up and gives her a hug and says, "Thanks, well done!"

"What for?" asks Nolitye.

"For the fatcakes, silly! I can't believe how much money we've made today. Are you sure you were selling only fatcakes?"

"Yes, Mama," Nolitye says, crossing her fingers that her mother won't ask any questions. She hates half-truths, like telling Moeder that she and Bheki have been laughing about a silly joke.

"Well, I had a good day at work too, so I decided to buy us some chicken to celebrate. It's not every day that we can afford to eat meat."

After their special treat, Nolitye goes outside to fetch water for washing the dishes. She passes MaMtonga's shack with the empty bucket. The door is open. "Nolitye," MaMtonga calls in a hoarse voice.

Nolitye stops unwillingly and peers into the semi-dark hovel. Even with a candle burning inside, the place still looks dim, as if there's just too much darkness in there.

"Yes, MaMtonga," Nolitye says, trying to find the old woman in the shadows. She can't understand why the candle doesn't make more light. Narrowing her eyes, she looks again and finally sees MaMtonga sitting on the bed in the corner. She is not wearing her usual head wrap, so her head, mostly bald but for a few tufts of short hair, is exposed. With the long forefinger of her left hand MaMtonga is scratching her head. The rasping sound gives Nolitye the horrors, but the strange smell in the room is worse, as if something is rotting somewhere in the dark.

Gradually, Nolitye becomes used to the dark and she notices that MaMtonga is stroking something on her lap with her other hand. Must be the snake she's heard about but no one has ever really seen, Nolitye decides.

"Why are you so scared, child?" MaMtonga asks, not unkindly.

"I'm not scared." Nolitye presses her hand tightly to her chest where the bag with the stone is hidden.

"So now you have the magic stone," MaMtonga says in the same matter-of-fact way as Ntate Matthews earlier. Nolitye's heart misses a beat. She tries not to show her surprise and doesn't say anything. How does the old woman know? Is she conspiring with Ntate Matthews? Did Bheki say something to someone? No, Bheki promised; he wouldn't do that.

"That stone is too powerful for a little girl like you."

"But it found me," Nolitye says without thinking. Then she realises that MaMtonga didn't say that she found the stone. And that must mean something.

"Tell you what, child, give me the stone and I'll let you have anything you want. You and your mother can live in a brick house and even drive a car if you want," the old woman says, ignoring what Nolitye said. "I can make it happen, you know. Tomorrow already you could win the Lotto."

Nolitye takes a deep breath. The stench hits her in the pit of her stomach, but she calmly says, "The stone is mine now." She waits a few seconds before she adds, "And I'm not going to give it to anyone."

MaMtonga presses her lips together and her face swells up. With a loud bang, the door to her shack slams shut behind Nolitye's back. An eerie wind fills the room and the candle at once grows into a big wavering flame. MaMtonga rises from her bed. The pupils of her eyes look like bits of glowing coal. For the first time, Nolitye notices the green-and-brown snake coiled around the old woman's neck like a living necklace. She lets out a terrified scream.

"Shut up, you naughty girl!" MaMtonga yells.

She really is an umthakathi, a witch, Nolitye thinks. Only a witch will live with a snake.

"Give me the stone," the old woman says in her hoarse voice, slowly coming closer. The horrible smell that fills the room is MaMtonga's bad breath, Nolitye realises, shaking with fright. Clutching the little bag in her right hand, crumpling the front of her blouse, she backs away from the old woman, desperately wishing that the door would open. And indeed, the door swings open quietly. Nolitye rushes out. Without warning, the door closes again, this time with a bang.

Nolitye's mother is waiting outside. "What were you doing at MaMtonga's?" she asks, concern in her voice. "I heard you scream."

"Mama, she was coming towards me with her green-and-brown snake!"

"Nolitye, how many times have I told you to stay away from MaMtonga?"

"But she asked me in, Mama."

"And I specifically told you never to listen to her or to go anywhere near that woman!"

Just then MaMtonga's door swings wide open again. The old woman shuffles into the opening. There is no sign of the snake, but her eyes are full of anger and contempt. She spits on the ground. Nolitye imagines hearing the earth sizzle as though MaMtonga had just spat out something very hot. A thin trail of smoke rises in the air and disappears.

"Your child is playing with something she shouldn't have," MaMtonga tells Thembi.

Thembi pretends not to hear. Instead she puts her arm around Nolitye's shoulders and rushes her back inside their shack.

"You dare ignore my warnings, Thembi! Your child is playing with something that can call all the evil out upon her!" MaMtonga shouts after them.

"What is she talking about?" Thembi asks Nolitye.

"I don't know." Nolitye tells another half-truth.

"You stay here. I'm going to talk to her."

"No, Mama, please. You can't," Nolitye pleads. "What if she puts a spell on you?"

"Then I'll have to be strong." With that Thembi closes the door behind her.

Alone in the shack, Nolitye becomes very scared. What if the stone really is too powerful for her? Gingerly, she takes it out of the little bag and tries to speak to it. But the magic stone doesn't respond. It must be because it is after nightfall, Nolitye decides. The stone specifically said it got lonely. Reassured, she walks over to the bed, bends down, pulls the bucket out from under the bed and puts the stone with the rest of her collection. In the half-dark, the stone starts glowing dimly. Nolitye stares at it. A soft, warm wind sneaks into the room. It gives Nolitye goosebumps that tickle her from the small of her back all the way up her spine. She shudders with pleasure and then she gasps. A pale white light, shaped like a woman, has appeared on the far side of the bed.

"Are you a ghost?" Her voice comes out so softly that she can almost not hear herself speak.

"Don't be scared," the ghostly figure reassures her in a soft, soothing voice.

Nolitye calms down a little. To her amazement she sees that the stone is flitting around the woman's head like a small sunbird. The apparition, she notices for the first time, is dressed in the traditional black-braided white skirt and wrap of a Xhosa woman, yet her faced is covered by a beaded veil.

"Who are you? What are you?" Nolitye whispers.

"I told you: I'm the Spirit of the Stone. I'm the Spirit of Women's Strength and now it is time for you to grow up and hear some difficult things."

"Like what?" Nolitye has not moved. She stands as if glued to the floor. "Why don't you sit down? It is a long story I need to tell you."

"Thank you." And Nolitye gratefully sinks onto the bed.

"There is something you need to know about this stone, child." The voice is calm and clear.

"A long time ago when Nkulunkulu of the Heavens was still completing his plans, all people were lacking in wisdom. One day Nkulunkulu thought that it would be good to give people knowledge so that they could lead prosperous lives. So he gave them a special stone which he placed in a sacred cave. He sent messengers from the Animal, Reptile and Insect Kingdoms to call all the tribes from far and near. Every year at the beginning of the harvest, Nkulunkulu said, they had to bring offerings to the cave where the stone was."

As the figure speaks, Nolitye loses her fear. She leans forward so as not to miss a word of what the woman tells her.

"To one tribe he sent agile Monkey, brave Lion to another and to yet another, ruthless Crocodile. And so the many tribes came to be known by the different animals that Nkulunkulu sent to them. Lizard was also tasked with the message because of his great speed. But when it came to the last tribe, only Chameleon, the Slow Walker, was left to take Nkulunkulu's message to the people.

"The Slow One took his time putting one foot forward and then pulling it back as though not sure if it was the right step to take. While all the other animals delivered their messages in good time, the Slow One took a very long time. The first harvest came and went without the Slow One alerting his tribe. So his tribe suffered while the others prospered."

With the magic stone still circling her head, the Spirit of the Stone continues, "When the Slow One finally arrived with Nkulunkulu's message, it was too late. Because the other tribes had obeyed and taken timely offerings to the sacred stone at the beginning of each harvest season, they had grown in strength and prospered, while the Slow One's tribe had diminished in number and wealth."

After a short silence, the soothing voice asks, "Have you heard of Ncitjana the Mean One?"

Nolitye is taken aback. Why the question? She was so completely carried away by the story. She frowns, turning the name over and over in her mind. Then she remembers that Ntate Matthews said something about a Mean One the other evening when he asked Rex about the missing children. She nods.

"Well, Ncitjana is a descendant of that tribe. When his great-great-great-great-grandfather heard about the special stone in the sacred cave, he travelled there and stole it and took it home with him, because he wanted the Slow One's tribe to grow and prosper even more than the other tribes. But Ncitjana's great-great-great-great-grandfather's five sons were even greedier than him. They broke the stone into five pieces and each one took a piece and they scattered across the land, each one to start his own tribe. But wisdom and wealth do not enter this way. The power of the stone was lost. And that, child, is why there is so much fighting among the different groups and individual people today. When it was in one piece, the stone used to keep people together."

For a moment the woman seems to fade to a duller shade, but then the soothing voice continues, "What you have found, child, is the heart of the stone, the most precious piece."

"Heart? You talk about it like it was a living thing," Nolitye remarks, full of wonderment.

"It is alive and powerful and full of mystery. Beware and treat it with respect."

"I am . . . I mean, I will."

"The other pieces will come to you, until all the pieces have finally come together. When that has happened, a very strange thing will occur. But I cannot tell you about it yet. You will see with your own eyes the power of the stone once all the pieces have come together again."

Nolitye doesn't know whether to be scared or feel good. Until now she hasn't realised how important her stone is. "And how will the other pieces come together?" she asks.

"That is not for you to worry about."

"But what about MaMtonga? What does she really want from me?"

"It's not you she's interested in. It's the stone. She's been looking for the central piece all her life and now that you have it, she wants it."

"But I won't give it to her because I know she wants to do terrible things with it!"

"Yes. She wants to use the power of the stone for black magic. She wants to use it to fill the world with evil."

"But how do she and Ntate Matthews know about the stone? Only Bheki and I knew, and I know Bheki can keep a secret."

"They are elders in the community. They know things about our people and culture that a young one like you cannot possibly imagine. All I can say is that they have ways of knowing things."

"So what do I do now? Because MaMtonga is never going to leave me alone."

"You are going to have to fight her with white magic."

"Me, with white magic?"

"Yes, child. You too have the gift. It was passed on to you from your father."

Nolitye's heart skips a beat. The Spirit of the Stone is saying the same thing as Ntate Matthews, that she has inherited her father's magical powers.

"But how? I mean how will I fight MaMtonga with magic?"

"Only a natural magician could figure out that there is power in stones. All these years, while you thought you were just collecting stones, you have been calling upon magical powers that were given to you at birth. That is why you were chosen to find the stone."

Nolitye would like to say something but can't find the words.

"You can make the stones speak, child," the shimmering figure tells her. "A long time ago the sacred magicians were so powerful that they could make huge rocks that weighed many tons move and float. It is said that this is how the ancient Egyptians built the pyramids. They used sacred stones to make those huge rocks float. The stone that you have is such a sacred stone."

Nolitye hears footsteps outside the door. Before she can move or say anything, the magic stone floats back into the bucket and the bright light that was the woman fades.

"Nolitye," her mother calls as she enters the shack. There is worry on her face.

"Mama?" Nolitye gets up from the bed and steps closer to where her mother is lighting a new candle at the table.

"I just spoke to MaMtonga and she had disturbing things to tell me. She says that you have been doing bad things. She says you stole money this morning."

"That's not true, Mama." Nolitye shakes her head vehemently. She can't believe MaMtonga would say such a terrible thing about her.

"Then how do you explain all the money in the condensed milk tin, when you and I know there's no way you could have sold that many fatcakes."

Nolitye doesn't say anything. She thinks fast.

"Did you steal the money?"

"No, Mama, I promise."

"Then where did the extra money come from?"

"Uhm . . ." Nolitye doesn't know what to say. She wishes she could ask the Spirit of the Stone for advice.

"Don't lie to me, Nolitye. You're not too big for a hiding."

Nolitye can see that her mother means what she says. But there's no way that she can tell Thembi the truth about the stone and the fatcakes. Something deep inside tells her that she should keep all knowledge of the stone a secret. She can't quite understand it. She has never before felt that she could not be honest with her mother, but the feeling is so strong that she can't act against it. "Okay, Mama, I picked up money," she says and crosses her fingers that her mother will believe her. "There was this man in a rush, going to catch the train, and he dropped his purse. I saw it and picked it up. Bheki and I ran after him to give it back, but he was in too much of a hurry. Before we could get close enough, he'd leapt on the train and was leaving the station. What else could we do? So we kept the money."

Everything is such a mess, Nolitye thinks to herself. It is dreadful that she has to lie to her mother.

"I see," Thembi says. "I knew that you wouldn't steal money. I was surprised when MaMtonga told me."

"She's just trying to get me into trouble, Mama. And I don't know why."

"Don't worry about that now." Thembi pulls Nolitye closer and gives her a hug.

Nolitye feels safe and happy. But then she remembers what the shimmering figure told her about having to fight MaMtonga with white magic. "Did you see the green-and-brown snake, Mama?" she asks with her mouth close to her mother's ear.

Thembi stands back. "What green-and-brown snake?"

"The one that's in MaMtonga's place. I saw it."

"Nolitye, now don't tell lies. I was there in her room and I didn't see any snakes."

Nolitye doesn't mean to say it, but the words just come by themselves: "She's a witch, you know that, Mama."

Thembi looks at Nolitye for a long while and then shakes her head. "Nolitye, that's a terrible thing to say about the poor old woman. She did nothing to you."

"I'm sorry, Mama. It's just that MaMtonga said some horrible things to me while I was in there. And I'm sure I saw a green-and-brown snake wrapped around her neck."

"Nolitye, there was no such thing! Now stop imagining things!"

Suddenly, Nolitye feels completely confused. Did her eyes play a trick on her, or is MaMtonga just good at hiding things? She's not sure any more, but she won't talk about it any more either, because it is just upsetting her mother.

With a sharpness in her voice, Thembi says, "Now pack away your silly stones before I throw them out." And she gives the enamel bucket standing next to the bed a nasty look.

Nolitye quietly does as she is told. Without saying a word, Thembi changes into her nightdress and gets into bed. Nolitye also changes into her sleep T-shirt and blows out the candle. Soon Thembi is snoring, with Nolitye dreaming deeply.

A terrifying scream suddenly echoes outside. Startled, they both sit up in bed.

"What's going on?" Nolitye asks, dazed.

"Hayi! Hayi!" a woman wails somewhere outside. She sounds heartbroken.

Thembi scrambles to find the box of matches they always leave on the table and lights the candle. She puts on her nightgown and slips her feet into her push-ins. "You stay here," she tells Nolitye as she unlocks the door and goes outside.

Nolitye puts on her sweater and remains standing in the doorway. She watches her mother walk to where a few people have already gathered around the wailing woman. It is about halfway to MaMokoena's spaza shop. MaMokoena and Ntate Matthews are coming from the opposite direction. They join the group of onlookers at the same time as Thembi. There are quite a number of people now, most of them dressed in their sleeping clothes. Some are yawning.

Nolitye tries to hear what is being said, but she can't make out anything, just the crying of the woman. She wishes she could go closer, but Thembi would be very angry if she left the house. She sits down on the doorstep and waits. At last two women break away from the group and walk back past the house.

"Please, Mama," Nolitye addresses the older of the two women, "what happened?"

"Oh, my girl, you don't want to know," the old lady says. "A third child has disappeared tonight. You better go inside and lock the door." They carry on walking, clucking their tongues.

But Nolitye does not go inside. She is too worried. Who could it be that was snatched so close by? She gets up and stands on tiptoes to try and see down the street. Something makes her look around. She almost swallows her tongue she gets such a big fright. MaMtonga is standing outside her hovel, listening intently as she scratches her bald head. Beastie, the terrible dog that almost killed Rex, sits obediently on the ground next to her. Nolitye can't see the snake.

When MaMtonga sees Nolitye looking at her, she starts laughing, cackling loudly. Frightened, Nolitye looks around to see if there is anyone else in the vicinity that could protect her. Fortunately there are. An old couple is returning from the commotion down the street. They are shocked by MaMtonga's cruel laughter and shake their heads in disgust. "She's probably behind it!" the man says, pointing at MaMtonga. His wife agrees. Suddenly they start shouting, "Umthakathi! Umthakathi!"

But MaMtonga is not concerned about being called a witch. She just turns her back on them and goes inside her shack, cackling as though someone is tickling her. As soon as the door closes, Beastie gets up and slinks away in the dark, just like a hyena.

Nolitye pulls her sweater tight around her body and waits for Thembi to return. She is too scared to wait inside, so she sits down in the doorway again. When Thembi arrives back, Nolitye flings her arms around her. "Mama, please tell me what happened?" she pleads.

Thembi strokes her dreads. "A little girl disappeared. It was her mother, MaKhoza, who cried like that. She says her daughter went to the toilet, but when she stayed away too long, she went to look for her. That's when she saw a large man putting her daughter into a sack. Another man was also there, helping him. Just an ordinary-looking man. They ran away when they saw her coming."

"Oh Mama, what did this man look like? Did the girl's mother recognise him? Did she know him?"

"No, she said she has never seen him before. But she could describe him very well. She says he was a giant of a man, hairy and barefoot, only wearing a loincloth. He had a panga with him, she said, because he cut the washing line as he ran away."

Thembi looks at Nolitye. "Ntate Matthews said he thinks it must be the Zim. Silly man, we all know the Zim only exists in stories for children." Nolitye stops breathing for a moment. Then it was the Zim, she thinks, her heart beating wildly. And it wasn't a panga he was carrying; it was the nail of the little finger of his right hand that cut the washing line.

Thembi puts her arms around Nolitye's shoulders. They listen to the night noises: the distant screeching of a car speeding down a road and the gunshots that soon follow, dogs barking nearby and others replying farther away, Mandla the donkey braying mournfully and then falling quiet.

Nolitye is shivering so much that Thembi says, "Let's go to bed. It is getting chilly."

Snuggled in behind Thembi's back, Nolitye at last feels safe again. Suddenly she sits up. "Mama, what is the name of the little girl that got stolen?"

"You won't know her, they moved in here very recently, only last week. I have not seen MaKhoza before tonight. Sleep now."

But Nolitye has jumped out of bed. "Is her name Mbali, Mama?" she cries. "Is this MaKhoza the mother of Mbali?"

Thembi gets out of bed and lights the candle again. "Yes, Mbali, that is her name. But how do you know her?"

"She also goes to Nka Thutho, Mama, but I spoke to her today for the first time. She bought a fatcake from us." To calm her down, Thembi makes Nolitye a cup of very sweet black tea. Then she tucks her into bed before she gets back in herself and blows out the candle a third time the same night.

Chapter Seven

THE DUEL

WHEN she wakes up the next morning Nolitye feels relieved that the night, like a bad fever, has passed. She opens the curtains and welcomes in the warm sunlight. It streams through the small room like a blessing. Thembi makes some porridge while Nolitye washes. When she's done, Nolitye takes the orange plastic dish and pours the dirty water on the tomato plant Thembi planted next to their front door.

"I'm hungry, Mama," she says as she watches a flock of pigeons swoosh past.

"I'm not surprised. With all the disturbances last night . . ."

Nolitye changes into her Sunday best: a red-and-yellow floral dress with matching yellow shoes that she only ever wears to church or on special occasions, such as Christmas Day. Thembi also changes into her best clothes and puts on make-up and a pair of high heels. Before they leave for church, Thembi reaches for the condensed milk tin on the top shelf and takes out some money for the collection.

They walk past MaMokoena's spaza shop, which is closed on Sundays, and past some Zionists in their blue-and-white attire. There is a sombre atmosphere in the narrow streets. Even the children who are usually loud and eager to get to Sunday school are subdued.

Not all people in Phola go to church. Some lounge outside their self-built homes, soaking up the sun on their day of rest, but when Nolitye and her mother walk into church it is already almost full, so they sit at the back. Nolitye notices MaMokoena near the front. She is sitting next to a woman who is sobbing softly. It must be MaKhoza.

Nolitye can't keep her mind on what the pastor is saying. She thinks of the cry in the middle of the night and of MaMtonga laughing so loudly that the old couple called her an umthakathi. And then she remembers the story the Spirit of the Stone told her. Instead of listening to the pastor, she is trying to imagine what other magical things the stone would be able to let happen, and whether they could use the stone to help them find Mbali. Just then a woman sitting two rows in front of them looks back at Nolitye and smiles. Thembi doesn't notice. Her full attention is focused on the sermon.

Nolitye smiles back at the woman. She seems to be wearing a dress made of soft white feathers! Nolitye takes a hard look at her, trying not to stare because that would be rude. The more she looks at the woman the more she thinks she is not an ordinary human being. She has pointy ears, but Nolitye can't think what exactly it is that is so unusual about her.

Nobody else in church pays any attention to the strange woman in the feathery dress, or even notices that she is looking and smiling at Nolitye. Nolitye rubs her eyes to make sure that she is not dreaming. Thembi pokes her in the side and says, "Stop yawning."

"I wasn't yawning," Nolitye whispers back.

Then something bizarre starts to happen. It is as if time slows down. The pastor seems to be talking and moving in slow motion, his voice slurring because he speaks so very slowly. Nolitye looks around in astonishment. Everyone else in church also seems to be acting in the same slow manner. In fact, all movement slows down even more until the pastor stops speaking altogether and just freezes in mid-sentence, his eyes open and his mouth too, but with no sound coming out.

Nolitye can't believe her eyes. Even Thembi next to her is frozen along with everybody else as if made of stone. The only person who is moving is the woman with the pointy ears. Without warning, she starts floating out of her seat towards Nolitye. Nolitye touches her mother's cheek and pulls back her hand in shock. Her mother's skin feels hard and cold like MaZwane's porcelain teapot, and she doesn't respond at all to Nolitye's gentle touch.

"What have you done to my mother?" Nolitye asks the woman when she gets close enough, trying not to sound accusing. The woman opens her mouth, but instead of speaking, she sings a few notes in the most beautiful voice. Immediately, Nolitye relaxes and a dreamy numbness settles on her eyes.

"Hello," the floating woman says, drawing even closer. As if in a dream Nolitye takes a good look at her clear green eyes, her delicate bare feet and the even brown colour of her complexion, smooth like chocolate. Her toenails sparkle as if they are made of gold.

"Hello," Nolitye finally says, delight and fear mingling in her voice. "Who are you?"

"My name is Nomakhosi," the woman introduces herself and bows her head. "I'm an ancestral spirit from the land beyond death where all ancestors live."

At a loss for words, Nolitye just nods her head.

"I'm the one who is going to be your guide and help you retrieve the other stones."

"But . . . how shall—"

"Sorry, we don't have much time," Nomakhosi cuts her short. "You must find the next stone. Like I said, I will be your guide and will tell you where to go."

"So I must go somewhere to find these stones? I thought they would just find me."

"No, you must find them. Only the heart stone has found you. The others you have to look for."

Nolitye sighs. "Don't worry, I will help you." Nomakhosi promises. "Now listen carefully. Today after church you and Bheki are going to go with Four Eyes."

"Bheki and Four Eyes? But how do you know them?"

"I know everything that I need to know about you. I know how you hate eating carrots, for example. But your mother is right carrots are very good for you. You must—"

Nolitye cannot help but interrupt the spirit from the land beyond death. "What about Four Eyes?" she asks. She must know what will happen after church - the last thing she wants to hear about from this all-knowing stranger is that she must eat vegetables.

"Four Eyes is going to take you to meet a woman who has the stone. I cannot tell you more than that."

Nolitye frowns. Until yesterday they weren't even friends with Four Eyes, and now he is part of the adventure of the stone!

"It is time for me to go," Nomakhosi says. A cool breeze sweeps into the church and the green-eyed woman disappears in a trailing grey-white shadow of mist. Nolitye blinks her eyes. But Nomakhosi has indeed vanished and time is speeding up again: the pastor starts moving and talking as before, and everyone else also comes to life. Nolitye prods her mother just to check if she is still a statue.

"What's the matter?" Thembi asks.

"Nothing," Nolitye whispers although she would very much like to tell her mother that all movement stopped right in front of her eyes and that a woman from the ancestral spiritual world, dressed in feathers, suddenly appeared from nowhere and hovered in the air, floated straight towards her and spoke to her. But she can't, because one isn't supposed to talk in church, and it would in any case sound like a lie; Thembi wouldn't believe her.

After church Nolitye goes home. Still bursting with excitement about meeting Nomakhosi, she changes into her day clothes. "Mama, may I please go and play at Bheki's house?" she asks.

"Yes, as long as you walk straight there and back," Thembi agrees. "I promised MaKhoza that I would come over after church and keep her company. So that is where I'll be if you need me."

As soon as she is alone, Nolitye is overcome with a strong urge to hold the magic stone. She gets down on her knees and pulls the enamel bucket from under the bed. The magic stone, lying on top, sparkles with a gentle purple-blue light. Nolitye stares at it. She can't believe how lucky she was to have found it. As soon as she takes it in her hand, the same tingly feeling makes her giggle. She puts the stone in one of the pockets on her day-dress and shoves the bucket with the other stones back in under the bed, locks the door and goes straight to Bheki's house.

Bheki is in the back garden with Khaya, who is trying to play with him, but Bheki looks very bored. "Why are you looking like a sour apple?" Nolitye asks.

Bheki points to Khaya, who is pulling out his shoelaces as always. "I have to babysit this little terror while my mother is having tea with her friends," he complains.

"He is just playing his favourite game," Nolitye teases him a little.

Bheki just gets a pained expression on his face. "Did you bring the stone?"

"And a lot more than that! I've got news for you."

So much has happened since she saw him the previous day that she has to think hard where to start, what to tell him and about what to keep quiet. She starts by telling him about MaMtonga and the green-and-brown snake and how the old woman hid it when her mother spoke to her.

"So she must be a witch," Bheki says amazed, and without even looking he takes a cookie from the plate stacked with crunchies which MaZwane must have left for her two sons. Embarrassed, he quickly offers Nolitye one.

Nolitye considers telling Bheki about Nomakhosi, but something warns her not to share the experience in the church with him. Even friends have to have their own secrets, she decides. However, she does tell him about Mbali disappearing. Then, to take his mind off the terrible news, she takes the stone from her pocket and puts it on the grass, remembering that it needed at least an hour of sunlight.

"Would you like something to drink while we wait?" Bheki asks politely after a few minutes. He finds it frustrating not being able to touch the stone. "Ma made a jug of Oros before she left."

Nolitye nods.

Khaya is happily amusing himself with Bheki's shoelaces, so they leave him in the garden while they quickly go inside to fetch their cool drinks. When they return, Bheki gets such a fright that he drops his glass of Oros on the steps. The glass shatters in a hundred pieces and the cool drink splashes all over his laceless takkies. Right there in the middle of the lawn Khaya is standing clutching the stone, the shoelaces forgotten at his feet. Only it is not Khaya as they know him; it is a little giant at least five times Khaya's size that stands there swaying on his feet.

Bheki rushes to Khaya and grabs the stone from his hand. The toddler lets out such a shriek that the birds in the two peach trees fly away in panic. And still Khaya screams. Bheki has to make soothing sounds and tickle him to distract him and make him stop shrieking. Only when Bheki dangles his shoelaces in front of Khaya's face does he forget about the magic stone.

"What will Ma say?" Bheki cries out in dismay. "This is a disaster."

Khaya is now sitting down, beating the grass with his fists, sending out little earth tremors. His hands have become much bigger than Bheki's.

Nolitye gulps down her juice without even tasting it. "Let's get him inside before anyone sees him," she urges Bheki and casts her eyes around. Together they try to pick up the small giant. But try as they may, they cannot move him one centimetre. They push him from the back with all their strength, but still Khaya doesn't move. He sits firm like a rock.

"How did this happen?" Bheki asks, his mouth dry with nervousness. "One minute Khaya is just a normal toddler, we turn our backs and the next minute he's a small giant."

"It must be the stone, Bheki!" Nolitye suddenly realises.

"What am I going to say to my mother?" Bheki is on the verge of tears. "Let's worry about that later. Let us get him inside first." Nolitye comes up with a plan: she steals the shoelaces from Khaya and puts them just out of reach in front of him. Every time he tries to grab them, she pulls them back a little. And slowly the little giant is being lured up the steps into the house through the kitchen door. He is so big that the kitchen table shakes when he bumps into it.

Bheki tries to calm him down by giving him his red tow-truck. Khaya reaches for the toy with shining eyes. Bheki turns his head and looks away because he fears his baby brother will crush his favourite toy into a bunch of metal scraps. The tow-truck looks very fragile and small in Khaya's hand.

"Nolitye, do something. Khaya can't stay this size. My mother will kill me," Bheki pleads.

Khaya struggles up and grabs a mug from the table and flings it across the room. It smashes into pieces against the wall.

"Come on," Nolitye says, and with the stone in her one hand and Bheki's hand in the other, she wishes for Khaya to go back to his normal size. They watch anxiously.

Nothing happens. Instead the Spirit of the Stone tells Nolitye, "First the next stone. Then your wish will come true."

Bheki can see Nolitye is listening to something, so he asks, "What is it saying?"

"It says I must first find another piece of the stone." When Bheki looks at her blankly, she says, "Didn't I tell you that this stone was part of a bigger stone?"

"No, you didn't!"

"Well, our magic stone was part of a bigger stone and I . . . Hm, well, I stumbled upon the most important piece. The heart of the original stone. So now the other stones are trying to get together with this central stone." When Bheki still looks confused, Nolitye says, "The stone says if we find the next piece our wish will come true."

"So it's kind of like a jigsaw puzzle?"

"Except the pieces are scattered all over the place."

"But Nolitye, what do we do about Khaya in the meantime?"

There is the sound of pieces of crockery clanking against each other. Nolitye swings around. "Oh look, Bheki. He's opened the cupboards!"

Just in time they duck, because three plates come crashing to the floor, much to Khaya's amusement. Bheki has to wrestle with him to get him to sit down.

"Tell you what, I'll go and fetch Four Eyes while you look after Khaya."

"You better hurry up or else there'll be nothing left in the house!" Bheki cries, now completely panic-stricken.

Nolitye rushes out. It is windy outside and bits of paper and torn plastic float on the road, but she hardly notices. She needs to get to Four Eyes as soon as possible because Nomakhosi said that he would help to lead her to the next stone, and until she finds that stone Khaya is not going to become small again.

She arrives at Four Eyes's house gasping for breath and knocks on the wooden front door. Four Eyes is happy to see her; he has been waiting for her. His father doesn't seem to be there and Nolitye is about to tell him what happened to Bheki's little brother when a tall woman in a dark cloak walks into the front room. She looks a bit like Four Eyes, except she does not wear glasses. Nolitye cannot help but stare at her. There is something very strange about her eyes.

"You must be Nolitye," the woman says and shakes her hand. Only then Four Eyes says, "Nolitye, this is my Aunt Vera."

Nolitye puts her hand in her dress pocket to try and find out from the stone whether this is the woman Nomakhosi was talking about. And then, without warning, it happens again: time slows down. Nolitye watches Four Eyes and his aunt's movements become sluggish till they seem completely frozen. Nomakhosi, with the green eyes and pointy ears, floats in out of nowhere, this time dressed in sparkling beads and a bright red-and-black-and-white Swazi cotton cloth. Her hair is combed into a spectacular fuzz decorated with small feathers. Her skin seems to shimmer as though it has been sprinkled with gold dust.

"What's going on? Why are you here, Nomakhosi?" Nolitye asks.

"This will happen every time I need to communicate with you."

"I'm very pleased to see you," says Nolitye anxiously. "We have a big problem with Khaya."

"I noticed," Nomakhosi says, and Nolitye thinks she hears a little laugh. "What did Khaya do with the stone? Bheki and I never grew from touching it."

"He licked it. So be warned of the consequences of putting the stone in your mouth."

"Won't you please tell us what we should do about Khaya?"

Nomakhosi explains that Four Eyes's aunt has the next stone Nolitye needs, then without warning, she fades away into a vapour of mist. The moment she has vanished, time speeds up again and Four Eyes and his aunt come to life.

"I have something for you, Nolitye," Vera says. "Four Eyes, won't you please wait in the passage?"

Four Eyes looks hurt, but he does as he is asked. Nolitye watches his aunt closely as she puts her hand in a large handbag and takes out a small bundle. This she unwraps, but inside is another piece of cloth tied into a knot. Vera unties the knot, but inside is yet another layer. Four times she unties pieces of cloth before she finally unwraps a small stone. She cautiously hands it to Nolitye. Nolitye takes the stone between her thumb and forefinger and takes a close look at it. It is slightly smaller than the magic stone and one side shines with a blue tint, while the other side glows purple.

"It's beautiful, isn't it?" Vera says. "I've waited all these years to give the crystal to the right person. We have known about you for quite a while now, Nolitye."

"We?"

"The Sisters of Light."

Nolitye doesn't understand. So much has happened in the last couple of days and she has met so many new and mysterious women. "Who are the Sisters of Light?" she asks, careful not to sound rude or stupid.

"You, child, are the Keeper of the Stone, the one who's going to restore the stone that once held everything that was pure and innocent. The Sisters of Light come from a long line of healers that in the beginning, before Ncitjana's ancestors stole it and broke it into five pieces, used to protect the stone."

Nolitye shivers at the mention of Ncitjana's name. "But what can I do? All of you call me child."

"Exactly. That's why you are so special - you are still pure and innocent."

"I don't know about being pure and innocent," Nolitye says rather cheekily.

"Well, no one said you are perfect!" And Vera gives her a teasing smile. Nolitye takes the first magic stone from her pocket. She opens her palm and watches it shimmer in the light. She places the stone Vera gave her next to it. The two pieces of crystal now sparkle as if touched by a magic light. Vera watches them as eagerly as Nolitye. Slowly her eyes narrow, she starts fidgeting with her hands. With alarm, Nolitye notices a greedy look creeping into the older woman's eye and just as Vera leans forward to snatch the stones from her palm, Nolitye jumps back. But Vera has already plucked both stones from her hand.

Immediately, as if compelled by an outside force, Nolitye pushes the old custom of being respectful to an older person from her mind and tries to wrestle the stones from Vera's grip. The woman is too strong, so Nolitye yells, "Give them back! They're mine, you said so yourself!"

Four Eyes comes rushing into the room. In a flash Nomakhosi with the clear green eyes and sparkling beads appears again. This time a fiery Xhosa skirt with thin bands of black binding round the bottom swirls around her ankles. Nomakhosi looks like a flame! And as before when she appeared, time starts slowing down.

"By the powers of light and day, I command time to remain the way it has always been, ever moving," Vera quickly intones an old spell-breaker before her parted lips stall.

To Nolitye's consternation the spell works and the next moment Vera starts moving about again. Four Eyes, however, remains frozen in time.

"Nomakhosi, we finally meet," Vera says.

"A Renegade," Nomakhosi whispers with her face turned away from Four Eyes's aunt. She speaks very softly and tells Nolitye how some Sisters who were originally of the Light have swapped over and now also work with the dark forces. So they are neither healers in the service of light nor witches under the command of the dark. "That's why they are called Renegades," she explains. "Sometimes they are good, and sometimes they are evil."

Aloud, Nomakhosi says, "By the power invested in me by the Sky King, our Sun, the Oldest Ancestor, you shall not have that stone, Vera."

In response Vera says, "I believe you have challenged me." Suddenly she unwraps her dark cloak to expose a dress printed with snakes all over green-and-brown snakes. Nolitye swallows. The snakes on Vera's dress look exactly like the green-and-brown snake in the house of . . . of . . . the nasty old woman staying next to her and her mother. Try as she may, Nolitye can't remember their neighbour's name. All she remembers is how awful she felt in the company of the old woman and her snake.

"Those snakes," Nolitye whispers to Nomakhosi, "they remind me of a woman I know, but I just can't remember her name . . ."

"And you will never be able to say her name, because I have eaten it from your memory," Vera says with a smug smile and quickly chants a spell: "Pig's tail and serpent's breath, I command life unto my little ones. Philani!"

Nolitye can hardly catch the words, but as she watches, all the green-and-brown snakes on Vera's dress come to life. They wriggle and slither onto the ground. Nolitye screams out loud and starts jumping about. Nomakhosi floats closer and picks her up in her arms. They hover just out of reach of the snakes with their forked tongues and black, beady eyes. Nolitye feels a little dizzy.

Vera doesn't seem pleased that her snakes stand on their tail ends, frantically trying but failing to reach Nomakhosi and Nolitye. "A delightful little trick, my dear, but how about this!" Vera says. She snaps her fingers and out of nowhere a swarm of bees appears. They swoop down on Nomakhosi and Nolitye, who still can't believe she's floating in the air. A split second before the bees reach them, Nomakhosi starts singing. She closes her eyes and a lilting melody flows from her mouth. The bees disappear as fast as they appeared and the snakes are swept away like limp pieces of string.

"MaMtonga!" Nolitye yells out as she suddenly remembers the name of the old woman who lives next to them. As soon as she says the words Vera starts turning into MaMtonga, letting out a terrifying shriek: her skin becomes old and saggy, her wig falls off and a bald head appears. Smoke is coming off MaMtonga's face as though the light is melting her. With trembling, claw-like hands she covers her face with the dark cloak. She lets out another frightening shriek which sounds as if it is coming from of the depths of darkness. And in a moment she has vanished. Only a pungent stench hangs in the air.

Nomakhosi puts Nolitye down, who is glad to be on firm ground again. They cover their noses and Nomakhosi picks up the two stones from the spot where MaMtonga vanished and gives them to Nolitye. "Nolitye, don't be confused," she says, "MaMtonga is actually a dark witch who this afternoon disguised herself as a Renegade. A true Renegade would never have tried to steal the stones from you, because a Renegade walks the thin line between light and dark, good and evil. Everything a Renegade does has to be carefully balanced, because they are influenced by both the light and the dark. The one force has to undo the other in order that they remain in balance, in equilibrium. One force can't be greater than the other. And for that reason there are very few true Renegades."

"So MaMtonga is a dark witch?"

"Yes, Nolitye, because a Renegade would never harm another soul by eating its memory like she did. The only way to deal with a dark witch is to use white magic against it."

"Well, I'm glad the fight is over."

"It's just the beginning, child. I'm afraid we're still going to see a lot more of MaMtonga."

Before Nolitye can answer, a moan from behind them makes them turn. A woman who looks like Four Eyes's aunt - except this time it really is Aunt Vera - is holding her head in her hands. She looks dazed like someone who has just woken up or has been under a deep spell. Nolitye turns to speak to Nomakhosi, but she has vanished without a trace. Time must be speeding up again, because Four Eyes lifts his feet one after the other, then rushes towards Nolitye.

"Are you okay?" he asks.

Nolitye chortles, thinking that Four Eyes has just missed a great fight between two powerful opponents. He notices that his aunt is moaning. She looks tired. In fact, she looks a bit drunk.

"Aunt Vera, what happened? And why are you wearing different clothes?"

Nolitye would love to explain, but there is no time. She's got a more pressing matter to attend to she needs to go back to Bheki's house at once. Who knows what Khaya has got up to since she left.

"Meet me at Bheki's place," she tells Four Eyes. "I need to get back urgently. I'll explain everything there." Before she rushes off, she pats him on the back and says, "Don't worry about your aunt, she'll be alright."

When Nolitye gets to Bheki's house, Bheki is just about pulling out his hair. His giant baby brother is swinging a chair above his head, ready to hit the light hanging from the ceiling. The desperation on Bheki's face makes Nolitye act fast. She takes out the two stones and, without knowing why, puts their purple sides together. A small spark jumps into the air when the stones touch. Then they start fusing together into one bigger stone. Nolitye stares at the new stone. It is impossible to see where the two pieces joined. Keeping one eye on Khaya and the chair above his head, Nolitye takes Bheki's hand. They look at each other and both take a deep breath before they silently wish that Khaya would go back to his normal size. As they watch, the baby giant shrinks and loses his strength. Bheki catches the chair just a second or two before it would have come crashing down on him.

Khaya is a toddler again and immediately starts crying. They do not notice MaZwane walking into the kitchen.

"Bheki what on earth happened in here?" MaZwane's eyes look like they are about to pop out of her head where she stands in the doorway, hands on her hips. Then she hurries to her crying baby, carefully stepping over smashed plates and mugs. Khaya stops crying as soon as he is in his mother's arms. MaZwane looks around dazed. Cupboard doors hang open and the kitchen looks as if a small tornado has gone through it.

Nolitye quickly puts the stone in her pocket. Bheki doesn't know what to say. "Uhm," he mumbles, and "Ah," but no word comes out of his mouth.

"I leave you just for the morning to look after your brother and this is what I come back to," says MaZwane, an angry frown on her forehead. She straps Khaya to her back with a shawl, takes a broom and starts sweeping up the broken crockery.

Just as well that she wasn't there to see her baby boy as a small giant, Nolitye thinks, imagining the alarm on MaZwane's face. She would probably have fainted.

"And you, Nolitye, where were you when all this was happening?"

"Me?" Nolitye is caught off-guard.

"She just came in, Ma," Bheki tries to come to Nolitye's rescue.

"I'm sure she can speak for herself," MaZwane says irritably. "Anyway, off with you two. I think you've done enough damage for one morning."

Bheki is only too happy to leave the house. At the gate they find Four Eyes. He's leaning against the post and looks rattled. "What's your problem?" Bheki asks him.

"It's a long story, but I think Nolitye knows more about it than she is telling."

Bheki glances at Nolitye and smiles.

Chapter Eight

A STRANGE DREAM

O N their way to the park at the crossroads near the school, Nolitye, Bheki and Four Eyes come upon Mandla the donkey, grazing on some wild grass on the side of the road. They stop, waiting for the usual complaints.

"I suppose you three have nothing better to do than watch me," Mandla grumbles, tearing at the grass.

"Always great to see you too, Mandla." And Nolitye gives him a bright smile.

"Well, some of us have to work," he grumbles.

"And some of us have to go to school," Four Eyes quips.

"But you like school. You can hardly compare it to drawing a cart and carrying sacks of coal all day."

To this, Four Eyes has no reply, and the other two also keep quiet. "So did they find the girl?" Mandla asks after a while.

How strange, Nolitye thinks, that Mandla should mention this, because Nolitye and Bheki have only just told Four Eyes that Mbali disappeared the previous night.

"Mbali? Not yet," Nolitye says, looking at her feet.

"If the Mean One has anything to do with it, they won't find her," Mandla says between chewing and chomping the next mouthful.

"Ntate Matthews says the Zim took Mbali," Nolitye answers. "But there was another man as well, MaKhoza, her mother, told the people. An ordinary man."

"It is true. The other man was Ncitjana, the Mean One," Mandla says, swatting flies with his tail. "That's the one I'm talking about. If he was there, the girl won't be found."

"Why not? What does this Ncitjana want to do with all these children?" Nolitye asks.

"The Zim wants to eat them, silly," Bheki says.

"But that doesn't explain why Ncitjana was there, too."

"Well, don't look at me," Mandla whines, chomping grass. "I'm just a dumb animal who transports a load all day."

"Well, isn't this a fine gathering?"

They all turn around to see who the owner of the gruff voice might be. It is Beastie. They didn't hear him sneak up on them. Mandla gasps and nearly chokes because he doesn't like dogs. They always bark and snap at him and sometimes his master has to crack his whip to make them scatter.

"You nearly gave me a heart attack," he stutters, spitting out grass.

"So sorry. But it's always good to creep up on prey, especially when you're as hungry as I am. The rubbish heaps have been cleared. A guy's got to eat, you know." Beastie licks his lips.

"He's joking, right?" Mandla brays.

"Wrong. I'm dead serious," Beastie snarls, showing his fangs. He slinks closer, sizing up Mandla.

Nolitye steps in front of Mandla. "Leave him alone," she says.

"Ja, just keep away!" Four Eyes adds. Bheki doesn't utter a squeak; he is too jittery with fear.

"You're a fine lot to speak. You get at least two meals a day. I have to go looking for food. Now move, before I make scrambled eggs of you," Beastie growls.

"I'm not moving," Nolitye says, her legs firmly planted on the ground. Four Eyes swallows his fear and says, "Me too."

"Uhm . . . Nolitye, Four Eyes . . ." Bheki begins.

"I know what I'm doing, Bheki."

"Yes, leave Nolitye alone. She knows what she's doing," Mandla says, so scared that he starts peeing.

"Perfect!" Beastie growls, irritated. "It's bad enough that I have to settle for a donkey, but one that has wet itself!"

"I don't like being the centre of attention," Mandla wails, his legs shaking, because Beastie has pulled his ears back, ready to attack.

"Not so fast, tough guy!"

They all spin around to see who has spoken, even Mandla who never moves fast has turned at a record speed. "More dogs . . . This is my lucky day," he brays, his big teeth clattering.

Rex trots up to Nolitye. "When the rubbish gets cleared, he always gets up to something," he says, indicating Beastie with his head. "So we followed him."

"Last time he killed two chickens and because we happened to be nearby, we got blamed," Shorty adds bitterly.

"Ja, and we got doused with boiling water," Ticks remembers.

"How unfortunate. But for your information, the chickens were tasty."

"Beastie, do us all a favour and just get lost!" Rex demands.

"Are you a sucker for punishment, Rex, or are you just plain stupid?" Looking Beastie straight in the eyes, Rex says, "Maybe a bit of both."

"Rex . . ."

"Don't worry, Nolitye, this time I've got back-up."

"And there's no way Beastie's going to do anything to Mandla as long as we're here," Ticks boasts, scratching an itchy spot behind his right ear.

"Oh, and I'm supposed to shiver a a fleabag like you!" Beastie darts Ticks a disdainful look. "Try your luck somewhere else, scumbag." And with that Beastie pounces on Rex and grabs him by the scruff of his neck. A scuffle breaks out. Shorty and Ticks each go for a flank. Whiskers, who can't reach much higher, seizes Beastie's tail, yanking it with all his might. Mandla doesn't move, but brings forth an ear-splitting neighing.

Bheki closes his eyes. Nolitye stands there panic-stricken, while

Four Eyes yells at Beastie to leave Rex alone. Rex's pack is hanging onto various parts of Beastie, but he doesn't show any sign of loosening his grip. He's still got Rex by the neck and he is not going to let go. A small cloud of dust hangs in the air.

"Mandla," Nolitye pleads, "please do something before one of them gets seriously hurt!"

"I'm just a donkey." Mandla looks horrified at the thought of getting involved in a dog fight.

"Mandla!" Nolitye screams.

Mandla hates being shouted at. He snaps out of his fear and turns his backside to the dogs. Exactly at that moment Beastie loses his balance and falls backwards. Mandla sees his chance and flicks back his hindlegs, kicking Beastie in the gut. The force of the kick sends Beastie flying across the road. He lands on the other side, moaning something awful.

Mandla's master, returning from wherever he has been, rushes over to the hyena look alike and with gusto applies his whip to the half lights-out beast. Beastie staggers up and runs off yelping, his tail between his legs. When they see Mandla's master walking towards them with his whip Rex and his pack too disappear down a side street.

"You filthy rats!" the coalman shouts, throwing stones after them.

"They were trying to protect your donkey from that other dog," Nolitye tries to explain.

"And what are you children doing here? If you don't make yourselves scarce I'll give you a whipping you won't forget. I'll . . ."

Nolitye looks at the coalman, not sure whether he is joking or not. "Nolitye, let's go," Bheki urges, tugging at her hand.

"But Rex and—"

"Let's just go!" Bheki starts pulling her away. "You too, Four Eyes."

The man grabs the rope tied around Mandla's neck and starts pulling him. Mandla brays, complaining of hunger, about being rushed, but he nevertheless follows his master.

"We didn't even have a chance to say goodbye to Mandla," Nolitye says as they carry on up the road.

"Sometimes you don't know when to call it quits, Nolitye," Bheki says. Before Nolitye can reply, Four Eyes notices Rex and his pack coming back up the side street. Apart from a few nicks and cuts they all look fine. "This time, I decided that four heads were better than one," Rex says to Nolitye.

"Well, I hope that's the last of Beastie."

"Me too," Bheki adds.

"Me three," Whiskers echoes in a small voice, which makes them all laugh.

"Well, like I said, the rubbish heaps have been cleared so we have to go scouting," Rex says, and the dogs trot down a footpath that leads to the railway line.

"So what was happening at Bheki's house that you had to leave my place in such a rush?" Four Eyes asks Nolitye as they finally sit down in the little park.

Nolitye and Bheki look at each other. They know they can't keep the magic stone a secret from him any longer. Four Eyes has proven his friendship by sticking with them. He could have gone back to the Spoilers, but he hasn't. Nolitye nods to Bheki, which is her way of saying, let's tell him. She begins by taking out the magic stone. She must still get used to it being almost double the size, but at least it is still the same soft purple colour.

Four Eyes looks intently at the stone. "So what's with it?" he asks.

"It is not an ordinary stone," Nolitye explains. "Actually, it's a crystal." Four Eyes reaches for the stone, but Nolitye pulls her hand away. "Like I said, it isn't an ordinary stone. It was once part of a bigger stone with special powers."

"Special powers?" Four Eyes screws up his face to understand.

"Yes, special powers."

"Just listen to what happened to us," Bheki boasts, eager to stress their role. But first, Nolitye tells Four Eyes and Bheki the story that the Spirit of the Stone told her about Nkulunkulu and the sacred stone and how it was broken into five pieces by Ncitjana's ancestors and how after all this time it has fallen to her to restore the stone.

Four Eyes listens respectfully. He knows it must be serious because Bheki, his arms folded on his tummy, has a grave look on his face.

"So up to now I've found the heart of the stone and the first piece. The other pieces will show up in time." She smiles. "But already the stone can do amazing things."

Nolitye and Bheki tell Four Eyes how the stone made them giggle, how it healed Rex, and how it filled the bucket with fatcakes when they wished for it to happen.

"You guys are having me on," Four Eyes says, shaking his head in disbelief.

"I'm telling you, the empty bucket was filled right to the top with fatcakes." Bheki takes Four Eyes by the shoulders and shakes him a bit to make him understand. "Just this morning my little brother Khaya turned into a small giant. That's why Nolitye had to rush back to my house from your place, if you want to know."

"If Khaya was a giant, then I'm Father Christmas," Four Eyes laughs. Nolitye puts the stone back in her pocket with an expression that says: Just you wait and see, Four Eyes.

"I'm sorry, guys, but I really find it hard to believe— "

"Well, it happened!" Bheki interrupts him and throws his hands in the air. "Wait!" Four Eyes says, suddenly looking interested. "Did the stone have anything to do with my aunt acting so strange when you came to our house, Nolitye?"

"You bet it had!" Nolitye says and winks. "And now I better go home or my mother won't know what has happened to me. See you guys tomorrow!" And off she runs to Phola.

Thembi is not home yet. Nolitye feels sorry for herself; she also feels frightened. It was one thing if Bheki and Four Eyes were around, but on her own she didn't feel so brave. She never expected her habit of collecting stones would get her into so much trouble. It was true, the magic stone had given her and Bheki a lot of fun, but they couldn't share the secret with anyone but Four Eyes, and he didn't even really believe them. And she couldn't tell anyone about Nomakhosi, not even Bheki. Even he would not believe her, because nobody else could see the mysterious woman who floats in from nowhere and makes time stop. It is only she who can see her, just like it is only she who can hear the stone talk.

If I dare tell anyone about everything that has happened the last four days, Nolitye thinks, they will say I am crazy.

She peeps out the door to see if MaMtonga is around. But their neighbour's place is closed up and looks deserted. Nolitye peers down the narrow street towards MaMokoena's spaza shop to see if Thembi is perhaps on her way home. Except for a few small children playing in the street, and some women talking to MaKhoza in front of her house, there is no one around. Nolitye sighs and locks the door and sits down at the table, resting her head on her arm. All this talk about witches and white magic and Renegades; it is all too much for her. What worries her more than anything else, though, is the business about having to find the other three pieces. How can she find them all by herself? She has not even told her mother about it, and that, while both Ntate Matthews and MaMtonga seem to know everything about the stone - MaMtonga even swore she would take it. There can be no doubt, MaMtonga is a witch, and she is not going to give up on the stone. Look how she turned herself into Four Eyes's Aunt Vera and almost managed to steal the stone! Compared to MaMtonga, Rotten Nellie and the Spoilers are small worries, even though they do make life unpleasant.

Discouraged and feeling helpless, Nolitye starts sobbing softly.

"Nolitye, what is it?" Thembi asks when she arrives home shortly afterwards and sees how puffy Nolitye's eyes are. Nolitye stops crying, but she doesn't answer immediately. She does not know what to tell her mother.

"Come, Nolitye," Thembi says. "Come and sit here next to me on the bed and tell me what is upsetting you."

Nolitye moves over, but she still doesn't know what to tell her. Thembi puts her arm around Nolitye's shoulders. "I know you are worried about MaKhoza's daughter who disappeared last night. But nothing can happen if you don't go out at night by yourself."

"Thanks, Mama." Nolitye smiles at her mother through her tears.

"You always want to know about your father," Thembi continues, and to Nolitye's surprise she puts her arm around her. "Perhaps it is time I told you more about him. You know, he came from a long line of traditional healers. His father, his grandfather, his brothers, even he himself, were healers."

"That is what Ntate Matthews also said," Nolitye says, all ears now.

"Oh, did he?" Thembi doesn't sound so chummy any more and gives her a strange look as she gets up and walks to the wardrobe. She stands on her toes and puts her hand on the top shelf, feeling under some old clothes and things that she keeps there. She returns to the bed with a small cloth parcel. She puts it on her lap, and unties the cloth. Inside is a bracelet made with beads and cowrie shells.

"Here, give me your hand," she tells Nolitye, and ties the bracelet around her wrist. "Your father wanted you to have this. He said you would know what to do with it when the time was right. I think the time is right for me to give it to you."

"Oh Mama, thank you!" With shining eyes Nolitye touches the delicate red and blue beads and cowrie shells. The shells are spotlessly white. Tears come back in her eyes.

Thembi gives her a hug. "Let's have supper and get ready for bed. Tomorrow is Monday and we have to get up early again."

Nolitye drifts into sleep and gets carried away by dreams. But they are not easy dreams. She turns restlessly from side to side until she finally gets up for a glass of water. Thembi is fast asleep, so she opens the curtain of their small window. The moon is already much smaller, but the tall street lamps cast a bright light outside. All is peaceful and quiet. Nolitye gets back into bed and snuggles in behind her mother's back. Thembi seems to sleep like a log.

After a while Nolitye's thoughts fade into dreams again. She finds herself walking alone along a riverside path. The path leads to a distant forest. A fish eagle flies above her, slowly swooping down. Nolitye looks up and realises that the eagle is diving towards her, its talons stretched out to grab her. She starts running as fast as she can and enters the forest where she is protected from the bird of prey by tall trees, dense bush and thick undergrowth. The eagle doesn't give up though. Its piercing cry disturbs the silence of the forest. With difficulty Nolitye struggles through the trees and prickly shrubs, scratching her arms and legs. Eventually, she stumbles upon a clear, narrow footpath. She senses someone's eyes on her, but every time she turns around to check, there's no one. She starts walking faster, her heart beating to the rhythm of her quickening steps. When she again looks behind her, she catches a glimpse of something moving between the trees.

"Who's there?" she demands loudly. No one answers.

She keeps walking, nervously looking behind her. In the shrubs and bushes next to the footpath, she can hear the rustling of leaves.

"Who's there?" she asks again. Now she hears footsteps, but whoever they belong to remains in the dense bush. She starts running. Whoever it is also starts running. Nolitye runs even faster. She changes direction and cuts into another part of the forest. Now she can hear something running right behind her. It is breathing heavily and from the sound of its footsteps it must be big. Nolitye wills herself not to look behind her again for fear of what she might see. The creature gets closer with every step she takes. Then she trips over a stone and falls to the ground. She jumps up, dazed, and looks around her. There is nothing.

"Come out whoever you are!" she shouts bravely, even though she is terrified. No sound. Not even a rustle from the trees and bushes around her. She feels smothered by them and looks up at the distant sky. When leaves start rustling nearby again, Nolitye steps backwards, bewildered. She screams in anguish as she topples backwards down a hole that burrows into the bowels of the earth. She tumbles down, down until she lies still in complete darkness. She scrambles to her feet, dusts herself off and spits out the dirt that somehow got inside her mouth. She feels her way in the dark through what seems to be a tunnel. It stinks, as if someone has left meat to rot.

She stumbles on a little further into the dark. Around her feet she hears squeaking noises. It must be rats that brush past her ankles. She bites on her lip so as not to scream. At the end of the tunnel a small light starts flickering faintly. She steps carefully towards the light, the rats now accompanying her. Light begins to flood the darkness. Strange-looking furry songololos fall on her head. This time she screams and shakes them out of her hair. She moves faster to get to the light. Near the end of the tunnel she finds a burning torch leaning against one side. She takes the torch and walks on until she comes to a fork in the path. Her instinct tells her to take the path to the right, but her curiosity makes her choose the left path.

The stench of rot gets worse the further she walks. She shrieks, terrified, and almost turns back when she sees bones scattered on the floor. And then, without prior warning, she hears grunting and a terrible growling. Her heart hammers in her chest. She whips around and starts running back, but the grunting gets louder and comes closer. Something is chasing her! She can hear hooves advancing. She tries to run faster but again she slips and falls. When she staggers up, she opens and closes her eyes a few times. Behind her, in the darkness of the tunnel, she faintly sees a bull with large horns and human hands, yet on his back legs he has hooves like all cattle. And instead of a snout, he has a human mouth with fierce-looking fangs sticking out. On the woolly forehead his eyes glow red as fire. Deep in the tunnel she can see a tail, thick and long, suspended in the air like that of a lion. This is Imvuvu, the terrifying night creature, she realises, remembering the tales the old people of Phola tell. A creature, they say, that lives in the depths of a tunnel only.

"What do you want in my domain?" the Imvuvu demands in the deepest voice Nolitye has ever heard. A red tongue flits from side to side behind the terrible fangs.

"I got lost," she says, her voice quivering. "I'm looking for my way home."

"Unfortunately, I have to eat you because no one is allowed in here," the Imvuvu grunts.

"But you can't eat me! I'm skinny and I'm sure I won't taste nice." Nolitye shakes so much she can hardly get the words out.

The beast touches her arms with his hairy human hands to feel how much meat there is. Horror-stricken, Nolitye can hardly keep still, but she allows the beast with its large hands and long unkempt fingernails to fondle her arms.

"You will do. I haven't eaten in a month," the Imvuvu says, licking his lips. Then it reaches behind his back and takes out a huge panga.

Letting go of the fire torch, Nolitye screams and shuts her eyes. But before the Imvuvu can deliver its fatal blow, she feels a hand grabbing her fast and firm. She opens her eyes and looks behind her, but it is too dark to see properly. She gets pulled through a secret door which she has not seen before and which immediately closes behind her again. In the tunnel the Imvuvu roars with anger and disappointment and starts banging on the door. Fortunately, it sounds like a strong, thick door, but in having dropped the fire torch she cannot see who has saved her though she can hear someone rummaging in his pockets, searching for something. Somehow, she knows it is a man.

"Shhh," the stranger warns as Nolitye tries to regain her breath.

She hears the reassuring sound of a box of matches being shaken. There is a quick flick and a flame leaps to life. The stranger lights another torch and now Nolitye can see his face. She peers at him, taking a step closer. He stands silent, not saying a word. Memories flood into her head when she realises that she knows the man before her.

"Papa, is it really you?" she asks hesitantly.

"Nolitye," the man says, as if caressing her name. "It's me, Xoli, your father. I missed you, my bubu."

No one has ever called her that except him. She has never forgotten his pet name for her even though she was only five when he got killed. She puts out her arms and hugs him. Suddenly they are surrounded by bright light. She won't let go of him.

He spots the fine scratches on her arms and legs which she got from running through the forest. With one arm holding her, he takes out a handkerchief with the other and wipes away the dirt and small drops of blood.

"I'm fine, Papa. It's just a few scratches," she says, feeling happier than she has ever been. All her father does is hold her close to him.

"I must be dreaming," Nolitye says. "Dreams are doors to the future."

She takes in her father's strange words, and then asks, "Papa, why did you leave me and Mama?"

"Because I was careless. I'm sorry, my bubu."

A soft patter of feet comes towards them. Suddenly afraid that the Imvuvu might still be around, she shouts, "Who's there?"

A second stranger steps into the light. It is her mother, looking very real and lifelike!

"Mama!" She lets go of her father. "But how is it possible that you can walk into my dream?"

"Because sometimes dreams are more real than life."

"My bubu," her father says. The serious tone of his voice makes her turn and look at him. "There is something you must know."

Nolitye touches her mother's hand. It feels real. But so did her father. "You'll have to be a big girl though," her father cautions, "because this is going to be hard for you to understand." In reply, Nolitye takes her mother's hand.

"This is not only a dream. The woman in Phola who says she is your mother is not your real mother. She is a witch, an umthakathi, who has disguised herself as your mother."

"But how can that be, Papa?" Nolitye is completely confused and bewildered. She drops the hand she is holding as if it is a hot coal. But the woman not only takes her hand again, she also puts her arms around Nolitye and holds her tight. Though utterly confused, Nolitye becomes aware of a wonderfully consoling warmth spreading through her trembling body.

"You were probably too young to remember, but on the day of my accident this woman who says she is your mother didn't shed a single tear. That was the surest sign that she was not Thembi, your real mother, the one who is holding you now."

The woman gives her a gentle little squeeze, but she doesn't say anything. "Now listen carefully, my bubu," her father continues. "The witch who has disguised herself as your mother and MaMtonga are working together to steal your magic stone. They want to give it to Ncitjana."

"To Ncitjana?" Nolitye doesn't understand what her father is trying to tell her.

"Yes, to Ncitjana. Remember, he is the one whose ancestors stole the sacred stone and broke it into pieces? Well, Ncitjana may look like an ordinary man, but he is a very powerful umthakathi and for a long time he has been trying to get back the pieces of the stone. When I found this out, I tried to put a spell on him to kill him, because I knew he was an Evil One and that he might harm you one day. He was working with MaMtonga then already, and he knew that you had been born and that with a name like 'Keeper of the Stone' it would be your task one day to restore the sacred stone's original power by collecting all the different pieces."

Nolitye looks from her father to the woman who is holding her, still not understanding.

"You could not be told any of this before because you were too young to know the truth, my bubu. But now I can tell you. It was Ncitjana who made the mining accident happen, and it was on that day that the woman who says she is your mother turned herself into Thembi and started acting as if she was your mother."

"So my mother in Phola is a witch in disguise!" Nolitye starts trembling again. She thinks about all the times this woman got angry with her for no reason.

"Just like Four Eyes's aunt. Remember when MaMtonga pretended that she was his aunt and looked just like her? You couldn't tell them apart, could you? Remember when you suddenly remembered MaMtonga's name and she changed from being Aunt Vera and became her old, ugly self again?"

"Yes, Papa, I remember. But how do you know that?"

"Nomakhosi comes to see us with news about you, even though we are trapped."

"So you are real," Nolitye says, and loosens the woman's arms and steps aside to look at the two people who say they are her father and mother. She pinches herself, and still cannot be sure if she's dreaming.

"The day I had the mining accident MaMtonga and that woman, whose real name is of course not Thembi, trapped us here in the underworld."

Both her parents hug Nolitye. "What you have to do is find out what that woman's real name is," her mother, the real Thembi, whispers for the first time, and now Nolitye notices how much gentler her face is than that of the Thembi she knows.

Her father adds, "It is urgent, because now that you have found the magic stone, her attitude towards you will change more and more. Before you were just a harmless little girl, but now you have a powerful stone which they all desire, and she won't be so kind any more."

"And if I find her name, what will that do?"

"It will break the spell that makes it possible for her to pretend to be your mother."

"So they keep you in this horrible place with a spell?"

"Yes. We are not dead, just trapped in the underworld."

"But how did I get to be here with you and Mama?" she asks, stealing a glance at the soft-eyed Thembi at her side.

"Because I'm also a good witch, even though I'm a Renegade," her father says. "Now that you have the stone I can summon its powers to let you be here."

She looks at her mother for a response. Thembi only nods.

"But listen, my bubu. You must be strong and as soon as possible find out what that woman's real name is. You'll have to be very careful though because she's a Night Rider."

"A Night Rider?" Nolitye feels tired. She never imagined that there were so many different powers at work in the world, some good and some evil, some evil but in the guise of good.

"I know it is all very confusing," says her father kindly. "But just remember that a Night Rider is a witch who only operates in darkness. During the day she eats the sun and at night she roams the earth. You will never catch her out, because Night Riders are too quick. They can play with shadows and make you believe one thing when in fact it is another thing."

"Is MaMtonga also a Night Rider?"

"Yes, and unfortunately of the highest kind," her father says.

It is all too much for Nolitye to take in. She hangs her head with weariness. "I don't understand all this," she says, her voice almost too soft to hear.

"Don't worry, I know you will succeed, my bubu," her father says. "Now you must go before that woman who pretends to be your mother realises that we have stolen you for a while."

"I don't understand why she doesn't just take the stone, if that's what she really wants," Nolitye says.

"That stone is guarded by Nomakhosi with special powers. If that woman tries to touch it, she will get burnt. And she knows this."

"Burnt?"

"Yes, bubu," her father says gravely. "The only thing she can do is to plot with MaMtonga to try and steal it and give it to Ncitjana who knows how to work its powers."

The bracelet on her arm catches Nolitye's eye. "Papa, who gave me this bracelet, my real mother or that woman? And is it true that you wanted me to have it? Is that true, Papa?"

Nolitye feels someone shaking her. "Is that true?" she repeats.

"What are you saying, Nolitye?" Thembi is bending over her.

Nolitye opens and closes her eyes a few times. She was dreaming, she realises. She gets out of bed feeling heavy, a headache dulling her thoughts. "Last night I had a strange dream," she says, rubbing her eyes.

"What happened to 'Good morning'?" Thembi asks. Nolitye looks into her eyes. Her dream rushes back into her head. She turns away, shivering. How can she be sure it was a dream and not reality?

"Come now! It's getting late! School is starting in half an hour's time and I need to get going," Thembi says impatiently.

The hot water for washing is waiting on the Primus stove. Nolitye pours some into the orange dish. She washes quickly and puts on her uniform. Thembi doesn't say anything. She seems to be in a bad mood.

Pretending not to notice the silence, Nolitye picks up the hand mirror to see if her hair looks tidy. Stretching out her hand, she notices fine scratches on her right arm. She looks at her left arm. It is also covered with scratches. She gets such a fright that she drops the mirror. It shatters into a handful of glass slivers.

"What's wrong with you this morning?" Thembi yells. "That's seven years of bad luck and I have enough to worry about already, thank you!"

"Sorry," Nolitye whispers. Thembi ignores her.

Now Nolitye is convinced that the woman with her is not the real Thembi. She runs her fingers gently over her bracelet, not sure whether she should wear it or not. The dream stopped before her father could answer her question.

"Come on, we have to get going!" Thembi repeats impatiently. "But we haven't even eaten," Nolitye pleads.

"Then take two slices of bread. You can eat them on your way to school." Nolitye is taken aback, but when she remembers her father's wish for her to be strong she keeps quiet. After all, this woman might just be a fake. Nolitye looks at Thembi, trying to see if there is anything that may suggest that she is not her real mother.

"What are you staring at? What's wrong with you this morning?"

"Nothing." Nolitye quickly cuts two slices of bread. There is no time to spread it with peanut butter, and certainly no time for tea.

"Hurry up, wena!" Thembi clucks her tongue.

Nolitye grabs her school bag and slings it over her shoulder and slowly traipses out the door.

Thembi swings round angrily and pulls her by the scruff of her neck. "Leave me alone!"

"What is wrong with you this morning?" Thembi asks again, this time in a dangerously quiet voice.

"Nothing!"

"If your friends are filling your head with ideas about talking back to your mother, I'll stop you from seeing them. And you're not too old for a hiding."

Suddenly very angry, Nolitye says, "You won't dare touch me, because you're not my . . ." Just in time she bites back the words "real mother". It would only give away her suspicion about Thembi's true identity.

They are already out the door when Nolitye remembers the magic stone. "Please wait, I forgot my stone," she says, coming to her senses.

"Forget that silly stone," Thembi says harshly, stretching out an arm as if to hold back Nolitye.

"I need it. I'm writing my test today and it gives me good luck."

"Fine, you can fetch it using your spare key. I'm going to be late for the taxi. Goodbye!"

There is definitely something odd about Thembi's behaviour this morning, Nolitye thinks as she turns the key to go back into the shack. She is never this irritable in the morning.

She looks up at the sky when she returns with the stone. It is unexpectedly covered with a grey blanket of brooding clouds. Nolitye feels a tinge of fear. In the dream her father said that she was dealing with a Night Rider. Could it be that the woman who claims to be her mother has eaten the sun? She clutches the magic stone tighter in her hand. Again she wonders about the bracelet. Should she take it off or keep it on? No, she'll keep it on. Perhaps Papa really wanted me to have it, she tells herself. She locks the door and takes a short cut to Bheki's house.

True to form, Bheki is eating porridge when she arrives. If only he knew that she had to eat two slices of dry bread on her way here for breakfast! Nolitye thinks. Bheki's mother, under the impression that she's had a proper breakfast, offers her only a mug of tea. With her tea Nolitye swallows the lump of sadness in her throat as she watches Bheki's mother fussing over him. She has straightened his shirt collar and is now wiping some porridge from his face.

"I know you're hungry, son, but do you have to eat with your nose as well?" she teases him.

"Where's Khaya?" Nolitye asks to take her mind off everything.

"For a change he's sleeping," MaZwane says. "He went to bed very early yesterday evening. For once he seemed to be really tired."

"I wonder why?" Nolitye says and winks at Bheki.

"It's probably got something to do with the mess in the kitchen yesterday," his mother says, still sounding upset.

"Ma, I thought you said you'd forgotten about that," Bheki pleads. "I said I was sorry."

"You're right. My turn to say sorry! You two better get to school," MaZwane says, and sees them to the door. "Bheki, don't forget Papa's picking you up after school to help him do some shopping."

"Yes, Ma." He gives her a little peck on the cheek while Nolitye walks on ahead.

"You're not going to believe what I have to tell you," Nolitye says as they turn out of the short driveway.

"Don't tell me you lost the stone!"

"No."

"MaMtonga didn't steal it, did she?"

"No."

"Ncitjana?"

"Stop before it gets any scarier, Bheki."

"Then tell me!" Bheki says as he distractedly watches their neighbour, old MaMkize, sweep the yard, a small puppy running between her legs, barking and tugging at the broom. "Sawubona, Mama," he greets her.

She waves back. " Sanibonani, my children," she says.

Nolitye doesn't say anything until they are safely out of earshot. "I had this really weird dream," she begins.

"You and your dreams. I should have guessed. What was it this time? Giant cockroaches? Cows with wings?"

"Would you just shut up and listen to me?"

"Okay, fine. I'm listening." Bheki sends a stone flying down the street with a mighty kick.

"I dreamt of my father . . . I actually saw him and my mother."

"What do you mean, you saw them?"

"Bheki, I saw my real mother. The woman I'm living with isn't my real mother."

Bheki scratches his head and rubs his chin. "Nolitye, you're not making sense," he says carefully.

She sighs with frustration. "Okay," she says, rolling up her sleeves. "Look at this."

She shows him the scratches on her arms. "So?"

"So! So I didn't have these when I left you and Four Eyes yesterday."

"And your point is . . ."

"I was still making my point! I was clawing my way through this bush in my dream." She looks closely at the scratches. She still can't believe that she got them from running through a forest in a dream.

"Wait, you got these scratches in your dream?" Bheki says, his eyes big with surprise. "Holy snakes!"

"That's what I was trying to tell you."

Bheki touches the scratches. "Ouch! Careful, Bheki."

"Sorry. So if these scratches are so real . . . then . . ."

"Then it means the people I saw in my dream were really my parents." Bheki shakes his head. He can't think of anything to say.

"I know, I couldn't believe it either. Especially when I saw the Imvuvu."

"Imvuvu! You mean like a night creature?" Bheki can think of lots to say, but his voice comes out high and squeaky.

"Yes," Nolitye says. "And it's true what people say. It is enormously ugly and big and has huge fangs."

"So what did you do? And what did it do - try to eat you?" Bheki sounds a bit more normal.

"It tried, but my dad rescued me."

"That's about the most amazing thing I've ever heard." And again Bheki is at a loss for words.

Nolitye too goes quiet as she tries to recall her father as he was in the dream.

"So what are you going to do?" Bheki asks after a while.

"Well, first I have to find out what this woman's real name is. My dad said it would break the spell that makes her look like my mother and that it will turn her back into her true self."

"You mean that's just a disguise?" Nolitye nods.

"Freaky," Bheki says. "I can't believe your mother is not your real mother."

"Me too. I'm just glad that now I know why my mother, I mean the other woman, is so nasty at times."

"So where're your real mom and your dad then?"

Nolitye sighs. It is not going to be easy to explain everything to Bheki, yet this is exactly what she does, all the way to school.

Chapter Nine

FIRE!

FOR once Nolitye and Bheki do not meet Rotten Nellie and the Spoilers on their way to school. Instead, Four Eyes is waiting for them at the school gates. Even though he got up early to study, he is worried about the Maths test they have to write. Moeder punishes anyone who fails their Maths test, and there's no way of getting out of writing her tests. Even if you're sick.

"At least now I can study and not feel like a cheese boy," he says.

"Why would you feel like a cheese boy if you study?" Bheki asks.

"You don't know Rotten Nellie. She calls you names if you study."

"That's the most ridiculous thing I've ever heard."

"You know why we haven't seen Rotten Nellie?" Four Eyes says. "Probably because she is bunking class to avoid the test."

Class is about to begin. Everybody settles into their seats and Bheki sits down next to Nolitye.

"Alright, children. I'll be handing out the question papers now. Remember, write in pencil so that you can rub out if you have to," Moeder says.

Just as she hands out the first paper the Spoilers walk through the door. It is an odd sight as all three have blood-soaked bandages somewhere on their right side: S'bu around his right wrist, Thabo around his right elbow, and Rotten Nellie's round her right arm, from her hand to her shoulder. Rotten Nellie moans a little and pulls a pained face.

"What happened to you three?" Moeder asks.

They all speak at once, grumbling under their breaths. It is difficult to hear what they say, but it sounds as if they were involved in a car accident.

"But I thought your parents don't have a car, Nellie?" Moeder says.

Nellie thinks for few seconds and then says, "Uhm . . . you see, Ma'am, it was my uncle's car."

"And you all injured your right arms in this accident?"

"I know, Ma'am, it was freaky," Rotten Nellie admits. The three look at each other, and Nolitye takes a proper look at them. The bandages are all sloppily put on.

"May I see your arm, Nellie?" Moeder asks.

Rotten Nellie moans before Moeder even touches her. Moeder catches Thabo off-guard when she unexpectedly grabs him by his right elbow. He forgets to act as though he is in pain and only moans when Moeder is already walking to S'bu's desk. It doesn't fool anyone, and, very angry now, Moeder gingerly touches the blood that has soaked through S'bu's bandage. She sniffs at the red liquid on her forefinger.

"Tomato sauce!" she explodes. "How dare you! That's it! All three of you are going to write this test right now and afterwards you're getting detention!"

The class cheers. Rotten Nellie looks miserable and when Moeder isn't looking she hits Thabo on the back of the head. When the commotion dies down Moeder finally hands out the test papers. As punishment, she does not allow the Spoilers to remove the bandages from their fake wounds.

Bheki can't help grinning every time he looks at S'bu, because the poor guy is forever scratching his head with his bandaged hand, and Thabo looks like he can't hold his pencil properly.

As for Four Eyes, he's only too glad to be rid of the Spoilers. He hated each time he had to fail a test on purpose just to fit in with them.

Nolitye writes fast and furiously. She loves Maths. She wishes everything was as simple as Maths. She didn't have time to study over the weekend and still she can work out all the answers. Which she can't say about any of the other questions and doubts she has.

Halfway through the period Moeder tells the class that she is quickly stepping out to the staffroom to get a book. "Please keep quiet, everyone," she asks, "and carry on with your test."

As soon as she leaves, however, trouble starts. Rotten Nellie, as usual, instructs the boy in the desk next to her to show her his answers. The boy tries to resist, but it is useless because Rotten Nellie is much bigger than he and simply takes his book by force. Soon Thabo and S'bu follow her example and bully the children next to them into showing them their answers.

Nolitye can't concentrate on the test questions because of the disturbance.

She stops writing and watches what is happening. All of a sudden she gets angry. So angry that she decides to teach the three Spoilers a lesson. She quietly takes the magic stone out of her shirt pocket and asks Bheki to take her hand. And then she wishes that the Spoilers would croak like frogs each time they look at someone else's answer.

That is exactly what happens and it gets worse as time passes. Each time Rotten Nellie or Thabo or S'bu tries to copy an answer, she or he starts to croak. At first everyone thinks the Spoilers are just trying to be funny, but when they see the panic on their faces they realise that they can't control themselves.

"Arrk, arrk. Ribbit! Ribbit!" Rotten Nellie tries to cover her mouth to stop the sound, but she can't. And she has the loudest croak because her voice is the deepest. It is not long before Thabo and S'bu start hopping around the room like frogs. The class falls about laughing.

When Moeder walks into the room the class try their best to suppress their giggles and laughter, but she senses something is not right. Then she notices Thabo and S'bu hopping around the room. She sees how distressed they look and bangs her book on her desk. "Silence!" she shouts. "The test is cancelled and will be written again tomorrow. But it will be a different test. In fact, there will be two tests: Maths and Spelling!"

Everyone in the class moans.

"What are you moaning about? If you're not careful . . ." Moeder takes out her cane. But the Spoilers can't help themselves; they continue croaking like frogs. "Arrk, arrk. Ribbit! Ribbit!"

"Will you three keep quiet before I give the class another test?" Moeder shouts.

But they can't help themselves. "Arrk, arrk. Ribbit! Ribbit!"

Moeder is ready to throttle Rotten Nellie who is making the most noise when Nolitye takes Bheki's hand and makes another wish to reverse the spell. She does it so discreetly that no one notices.

It works! The Spoilers stop croaking and Moeder's frown fades from her face. In a pleasant voice she says, "Well, perhaps it isn't necessary to write another test after all. I think you have all learned a lesson . . ."

After school Bheki's father picks him up in his bakkie and they go to town. Her school bag on her back, Nolitye goes to the library next to the headmistress's office. It is housed in a small room and there aren't that many books. The school depends on book donations mostly. It is always nice and quiet in the library, with no shouting, loud talking, music or traffic noise. Nolitye finds the silence calming, like the atmosphere in a church.

A few other children are already sitting at the tables doing homework; the librarian is reading a newspaper at her desk. "Please, Ma'am, can you help me find a book on shells?" Nolitye asks her.

"Shells?" Miss Kunene says, rubbing her nose.

"Yes, like these kinds of shells." Nolitye shows the librarian her bracelet.

"That would be cowrie shells," she says, putting the newspaper aside.

"And I don't think we have any books on those." Nolitye is disappointed. "Are you sure?"

"Sweetie, trust me, we don't have anything on shells."

"Okay, I'll just look around," Nolitye says, but the librarian has already gone back to reading her newspaper and hardly hears what she says.

Nolitye wanders through the few rows of books, not quite sure what she's looking for now that she knows there's no book on shells and she doesn't feel like using the encyclopedia. She stops in front of the small window in the furthest corner and stares out onto the playground. *If only I knew what to do with this bracelet,* she ponders to herself.

As if in response to her question, a book falls from the top shelf, hits her on the head and lands on the floor. Nolitye peers round the bookshelf to see if there is someone on the other side. There is no one. The librarian is still sitting at her desk, engrossed in the newspaper, and the other children are quietly doing their homework. *Odd,* Nolitye thinks, picking up the book. It is old and dusty with a grey jacket. She looks at the spine and notices that the book doesn't have a number like all the other books. In fact, it doesn't even have a title.

She opens the book. On the first page she finds a small inscription written in faded ink near the bottom. *The road is long and interesting,* the inscription says.

She turns to the next page. Nolitye starts reading the single short paragraph: *the journey starts with a single step. But you have to be curious to read on. Yes, you reader, standing there looking lost. But it is no surprise that you are reading these words.*

Nolitye looks around her, surprised that the book should speak to her so directly. She carefully turns another page: *You are wondering about something, which is why you are reading this book.*

One of the children gets up from the table, walks over and reaches for a book near Nolitye. She stops reading and looks at him suspiciously. But the boy hardly takes notice of her. He removes a large book from the bookshelf and returns to the table. Nolitye turns back to the small window and, hidden from everyone by the rack of books, she reads on: *This is the Book of Questions and Answers. But you already know what you want to ask, which is why you are reading. In fact, the truth is that you already know the answer to your question you just have to listen to yourself.*

Listen to myself? Nolitye thinks. What does that mean? She carries on reading: *If you listen well enough, you will hear a voice trying to tell you something. It is your own voice, instinct if you like. A feeling that won't go away.*

Nolitye thinks about what she has just read. She looks at her bracelet. She can't shake off the feeling that she feels uncomfortable wearing it. If only her father had told her what to do with it.

Feelings are like doors, she reads. *They can open up new worlds and show us things we do not ordinarily see, such as the mysteries that surround us. The shells you are wearing around your wrist are full of mystery.*

Nolitye drops the book she is so shaken by the last sentence. She looks around her again, but no one is watching her. For a while she stares at the book on the floor. Could the magic stone have anything to do with the book, she wonders. Since she found the stone everything has become strange, out of the ordinary, like an ever-changing story that never ends. Could MaMtonga's witchcraft have anything to do with the book? She bends down cautiously and carefully picks it up again.

But before she can open the book again, Miss Kunene rings a tiny bell and says, "Okay, children, I'm closing in five minutes." The other kids start shuffling in their chairs as they pack their books away. Nolitye turns back to the page she was reading: *It is said that once upon a time shells were used as money, but before that they were used by ancient magicians and witches to cast spells.*

Someone taps her on the shoulder and she nearly drops the book again.

"I'm sorry, I didn't mean to scare you," the librarian says. "I just need to put away all the books."

"It's fine," Nolitye says. She reluctantly hands the librarian the book. Miss Kunene looks at it quizzically when she sees that it doesn't have a title or a number on the spine.

"Where did you find it?"

"Uhm . . . actually . . . it was just lying on the floor," Nolitye says.

"Strange . . . Probably a donation that slipped my attention."

"May I take it home?" Nolitye asks.

"Not now, sweetie. I first have to register it and give it a Dewey number. You can come back tomorrow, though. I'm closing up now."

The librarian walks over to the window with the book and closes the curtain. Nolitye fervently wishes she could finish reading the book. Full of frustration she watches the librarian go back to her desk and put the book in the tray. The other children file out. Nolitye soon follows.

A light breeze is blowing outside. On the playground a small whirlwind gathers dust in a dancing spiral. Nolitye watches it and can't help thinking about what she has read. What spell is Thembi trying to cast on her with the bracelet, she wonders. Yet she can't bring herself to take the bracelet off. She is too curious and wants to see what happens if she keeps it on.

She takes a short cut home by walking across a piece of open veld. Just as she turns into a narrow alley leading to MaMokoena's spaza shop, she spots Rex and his pack huddled together in a corner. "What's up, guys?" she calls to them.

Rex growls but relaxes when he sees who it is. She goes closer. The dogs are protecting a small moving bundle.

Nolitye bends down to take a closer look. "This is the cutest thing I've ever seen," she coos at the three tiny brown puppies, still with their eyes closed, wriggling to lie one on top of the other.

"Ticks spotted them this afternoon," Rex says. "We think their mother has abandoned them." He gently licks the helpless little puppies with a long pink tongue.

"I didn't think dogs abandoned babies."

"You think only people do?" Whiskers yelps in a squeaky voice. "You'll be surprised."

Nolitye keeps quiet and watches Rex licking the brown squiggling mass. "Guys, we better move them, otherwise they won't survive the night," he says.

"Where will you take them?"

"To one of Shorty's girlfriends," Ticks says, pointing his snout at their handsome long-haired companion.

"What can I say? Bitches love me," Shorty snorts. Turning to Ticks he says, "You know, maybe if you stopped scratching yourself and had a dip in the river I might fix you up with a nice lady."

"And be a pet? No thank you. I'm a street dog and that's how I like it. If the women don't, then tough luck."

Rex picks up a puppy in his mouth and trots on ahead. Shorty picks up the next one, and Ticks stops scratching and follows with the last puppy.

Nolitye watches them disappear round a corner. She would have loved to take one of the puppies. She would have called him Lucky, like she has always wanted to do. But after last night's dream she dares not. Not until she's sure whom she is living with will she be able to ask permission.

Near the clinic Ntate Matthews comes ambling down the road with a spring in his step. He's dressed smartly and seems to be in a good mood.

"Dumela, Ntate Matthews," Nolitye greets him.

"And a fine day it is," he says. "I've just won three games of morabaraba. And you know what that means?"

Nolitye shakes her head.

"It means with my good winnings under my pillow I will sleep peacefully tonight." He goes on his way again.

Nolitye walks cautiously past MaMtonga's home, but her door is still shut and the curtains drawn. At home she remembers that she didn't put the magic stone in the sun today because she didn't go to Bheki's house after school. So she puts it in the bucket with her other stones, takes off her gym and starts doing her chores. First she washes some dirty socks, her school shirt, the sheets and two pillow cases and hangs them on the washing line, then she sweeps the floor. Finally she settles down to do her homework. It is still warm, so she leaves the window open.

When Thembi gets back just after sunset, Nolitye is already ironing the things she washed. Thembi is still in a foul mood. She grunts at Nolitye rather than greeting her properly and shoves her merchandise in the corner.

"How was your day, Mama?" Nolitye asks, surprised at the sudden dryness of her mouth.

Thembi just clucks her tongue, mumbles an okay, bangs a plastic bag down on the table and takes out a loaf of bread and a tin of beans. Nolitye stops ironing and gets supper ready, slicing the bread and warming up the beans. They eat without talking, their eyes hardly meeting.

While Nolitye is heating the kettle to wash the dishes, a loud shriek shatters the silence. "Fire! Fire!" someone yells. Soon people are banging on doors, repeating, "Fire! Fire!"

"Nolitye, quickly! Get all our stuff," Thembi shouts. She reaches for their two suitcases on top of the wardrobe and drops them on the floor. Nolitye flings open the wardrobe and starts throwing their belongings into the suitcases. Fire is a common occurrence in Phola. Every so often a shelter catches fire because a Primus stove tips over by accident, or a burning candle sets a tablecloth or curtain alight. And once one shack catches fire, the rest are also in danger as fire spreads quickly between the tightly-packed shanties. Everybody knows what to do when they hear "Fire! Fire" - save their clothing and bedding first.

"My stones," Nolitye says, reaching under the bed as Thembi pulls off the blankets and sheets.

"Forget your stones!" her mother yells. "Pack!"

Nolitye abandons the bucket of stones but hastily slips the magic stone into the little patchwork bag, which she now keeps with her stones, and slips it round her neck. Thembi seizes the Praying Hands and their clock, and chucks the condensed-milk tin with the money into an already full suitcase.

With their meagre belongings stuffed into the two suitcases, they open the door. A swarm of people are running past with buckets of water. They cough and cover their faces with wet towels or clothes as thick smoke fills the air.

Thembi drops the suitcase inside the door and runs fill a bucket of water. The fire rages about six shacks to the left of them and has already consumed three shanties. Most of their neighbours stand around powerlessly, holding on to mattresses, radios and whatever they had managed to salvage, while a line of men work efficiently, passing buckets of water between them. Children operate the six public taps, while some women are scurrying away from the fire with odd bits of furniture and other possessions.

With everyone working together, the fire is eventually extinguished. But six families are homeless and a cloud of smoke hangs above Phola, soot settling on everything and everyone.

In the commotion a woman has lost her youngest son. She starts panicking. Everyone is jittery about children disappearing. She grabs Nolitye who is nearest to her by the shoulders. "Where's my son?" she demands.

Looking around for the boy, Nolitye says, "I don't know, Mama. He was with us at the taps just now."

"But where is he now?"

"I don't know where he is."

"What do you mean, you don't know where he is?" The woman starts shaking Nolitye violently.

"What's the problem?" Ntate Matthews says, stepping closer. The woman takes control of herself and lets go of Nolitye.

"I don't know where my Lundi is," she says and starts sobbing.

"It's okay, we'll find him," Ntate Matthews says. He instructs the boys and men to look for the boy. Before he joins the search, he pats Nolitye on the back. "Good girl," he praises her.

"Lundi! Lundi!" everyone shouts, while the crying mother is consoled by some women.

"Why's everyone shouting? I'm here," a wide-eyed boy says, struggling out of the shadows with an old blanket in his arms.

His mother tears herself free and runs to him. "Be careful," the young boy says as she tries to hug him. He bends down and puts the blanket on the ground. "I found them at the back of the shelters. They would've burnt to death," he says, stroking the three small brown puppies.

They are the same puppies Nolitye earlier saw Rex and his pack carry to safety!

"Don't ever disappear like that again without saying a word," Lundi's mother scolds him, but she holds him close. "We'll have to find a home for the puppies," she says, eyeing the little creatures. "Maybe the SPCA . . ."

Everyone is relieved that Lundi has been found and that he did not disappear like Mbali, and Sara before her. But soon a woman who lost her house in the fire realises that her son has gone missing too. An older boy who helped to look for Lundi runs and calls Ntate Matthews back, and Ntate Matthews organises another search. Again the men and boys go all over the neighbourhood looking for the boy, shouting his name, "Vusi! Vusi!"

The boy is nowhere to be found. The men and boys return with empty looks on their faces; they shrug their shoulders and throw their hands in the air. By the time all the people who have lost their homes have been put up by friends or family, the search is called off. In the chaos of trying to extinguish the fire, another child has been stolen.

"Come on, Nolitye, let's go home," Thembi says to Nolitye, who has tried to help by just hanging around the frantic mother.

"Mama, they say the Zim and Ncitjana stole Vusi." There is fear in Nolitye's voice. "They say it was them who started the fire in the first place!"

"What nonsense! It's not our problem. Come on!" Thembi pulls Nolitye by the elbow. Nolitye, overcome with uncertainty about who the woman who says she is her mother really is, hangs back. She doesn't feel safe at home any more.

"Don't make me hit you in front of all these people," Thembi threatens, holding her firmly by the arm. "I don't know what has gotten into that little head of yours lately. Now move!"

Nolitye unwillingly turns her back on the weeping mother and walks home with Thembi. Thembi slams the door shut behind them and puts their water bucket back in the cooking corner. "Take these things out of the suitcases and put them back in the cupboard," she orders. "And if you ever again go against my instructions in public, I'll tan your bum so you can't sit for a week."

Nolitye does as she is told, convinced that this Thembi is not her mother. When Thembi takes out her washing rag and wipes the soot and ash from her face, Nolitye watches her closely. But she gives up. If this woman uses strong magic to assume the identity of her real mother, she would not be able to see the difference between them, she realises. Yet she remembers a gentleness in the face of the Thembi in her dream.

"Stop staring. Put away my blouses. And not like that, they'll crease." Nolitye grits her teeth and swallows the lump in her throat and neatly puts everything back in their place. She tells herself that things will not always be like this, that soon something will happen so that she will always be with her real mother.

When Nolitye gets into bed, she lies with her back to Thembi. She doesn't snuggle up and put her arms around her like she usually does.

Chapter Ten
THE TEST

ALMOST three weeks go by, and Nolitye becomes used to the power of the stone. She learns to leave it out in the sun, but not while little Khaya is around. There is no way she is going to allow the little-giant mistake again. She learns not to play with the stone for fun, for she has discovered that for every naughty thing she does, such as making the Spoilers croak like frogs, she has to do a good deed, such as heeding an inner voice calling on her to help an old lady across the street. The good must cancel out the bad, she learns; also a balance between good and bad is part of the responsibility that comes with having the stone. She begins to see that she is a Renegade, having to walk the fine line between doing good and being naughty. She spends a lot of time with Bheki and Four Eyes. By the end of the first week, Four Eyes has become close to them, hanging out with them during break, and after school drinking juice and playing cards with them at the bottom of Bheki's garden.

At night Nolitye wishes she could dream about her parents again, but it never happens. Instead, she becomes more and more suspicious of Thembi. She tries to act as if nothing has changed, but she keeps a constant eye on Thembi. She has found out that Thembi says one thing and does another. On her way to fetch water from the communal tap one evening, Nolitye catches her talking to MaMtonga. As she passes MaMtonga's door with the water bucket, she hears soft whispering. The door is ajar. Nolitye sneaks a peek. And there, as clear as day, she sees Thembi sitting on the bed listening to MaMtonga, while MaMtonga is caressing the green-and-brown snake.

"I'm telling you, MaMtonga," Thembi says, "she's got to recover more stones before the sacred stone can be whole again."

"You better watch her!" MaMtonga hisses.

"And you better stop trying to steal the stone from her, MaMtonga. The easiest thing would be to steal the stone from her once she's found all the pieces."

MaMtonga shakes her bald head with the few tufts of hair. "But what you don't understand is that each stone has its own power, and who says that little brat is going to find them all?"

"You don't know Nolitye," Thembi says. "She's a very determined girl." MaMtonga sniffs the air.

"What's wrong?"

"I smell young flesh. Who's at the door?"

Nolitye hugs the bucket to her chest so that the handle doesn't make a noise and quickly slips round the corner to hide behind the shack. And as luck would have it - or was it luck? - a stray cat walks past the door just as Thembi looks out of the door to see if there is someone.

"It was only a silly cat." Thembi sounds relieved that no one has been listening, but Nolitye has heard all she needed to.

One Thursday, in the middle of class, Nomakhosi enters the room in a rustling reed skirt. As usual, time suddenly slows down. Moeder's hand, writing on the blackboard, slows down until it stalls, pressing the chalk onto the board. Rotten Nellie freezes with an ugly scowl on her face because she was pulling a face at Four Eyes. The other children stiffen in all sorts of positions. One boy has his finger up his nose; another has his hand in the air to ask Moeder a question. All shuffling has stopped.

Nomakhosi tells Nolitye it's time to collect the third stone. The magician, who is coming to school that afternoon to entertain them with a magic show, will have the stone.

Nolitye feels a little anxious, but there is no time to tell Nomakhosi because she vanishes as unexpectedly as she arrived.

After class the whole school gathers in the hall. Everyone sits on the floor. Usually the headmistress has to tell them to be quiet, but today there is no fidgeting. The only sound is the rumbling of Bheki's stomach; he hasn't eaten anything since break. Suddenly loud drumbeats roll from somewhere and a hand in a white glove peaks out between the drops of the deep red curtains on the stage. The children gasp with excitement. They follow the hand dancing between curtains. Most have never seen a magician before and don't know to whom this curious hand belongs. The music reaches fever pitch. A leg clad in black pants pushes a black pointy shoe through the opening in the curtains.

Without warning, a cracker goes off, exploding in a cloud of smoke. Some children cry out, others giggle nervously. Soon it is quiet again.

Then the curtains are flung open and a tall man in a top hat and long trench coat steps to the front, holding a walking stick. He stands still while the smoke cloud clears. The children clap wildly and cheer. The tall man bows to them. He puts a finger to his lips. A hush fills the room as everyone watches, wide-eyed with suspense. Even Rotten Nellie, who usually looks bored, watches with interest.

"I'm Monna the Magician." And the tall man grandly stretches out both arms.

"But you look like a gangster!" Rotten Nellie yells. The hall erupts in laughter.

"If you're not careful I'll turn you into a frog," the magician says, pointing his walking stick at Rotten Nellie. The smile disappears from Rotten Nellie's face and the rest of the audience falls silent. Everyone remembers how the Spoilers started croaking like frogs not so long ago. It is so quiet that the magician's footsteps can be heard as he crosses the stage. From behind the curtains he pulls out a large red box on wheels, which he pushes to the middle of the stage, where he parks it next to a table, the only other prop. The magician taps the red box with his walking stick and whoops! the top pops open.

With his white-gloved hand, Monna the Magician takes a silver bucket from the box and turns it up and down and sideways until everyone is satisfied that it is empty. Even the teachers are now standing along the walls, watching the spectacle.

"Nogwatsha, the Clever One, is always up to mischief, but today I have him," the magician says, standing the bucket on the table. "Do you want to see Nogwatsha?"

The children all nod.

"No, you don't want to see him." Monna shakes his head. "I'll just put this bucket away," he says, lifting it off the table.

"No! No!" the children all shout at once, pleading to see Nogwatsha. "I said, do you want to see Nogwatsha?" Monna repeats.

"Yes!" a loud chorus insists. A little girl jumps up and down with excitement until her friends pull her down on the floor.

"Well then, come out from wherever you are, Nogwatsha!" Monna taps the bucket with his walking stick. Then he puts his hand in the bucket. He seems to struggle with something.

The children all jump up to try and see what's going on.

"Sit down!" the teachers order. They reluctantly sit down again, some of them remaining upright on their knees.

"Here's Nogwatsha!" And Monna pulls a white rabbit from the empty bucket.

The children cheer, all jumping up again and clapping. They looked completely baffled and start whispering.

"Sit down, or I'll pull out a crocodile!"

The children immediately flop down on the floor.

"Bim sala bim!" Monna says and does a quick hand turn and flings Nogwatsha at the children. The hall echoes with screams. But it is not Nogwatsha who lands on them; it is a cloud of confetti. The little paper flecks drift down on them, clinging to their hair and clothes. The children clap and laugh at each other for having screamed.

The magician does some more magic tricks; he turns a silk scarf into a pack of cards and makes two silver rings disappear. But Nolitye hardly notices. All she can think about is how she will get the next stone from him, and when everyone goes home after the show, she asks Bheki and Four Eyes to go with her to meet him. Shyly they climb up onto the stage. Nolitye puts out her hand and introduces herself.

"I know who you are," the magician says, taking off his top hat. His head is bald and shines like a polished stone.

Nolitye pretends not to be surprised. "These are my two friends, Bheki and Four Eyes," she says and pushes the boys forward. "Say something!" she hisses.

"What happened to Nogwatsha?" Four Eyes asks.

"He's probably up to his tricks again." Monna gives him a bright smile and says to Nolitye, "I guess you are here to get the gift."

"The gift?"

"Yes, the gift."

"You mean . . . the stone?"

"Yes, little Keeper of the Stone. It's a precious gift from the ancestors. I've hidden it somewhere and it's up to you to find it. Think of it as a little test."

"But Nomakhosi said nothing about a test."

Bheki and Four Eyes look at each other and then at Nolitye. They don't know who she is talking about.

"That's because she's not the one who has the stone. I've been guarding this stone for years and years and there's no way that I'm just going to give it up like that. I have to be sure that you will look after it."

Nolitye sighs so despondently that Monna the Magician looks deep into her eyes. "Okay, I'll help you," he promises. "If you go to the soccer field you'll find some molehills. The stone is hidden in one of these mounds. But which one is the question!"

Nolitye wants to protest that she has to go home and do her chores, but Monna has already turned his back. He leaves, loud footsteps and the sound of rolling wheels fading away down the corridor.

"Whew!" Bheki whistles, his shoulders already drooping. "The soccer field is covered with hundreds of molehills!"

Nolitye realises that they are in for a challenge, and the best way to meet a challenge is with a little help from the magic stone. She looks around to make sure that nobody except Bheki and Four Eyes are watching before she takes the stone from the breast pocket of her gym dress where she now constantly carries it during the day.

The strange tingly feeling that comes with touching the stone washes over her. She rubs it gently, holding it to her face. "What should we do to find the other stone?" she whispers. She waits a moment, but the stone remains quiet.

Four Eyes watches curiously. He has heard so much about the stone but he has never seen its power in action. Nolitye looks at the other two and shrugs. She puts the stone back in her pocket.

"Don't worry, we'll help you find it," Four Eyes promises.

They leave the hall. The school is deserted except for the school caretaker who is spearing the empty chip packets and ice-cream wrappers in the quadrangle with his spike.

They make straight for the soccer field near the station. Nolitye throws her hands in the air when she sees the many small molehills scattered all over the field.

"Don't give up, this could be fun, you know," Four Eyes consoles her.

She looks around and takes a deep breath. It is hot, with the sun beating down from a cloudless sky. They dump their school bags at the base of the nearest goalpost and roll up their sleeves. Nolitye tells herself that her chores will have to wait, no matter what Thembi will say.

"Let's split the field into three," she says. "I'll cover this side and you guys do the rest."

Bheki and Four Eyes walk to the other side of the field. They startle a hadeda that flies up with a flutter, squawking loudly.

There is no other way to go about finding the stone than getting down on their knees and sifting through the mounds with their hands. Four Eyes is enjoying himself. He doesn't mind getting dirt under his nails, but Bheki winces every time he has to stick his hands in the loose, warm soil.

Nolitye digs quickly like a rabbit burrowing a hole. Her cowrie shell bracelet gets dirty but she doesn't take it off. She begins to work up a sweat and has to wipe her brow with the back of her hand to keep the perspiration out of her eyes. But she keeps going.

Bheki works slowly, obviously afraid of touching any wriggly objects. Unnoticed, Four Eyes sneaks up on him and stuffs a cricket down his shirt. "Take it out, take it out!" Bheki screams, jumping up and down as though his shorts were on fire. He runs around the field wriggling and screaming like a crazy bull. Four Eyes folds double with laughter when Bheki eventually furiously unbuttons his shirt. The poor cricket falls on the ground and crawls in under some loose earth.

"That wasn't funny," Bheki complains.

"You should have seen yourself. Screaming like a girl," Four Eyes laughs.

"We don't have the whole day," Nolitye tells them, hands on her hips. They all go back to digging, with Bheki keeping a wary eye on Four Eyes. They have gone through about half the mounds when Nolitye starts worrying. What if Monna didn't put the stone in one of the mounds? What if he was just playing the fool? She notices how dirty her gym dress is, but she couldn't care less, not even at the thought that Thembi might be angry because she messed up her uniform as well as not doing her chores. She moves on to the next molehill.

"Guys, I think I got it!" Four Eyes suddenly shouts, holding up a stone. Nolitye and Bheki run over to him. Four Eyes is proudly cleaning the stone on his shirtsleeve.

Bheki is the first to reach him. "That's just a piece of ordinary granite," he says. "We're looking for a crystal." Since Nolitye told him about the encyclopedia he has visited the school library a few times to read up on stones.

"Where is it?" Nolitye asks when she catches up.

"Sorry, false alarm." Bheki hands her the stone.

"Nice try, Four Eyes," she says and chucks it away.

They go back to their digging. After another hour or so, Bheki calls Four Eyes and they walk over to Nolitye who seems to be just short of pulling out her dreads. "What are you doing here? You should be digging," she scolds them while she carries on sifting through a heap of sand.

"Listen, I've got a plan," Bheki says, wiping his hands on his shorts. "Ooh, my mother is going to kill me," he says when he looks at his soiled shirt.

"And my dad is going to eat me for supper," Four Eyes says, pushing back his dust-clouded spectacles.

"Sorry guys." Nolitye is close to tears.

"I know you tried asking the Spirit of the Stone to help us and it didn't work. But what if you just took out the stone and walked around the mounds with it? Maybe it'll give us a sign."

"That's a stupid idea," Four Eyes says.

Bheki gives him a superior look. "You don't have a clue how powerful the stone is."

"He's right, Four Eyes. It's worth a try." Nolitye gets up, dusting the dirt from her hands and shaking out her hair. They make sure that no one is around before Nolitye takes out the stone. It glistens in the sun, sending a thrilling feeling through her. She crouches and holds the stone above the next mound on her side. She moves her hand in a circle. Bheki and Four Eyes watch anxiously. Nothing happens, so she moves on to the next mound. This time she takes her time and makes the circular movement very slowly. Still nothing happens. So she moves to the next mound. And the next one. She goes through five mounds, but nothing happens.

"Well?" Bheki asks.

Nolitye shakes her head. "Let's go to the other side of the field where you guys were looking," she suggests.

She holds the stone above a mound near the goalposts.

Four Eyes looks on with a bored expression. "Do you really need this other stone?"

"Yes!" Nolitye and Bheki both yell at him. "Okay, don't bite my head off."

But Nolitye too feels discouraged.

"Here let me try," Bheki suggests. She hands him the stone. Bheki giggles softly and looks around before he randomly picks a mound near the corner of the field. He walks over and places the stone on top of the mound and watches it. Nothing happens. Crouching like a frog about to jump, he moves to the next mound and again puts the stone on its top. A big red ant walks over the stone, but nothing else happens.

"You try, Nolitye," Bheki says and hands the stone back.

Clutching the stone to her heart, Nolitye walks to the other side of the field, Bheki and Four Eyes traipsing behind.

"Come stone, don't let me down," she whispers before placing the stone on top of a mound that looks bigger than the rest.

"Look! Look!" Bheki says, rushing closer and pointing to the mound. The stone is moving by itself and it looks as if the soil is boiling up from underneath the surface.

"This must be it!" Nolitye says excitedly. She picks up the magic stone, rubs it clean and puts it back in her breast pocket. The three flop down on their knees and eagerly start sifting through the soil. Nolitye uncovers a stone the size of a big hailstone. It is encrusted in dry mud. She can hardly breathe. "I've got it!" she whispers. Very carefully she chips off the dirt.

"Let's just be sure," Bheki says.

When Nolitye has removed all of the dry soil, a blue-and-purple crystal glistens in the sunlight. With the stone firmly clutched in her hand, she throws her arms around Four Eyes and Bheki, and gives them a hug almost as strong as one of Bheki's mother's hugs. The three look at each other and start cheering. They leap up in the air, laughing and shouting.

From nowhere a cloud moves over and covers the sun. Nolitye shivers a bit but she is too pleased to have found the third stone to pay any notice to the weather. They grab their school bags and walk to the nearest tap at the station. While the other two keep watch, Nolitye washes the stone. It doesn't make her tingle like the main stone in her breast pocket, but it sparkles with the same purplish-blue light. It is truly magnificent to look at.

"May I hold it?" Four Eyes says. He takes off his smudgy glasses and inspects the stone closely. Then he passes it to Bheki who also marvels at it. Nolitye pulls her school bag closer and carefully puts the stone inside a side- pocket.

They walk to Bheki's house with smiles the size of a new moon on their faces.

"My goodness, you look like you crawled out of the earth!" Bheki's mother says when she sees them.

"Ma, we uhm . . . we had a mud fight."

"That's it, young man. Today you wash your own shirt and shorts," MaZwane says, folding her arms. She goes to the sink and hands Bheki a box of washing powder. Bheki looks at the Omo and then at his friends.

"Ma, can I do it later? Please," he pleads. MaZwane looks at her son and then at Nolitye and Four Eyes.

"Okay, but you're not getting any supper until you've done it."

Bheki nods. He hates lying to his mother but there was nothing he could do. A secret is a secret and he made a promise to Nolitye. They walk down to the bottom of the garden. A slightly nippy wind has come up and blown the cloud away; there is a tinge of autumn in the air.

In the last rays of the sun, Nolitye takes the main stone from her breast pocket and puts it on the grass. She opens her school bag and takes out the stone they have just found. Four Eyes and Bheki lean forward to watch as Nolitye puts the stones next to each other.

They shimmer with the same dull light.

Nolitye, Four Eyes and Bheki watch excitedly as the two stones move towards each other like magnets. When they come together, a small spark jumps into the air and grows into a halo of purplish-blue light.

The two stones have melded together. "That's the best magic trick I've ever seen," Four Eyes marvels.

"I'll say. Better than watching Nogwatsha coming out of that bucket," Bheki adds.

Nolitye picks up the stone and weighs it in her hand. "Soon it will be too big to put even in my gym's breast pocket," she says. She gets the giggles and quickly puts the stone down on the grass. "Tomorrow we are going on an adventure," she announces solemnly.

"Oh, oh, this sounds like trouble to me!" says Bheki.

"Come on, Bheki, you know that we have to find out what that woman's real name is. I now know for certain she's not my mother."

Four Eyes's face clearly shows he's in the dark, so they tell him about their suspicion that Nolitye's mother is a Night Rider, pretending to be her mother. They even tell him about MaMtonga and her snake.

"So what's the adventure?" Four Eyes asks eagerly.

"It's a surprise. Just remember to bring some money along."

Nolitye leaves with her stone safely hidden in her breast pocket. When she gets to Phola she tiptoes past MaMtonga's house. The door is closed but something tells her that MaMtonga is in there brewing some evil spell. A strange, bitter smell is seeping through the door. Nolitye also hears some chanting. She considers going to the window to peep, but resists the temptation. That would really be looking for trouble, she tells herself. So she goes home. Thembi is not in and she unlocks the door with her spare key.

She puts the much enlarged magic stone in the bucket with the other stones, takes off her dirty school clothes and cleans her gym shoes as best she can. The shirt and socks she quickly washes. Then she takes a new candle from the cupboard, lights it and sits down at the table with her schoolbooks. But she can't concentrate on the reading

Moeder has given them for homework. She is too hungry. Thembi does not seem to have cooked and there's nothing in the cupboards to eat either. No bread, no peanut butter, only empty jam jars. Now that she thinks about it Nolitye realises that Thembi has been coming home rather late at night the last few days. And she never asks Nolitye if she's had any supper, like she used to do. Nolitye has had to go to bed without any food.

Nolitye forces herself to read. She reads a few lines but soon forgets what she has just read and has to start all over again. Her stomach groans. After a while she gives up and goes to the window. She peers into the night, just in time to see the full moon rise into the sky like a silver balloon. She closes the curtains and returns to her reading.

Thembi walks in with her supplies and immediately moans about how hard it was in town today and how few things she managed to sell. "You know, I didn't even have enough money to buy something to eat," she complains.

The lie hurts, because Nolitye can see crumbs and smudges of fat at the corners of Thembi's mouth. "I'm going to bed early tonight, Mama," she says.

"What about your homework?"

"I've already done it." Nolitye changes into her oversized T-shirt and crawls into bed. Thembi gives no sign of hearing her stomach rumble.

A tear rolls down Nolitye's cheek and soaks into the pillow. She falls asleep, longing desperately for her real parents. Late in the night she wakes up feeling thirsty. When she rolls over she notices that Thembi is not there. She is not really surprised. In the dream her father did say that she was a Night Rider and that she did her work in the dark. And since it was full moon, it must be the perfect time for Thembi to be spreading evil.

Nolitye searches for the box of matches which is always next to the candlestick. She strikes a match and gasps with fright. There is someone in the room with her.

"Who's there?" she says, trying to sound brave.

"Sorry, I didn't mean to scare you," Nomakhosi says.

"It's okay."

"Why are you up this time of night?"

"I was just looking for Mama . . . I mean that woman who pretends to be my mother."

"I came to fetch you. She is out there looking for the fourth stone. They are trying to put a spell on it so that you won't find it. You see, the more stones you find, the stronger the main stone becomes. And this they can't allow. So come on, put on your clothes."

"But what if my . . . if that woman comes home and finds me not here? She'll punish me."

"Don't worry, she's going to be out all night with MaMtonga spreading evil with the help of other Night Riders."

"We must stop them! I've been thinking a lot about Papa and my real mother caught in the underworld with that horrible Imvuvu monster."

"Don't worry, they are fine."

Nolitye brightens up. She puts on her second-hand jeans and old sweater with the holes at the elbows.

"Are you ready for a magic trick?" Nomakhosi asks.

"What kind of a trick?"

"One that will make us as invisible as the night."

"Yes!"

"But you must relax and rid yourself of all fears. The invisible spell only works when you are not afraid. As soon as you have fear in your heart, the spell will fall apart. Are you ready?"

Nolitye nods eagerly. She has just remembered that Ntate Matthews said her father could make himself disappear.

"Peaches and plums, amadlozi with light, ikhanya becomes night, you see us no more!" Nomakhosi chants in her sing-song voice.

In an instant they become invisible. Nolitye blinks. She can't see her own body, even though the moon makes the room bright.

"Nomakhosi, are you still there?" she whispers a little anxiously. Nomakhosi doesn't answer. Instead, Nolitye feels a warm hand gently grasping hers.

"Boo!" Nomakhosi says.

Nolitye jumps a little and clutches her chest. "You gave me a fright," she says laughing. She can't believe how much fun it is to be invisible. As an experiment, she takes the enamel mug from the shelf in the cooking corner. It seems to float on its own. Even the candlestick she holds seems to hover in the air.

"I'm sorry to spoil your fun, but we must hurry up as Night Riders go all over the township when the moon is full," Nomakhosi reminds her. "But first we are going to the Amanzi Mnyama, the Black Waters river near the soccer grounds."

Nolitye waits for Nomakhosi to float outside before she locks the door. She tiptoes and takes a peep at MaMtonga's shack. The place is dark.

"Come on." Nomakhosi takes Nolitye firmly by the hand. She chants something that Nolitye can't quite make out and soon she too is suspended in the air. Nolitye gazes about her. The moon has turned a pale red colour and hangs like a giant peach in the sky. It bathes Phola in golden light. Below them she spots Rex and his pack howling at the moon; Whiskers looks especially ridiculous with his long thin body and big ears.

Nomakhosi flies higher and higher with Nolitye. Nolitye is nervous, but she holds tightly onto Nomakhosi's hand. The shanties in Phola become smaller and smaller. They fly over the freeway. Nolitye smiles. If only Bheki and Four Eyes were here to see her!

Nolitye recognises the Amanzi Mnyama river by the thin and tall reeds that sigh in the mild wind. Nomakhosi puts her down gently. After the fresh air, the stench of something burning fills Nolitye's nostrils. And it is cold.

Nomakhosi whispers to her to walk carefully as her footsteps could give her away. "I can't go closer than this," Nomakhosi says softly. "But

I want you to see for yourself what MaMtonga and the woman who calls herself your mother are up to. I'll be watching over you."

"Nomakhosi," Nolitye whispers. "Nomakhosi . . ."

But Nomakhosi is no longer there. Nolitye is on her own.

She tiptoes ahead, careful not to make the reeds rustle too much. A very short distance away she hears voices, so she stops. A group of people in dark clothes - they must be Night Riders - have made a fire. She creeps closer. In the light of the fire she can clearly see Thembi. It is no surprise, but now she knows for certain.

It seems that Nomakhosi has brought Nolitye here just in time.

"Sisters, brothers, fellow fiends, I come to you with the light of the moon," MaMtonga starts. She clearly is the leader, the main Night Rider. She holds a black walking stick, her green-and-brown snake loosely coiled around her neck. There are nine Night Riders, moving in a circle around the fire. They wear cloaks that look more like rags, and their faces are painted in strange green-and-brown patterns.

Flames dance in the air as though the fire is a living thing. Every once in a while MaMtonga throws some mixture into the flames which makes it hiss louder and causes the flames to jump higher.

"The girl child is getting stronger. The more stones she finds, the more the power of the magic stone and her own power will grow. We must put a stop to it before she finds all the pieces!" MaMtonga howls. "Fellow fiends and Night Riders, we are going to have to use all our power to stop her!"

The rest of the Night Riders cheer, raising their fists in the air. Nolitye shivers with a mixture of cold and fear. She starts sniffling.

"I smell young flesh!" MaMtonga says, and licks her lips as though she would like to eat the young flesh.

Nolitye gasps. The Night Riders all look in the direction of the sound. Nolitye steps back in panic, making the grass rustle. She tries hard, but she can't keep calm. Her heart is beating in her ears. She starts shaking with fear and in the wink of an eye she becomes visible, as Nomakhosi warned would happen. She looks for Nomakhosi, but she is nowhere to be seen. Nolitye spins round, confused and frightened.

She knows she can't just stand there, so she makes a quick dash for the path along the river, hoping that she has not been seen.

"After them!" MaMtonga shouts. "That direction!"

Two men sprint after Nolitye. She thinks quickly. Instead of simply running into the night, which would make it easy for the men to catch her, she stops in her tracks, moves aside and burrows into the tall reeds along the path.

Seconds later the two men rush past her. But she stays put, shivering with cold, her feet stuck in mud. She forces herself to take deep breaths and slowly she becomes calmer. About the cold she can do nothing, the wind has in fact become stronger. She keeps shivering. I should be in bed, she thinks. I should never have agreed to come out with Nomakhosi.

One of the men comes back and tells MaMtonga, "Whoever it was got away."

"Did you get a look at who it was?"

"No," says the man.

"Imbecile!" MaMtonga yells.

The Night Riders are nearby, but none of them notices Nolitye hiding in the reeds. MaMtonga takes out more of the dried-plant mixture and rubs it between her palms.

"Hyena's tail and owls that prowl at night, I make this offering to flush out whoever is upon us. Protect us from the potent smell!" she chants in a dreadful, hoarse voice and throws the herbs into the fire. A large flame with a trail of black smoke hisses into the sky, and a pungent smell fills the air.

The smell makes Nolitye's nose itch. She has to block her nose with her thumb and middle finger not to sneeze. The smell becomes stronger and the trail of smoke billows out into a dark cloud. Nolitye desperately needs to breathe. When she lets go of her nose, she can no longer control the itch. She barely manages to smother the sneeze.

But MaMtonga's sharp ears have caught the suppressed sound. "Over there!" she yells, her eyes glinting in the fire light. She points in the direction of where Nolitye is hiding.

Nolitye keeps dead still. If they should catch her here, it will be all over.

Two other men rush towards Nolitye. She is sure that this time they'll find her. Do something! she tells herself, but there's nothing she can think of. The men are only a stone's throw away. She feels weak at the knees as she looks around her, shivering and hugging her arms. She closes her eyes and waits. A cold breeze rustles through the reeds. Suddenly something scurries out of the undergrowth right under her feet. Nolitye gets such a fright that she has to put her hands over her mouth to keep herself from screaming. Whatever it was scuttles away through the reeds.

The two men stop in their tracks. "It was just a cat," one of the men says relieved, and they turn back.

"Well, did you kill it?" MaMtonga asks vengefully. "No, it ran away."

"Imbecile! You have a cabbage for a brain."

The Night Riders all move back to the fire. Nolitye has seen enough. As soon as everyone is moving in a circle again, she parts the reeds, careful not to make a noise, and makes her way home. Her feet are heavy for her shoes are caked in mud. She trudges quietly, the moon illuminating the path back to the freeway. Thembi doesn't allow her to walk outside alone at night, and she is scared out of her senses, but her desire to get away from the foul-smelling river and the circle round the fire is stronger. When she is sure that she is out of earshot of MaMtonga and her cronies, she starts running. It is not necessary, because she unexpectedly finds herself on the shoulder of the freeway. She looks left, right and left again before she sprints across, even though there is not a car in sight at this time of night.

At the first tall street lamp she stops. Through a small window she can hear a light snoring coming from inside a shack. She takes off her takkies and with a piece of stone from a rubble-heap next to the shack, she scrapes off the mud. She has stopped shivering because among the shanties it is not as cold as down by the river. Not able to decide which way to take home, she stands and watches a black cat ambling up to her. The cat sits down and starts licking its paws.

"Hey you," someone says softly.

"Who's there?" Nolitye asks, trying to sound unafraid. She peers at the small window.

"It's me, silly. Down here."

Nolitye looks down. The cat looks up. It is the cat who spoke to her!

"It's me, Nomakhosi," the cat says, preening her whiskers. "I'm a shape- shifter and since no one but you can see me in my human form at the moment, I have to either slow down time or change into an animal when I'm with people."

"How could you just leave me like that?" Nolitye reproaches her. She can't keep the sulk out of her voice. "I thought I was toast back there!"

"Well, you should learn to trust me. I was watching over you all along."

"That was a very close call," Nolitye repeats, but in a better mood. "But tomorrow I'm going to need your help. Please, I must find out what that woman's name is so I can break the spell and bring back my parents. It is very hard. That woman hardly gives me food these days."

"You will find her name, my dear. Now come on, let's go before you catch a cold. Put on your shoes," Nomakhosi says.

In the shape of a black cat weaving about her feet, Nomakhosi leads Nolitye home. Near the clinic, they see a pair of men staggering towards them. One of them falls over. The other tries to help him up but he too almost topples over. Nolitye rushes forward because in the light of the tall street lamp in front of MaMokoena's spaza shop she sees that it is Ntate Matthews. As always on a full-moon night he has drunk too much umqombothi. "Ntate Matthews," she offers, "can I help you?"

"Oh buzz off, you silly girl!" he slurs angrily. "Do you think we're not capable of getting where we want to on our own? Leave us alone!"

The black cat rubs against Nolitye's legs. She looks down and the cat quietly shakes its head. Nolitye steps aside so that the two drunken men can pass, but Ntate Matthews teeters towards her. "Who are you anyway?" Then he recognises her. He tries to stand up straight. "Oops! My friend Xoli Dube's daughter," he says, sounding much soberer. "You do what you have to do, my girl. You just hold onto that stone."

The black cat has run on ahead and Nolitye quickly says goodbye and follows it.

"Hey, Nolitye, come back here. I want to tell you something," Ntate Matthews calls after her. She pretends not to hear, because the black cat is already strolling past MaMtonga's dark hovel, and she runs to catch up with it.

Nolitye takes out her spare key to unlock the door. "Sleep tight," Nomakhosi purrs and trots off into the night. Nolitye slips inside and locks the door. She leans against it, clutching her hungry stomach. We have to find out what that woman's name is, she thinks. Living with her has become too much of a pain.

Chapter Eleven

A DOG CALLED MISTER

THE next morning Nolitye is up and dressed early. She takes a good look at Thembi who is still snoring lightly. Even as she lies sleeping she looks tired and haggard. Nolitye quickly looks for her purse and takes out some money. The old condensed-milk tin hasn't had any money in it for days and days now.

Thembi stirs. "What are you doing?" she asks, bleary-eyed. "Oh I, I. . . thought I'd make you some coffee."

"We don't have coffee. What are you talking about?"

"Did I say coffee? I meant tea."

"You know we ran out of tea bags." Thembi sits up irritably. "What's with you this morning?"

"Nothing. I guess it'll have to be hot sugar water then," Nolitye says, playing dumb, and slips the few coins she has taken into her shoe.

Thembi takes her time getting up. Her eyes are sunken in her head and her clothes smell of smoke. When Nolitye asks her, trying to sound innocent, why her clothes smell of smoke, she says, "Why don't you stop talking so much and go and fetch a bucket of water?"

"But the bucket is full."

"Well, I want fresh water!"

It is a cool morning. A blanket of smog hangs over Phola. Nolitye drags her feet as she walks to the tap. Inside their houses people cough; outside dogs bark.

"Sawubona, Nolitye," Mamani greets her. She walks fast with her usual huge basket on her head. The basket is full of mealies.

"Hello, Mamani," Nolitye says cheerfully. "Are you going to sell your mealies at the station?" Mamani nods and hurries along. Nolitye wishes one of the mealies would drop from the basket so she can pick it up. Her stomach is rumbling with hunger just at the thought of a delicious hot mealie. If it were not for the plate of food MaZwane insists she eats whenever she visits Bheki's house, she would have fainted with hunger long ago.

When she gets back to the shack with the water, Thembi is dressed. She is wearing a bright yellow turban Nolitye has not seen before. So much for wanting to wash in fresh water, Nolitye thinks.

Thembi has boiled some water and takes a plastic bag with half a loaf of bread from the cupboard. They drink hot sugar water with the dry bread. Afterwards Thembi takes her box with provisions and Nolitye takes her school bag. The magic stone she put in her breast pocket while Thembi was still asleep.

Thembi doesn't ask Nolitye if she has made sandwiches for school, and it is more than two weeks since she has made any peanut butter sandwiches for her. She gives Nolitye a hurried hug.

Near MaMokoena's spaza shop Nolitye bumps into Ntate Matthews. He looks terrible. His clothes are dirty and he has a wound on his forehead.

"Ntate Matthews, what happened to you?" Nolitye asks.

"It's those witches. You won't believe what they did to me early this morning. They're trying to destroy me."

"Who?"

"You know who I'm talking about. MaMtonga and her cronies." Ntate Matthews coughs. The sound makes Nolitye's stomach turn.

"I better go now, Ntate Matthews," Nolitye says, remembering how Nomakhosi shook her head when she wanted to help him last night. And she can smell that he has been drinking heavily.

"Take care," Ntate Matthews says. Nolitye is touched by the concern in his watery eyes.

Bheki is already at their front gate, waiting impatiently. "So what's the big adventure? I could hardly sleep last night," he says.

"What adventure?"

"Nolitye, don't play the fool with me!"

"Okay," she says, "there's still an adventure waiting. I'll tell you after we've met up with Four Eyes."

Four Eyes is waiting outside the school gate. From a distance he looks lost and lonely, but when he sees them he breaks into a smile. "Hey, what's the big adventure?"

"So you also want to know?" Bheki says. "That's all I could think about last night."

"Now come on, Nolitye, tell us," Four Eyes begs, jumping from foot to foot.

Nolitye takes a good few seconds before she speaks. She decides against telling them about her experience of the previous night. Bheki will in any case think it was just another of her weird dreams. "What if I said today we're bunking school?" she begins.

"I don't like the sound of that." Bheki looks to Four Eyes for support, but Four Eyes doesn't notice. His eyes are glued on Nolitye's face. "But what if I said we're going to be secret agents for a day?"

This time Four Eyes and Bheki dart a quick look at each other, but neither of them says anything.

Encouraged by the intrigued look on their faces, Nolitye continues, "We take the bus to town and find out what my 'mother' Thembi's real name is. I already told you that once we know that, the spell which she's put on me will be broken. Then we'll also see who she really is."

"What about your real mother?" Bheki at last asks.

"One thing at a time," Nolitye says, making the most of being in charge. Certain that nobody is watching them from the school building, the three hastily leave for the bus station, because Nolitye reasons that with school uniforms on they will attract less attention on the regular bus than in a minibus taxi.

But they don't get far. As they turn the first street corner, they run into the Spoilers. Rotten Nellie immediately starts laughing like a mad hyena. "My favourite idiots," she shrieks. "The three of you just make me sick."

"Ja, you guys belong in a zoo," Thabo agrees.

"Where are you going anyway?" S'bu chips in. "School is that way, stupids."

This makes Bheki so angry that he blurts out, "Well, we're not going to school! We're going to . . ."

Nolitye gives him a rough nudge. "What he meant . . . was that we're going to pick up Four Eyes's book. Right, Four Eyes?"

"Really? Oh yes . . ." Four Eyes looks bewildered and Nolitye thinks that for a smart guy he can really be slow at times.

"Something tells me you rats are lying." Rotten Nellie glares at them in turn.

"Well, are you going to take our lunch or what?" Nolitye says, trying to get Rotten Nellie off track.

"Shut up, you! It's supposed to be fun for us and terrible for you! And in any case, you haven't had sandwiches for I don't know how long."

Without another word, Nolitye turns and walks away, with Bheki and Four Eyes following her. This infuriates Rotten Nellie. "Hey! Hey, come back here! I'm not finished with you idiots," she screams after them. "And you two, don't just stand here! Go after them!" she adds. But Thabo and S'bu remain where they are.

Without looking back, Nolitye and Four Eyes carry on walking to the bus stop in the main road. "That was close," Nolitye says. "You and Four Eyes nearly gave the game away."

"It was your fault," Bheki and Four Eyes say simultaneously, pointing at each other. Nolitye just shakes her head and laughs.

They have to wait only a few minutes at the bus stop before the grey-blue bus to the city centre arrives. Nobody is paying them any attention and it is clear nobody from Nka Thutho is going to arrive looking for them. Even Bheki is getting excited and has stopped glancing back, because he, like the other two, has never gone to town without a grown-up. Nolitye pretends to fasten her shoe to get out the money she took from Thembi's purse. When the bus stops, she pays and they hurry to the very back, taking care not to push or shove, because when Nolitye spotted the bus approaching, she very firmly said, "We're naughty skipping school, so we must be very good on this trip. We'll have to be very polite to older people so our bad behaviour can be balanced out."

They squeeze in next to an old man, very pleased with the good seats. "Shouldn't you be at school?" the old man asks just as Bheki, a broad smile on his face, pushes his elbow into Four Eyes's ribcage.

Nolitye smiles at him and patting her school bag says, "Baba, we go to school in town."

The old man doesn't look convinced, and when he gets off at a stop near the city he waves his finger at them and in parting says, "Don't get up to mischief, my children!"

"There's something that always makes old people want to spoil one's fun," Nolitye says.

"Not my mkhulu," says Four Eyes. "When I stay with him he lets me watch TV till very late."

"You lucky fish!" Bheki sounds envious, but not too much. "My gogo makes me drink warm milk before I go to bed. You know how terrible that is? Yurgh! It tastes like medicine."

Nolitye and Four Eyes laugh at the comical face Bheki pulls, but Nolitye wishes that she had grandparents. She only vaguely remembers Gogo, her mother's mother, and whenever Nolitye asked Thembi about her father's parents, she started talking about something else.

"Hey you guys, we need to get off!" Nolitye says when she notices the minibus-taxi rank coming up. She went to town with Thembi not too long ago and realises that they have to get off at the next stop.

For a moment they remain standing where they jumped onto the pavement from the bus. There are so many people around, it looks as if they've been poured from a huge bucket and are now spilling down the various streets. Everywhere the three look there are people walking, selling things, yelling to each other or to passers-by. Cars rush by, some drivers hooting, others concentrating on not hitting a pedestrian or another vehicle.

"Guys, let's all hold hands so we don't get lost," Nolitye says and starts walking, more or less dragging the other two along behind her. She's never been to where her mother sells her stuff, but every time she's been in town with her, Thembi pointed out the spot. This is where she is heading with Bheki and Four Eyes. But the going is not easy. They get shoved aside by impatient men in business suits and bumped into by delivery boys pushing trolleys loaded with parcels; their school bags get snagged on women's shopping bags and Four Eyes's glasses get knocked down his nose.

"Is it still far?" he asks, pushing his spectacles back into place. "We're almost there," Nolitye consoles him over her shoulder.

At last they get to the phone booth Thembi had pointed out on their trips to town. Nolitye looks around. Yes, it is the right place, and the stall is there, right next to the booth, but it is occupied by a stranger. Nolitye steps up to her. "Dumela, Mama, do you know where Thembi is?" she asks politely.

The woman shakes her head. "I don't know anyone by the name of Thembi."

"The woman who sells things people need but always forget to buy," Nolitye explains.

The woman keeps shaking her head and asks Nolitye if she wants to buy some fruit. When Nolitye says no thank you, the woman says, "Then move off, you're wasting my time."

Why are people in town so rude, Nolitye wonders, and turns to the other two. "We'll have to be on the lookout ourselves, because that woman says she hasn't seen the woman who says she is my mother. I should be able to recognise her easily, because she is wearing a yellow turban today."

They wander around the taxi rank, but Thembi is nowhere to be seen. They are just about to give up, when Four Eyes whispers, "Hey, isn't that your mother over there?"

In the swirling crowd Nolitye spots the yellow turban. "You're a genius, Four Eyes!" she says excitedly.

"It has to be those spectacles he wears!" Bheki jokes.

They keep a safe distance behind the yellow turban. The woman who says she's Nolitye's mother crosses the street unaware that the three are following her. She goes to a fruit seller and buys three bananas, which she starts eating while talking to the fruit seller. The three keep stealing a look at the two chatting women while they pretend to be looking at the second-hand paperback books on a trestle table near the fruit seller. They are careful always to shelter behind some large grown-up so that Thembi won't see them if she turns round and looks in their direction.

After a while Thembi continues a few dozen steps up the busy street and disappears into a muti shop where they sell traditional herbs and medicines.

They wait and wait. When it is clear that Thembi is not going to come out of the shop any time soon, Nolitye and the other two walk over to the fruit seller. They also buy three bananas from her. This time Bheki pays. Nolitye takes the magic stone from her pocket and clutches it in her hand.

"I guess you must sell a lot of fruit every day," she says, trying to make small talk with the fruit seller.

"You'd be surprised, my girl," the woman replies while she serves another customer. "At least four boxes of these bananas."

"I can see why. They are too delicious for words."

The fruit seller looks pleased with the compliment and gives Nolitye a smile.

She rolls the stone in her hand, for she urgently needs courage. She must ask the question before Thembi comes out of that muti shop and sees them. She doesn't know how to begin, but the strange, tingly feeling she always gets from the stone comes over her and she says, "That woman who was here just now . . ."

Bheki and Four Eyes cross their fingers for good luck. "Which woman? I serve a lot of people every day."

"You know, the one who was chatting with you just now. The one with the yellow turban."

"Oh, that one! She's a regular customer. She's a traditional healer, you know."

You mean a Night Rider disguised as a traditional healer and pretending to be my mother! Nolitye thinks to herself.

"Anyway, what about her?" the fruit seller asks.

"Well, she looks like someone I know, one of my mother's friends. But I've forgotten her name," Nolitye says slyly. "I just can't remember it."

"You mean Sylvia?"

Bheki and Four Eyes look at each other.

"Of course! It's Sylvia. I knew it was something like that, a name that starts with an S," Nolitye says, chuffed with herself.

"Yes, she comes here almost every day. She works in the muti shop up here." And the fruit seller points to the door through which they saw Thembi enter.

"Well, we'd better get to school," Nolitye says solemnly, trying hard not to show her joy that they now know Thembi's real name and that the spell she has cast over her can soon be broken.

"Imagine what will happen when you call her Sylvia," Four Eyes says. They walk across a bridge to get to a park they can see in the distance, because that is where Nolitye said they should go. A train hums underneath them.

"I bet Nolitye's mother's face will melt away and the true Sylvia will show herself," Bheki predicts.

"No," Four Eyes says, "she will evaporate and disappear from sight!"

"Listen, the important thing is to find the next stone," Nolitye says. "I'm sure that to break the spell we'll need the added strength it will give us."

They come to a street lined with trees where traffic cops monitor the hooting taxis, all vying for the attention of possible passengers. There is little space to walk as stalls are scattered all over the pavement.

Everyone has something different to sell: T-shirts, pens, shoelaces, toys, umbrellas that have been in the sun too long and are faded to pale pink and the colour of very milky tea. There are long queues of passengers hanging onto large suitcases, blankets and bundles, waiting to board taxis. The smell of roasted mealies and fish and chips wafts about in the air. Music blares from where travelling salesmen sell CDs and tapes.

Everyone is in a hurry. Nolitye and Bheki have to stop a few times while Four Eyes fixes his spectacles that keep slipping forward. They enter the park through big gates. A photographer offers to take their picture for ten rand. Nolitye declines and he brings down his price to eight rand, but Nolitye still shakes her head. He gives up on them and goes in search of other clients.

People lie in the sun or under trees. An ice-cream vendor rings his bell as he rides his tricycle through the park. A few hobos are scratching in dustbins. Children sing from a nearby crèche. Nolitye, Bheki and Four Eyes sit down on a bench near the public toilets. Nolitye is tempted to tell them that the only way they can find out where the next stone is going to come from is by asking Nomakhosi, but she can't - Nomakhosi is her biggest secret.

They are gazing at the stream of people walking past when a dark-grey dove hovers for a few seconds above them before it lands at Nolitye's feet. It doesn't make a sound, but it tilts its head and looks at Nolitye as though it knows her.

"Hey guys, check out this dove," Bheki says. Nolitye says nothing as they watch it hop onto her lap. She strokes it gently. Then it hops onto her shoulder and starts flapping its wings. Now Nolitye knows for certain. Nomakhosi has turned herself into a dove before - a white one on the day Rotten Nellie took her sandwiches - and when she and Bheki bought fatcakes from Mamani. This dark-grey dove must also be her. The dove flies off and lands near the fountain and starts pecking at the ground. "Listen," Nolitye says, "I'll be back, I just need to follow that dove."

Bheki and Four Eyes do not ask why she wants to follow the dove; they've got used to the strange things Nolitye does and tells them.

When Nolitye gets close to the dark-grey dove, it flies off and disappears into the women's toilet. Nolitye rushes in after it. A woman on her way out screams when the dove, with Nolitye just behind it, enters the building.

The toilets are empty, except for a little girl who is washing her hands at the basins. From the way her movements are slowing down Nolitye realises that Nomakhosi has changed into her usual self, even before she sees the green-eyed woman with the pointy ears. This time she is dressed in the short traditional striped skirt of the Shangaan, stuffed with bits of material that make her waist look bigger. Draped over one shoulder she wears a bright orange sarong.

Nomakhosi seems to be in a big hurry. "Now that you know Sylvia's name," she says without any ado, "you can move on to find the fourth piece of stone. Only the power of the stone can destroy Sylvia, and break the spell she has over you, but it will have that power only once all five pieces have come together."

"Where will I find the next piece?"

"You'll have to go back to the townships again, to a place called Phiri. There you'll find Vilakazi's Butchery. At the back of the butchery is a dog who's been guarding the stone, but he'll only talk if you call him Mister."

Nomakhosi turns back into a dove and flutters out of the toilets. The water starts running from the tap again and the little girl blinks her eyes and continues washing her hands as though there has been no interruption.

Nolitye finds Bheki and Four Eyes patiently waiting for her on the bench. "Where did you go?"

"I just quickly went to the loo."

"So what's the plan for the rest of the day?" Four Eyes inquires.

"We have to get the next stone. It's in Phiri. And it's being guarded by a dog."

"But do we have enough money left to go to Phiri?"

"That's why we have the stone, Bheki," Nolitye says, not worried at all. Each one of them takes out the few coins they have. Nolitye puts all the money in her already bulging breast pocket with the stone. Then the three hold hands and wish for more money. But instead of her pocket suddenly swelling with more money, a business man in a fancy suit drops a twenty-rand note as he rushes past. Bheki scoops up the money and tries to run after the man to give it back to him, but Bheki is too chubby to move fast and the man is already driving off in a taxi by the time he gets to the taxi rank. Bheki returns with a hangdog expression on his face.

"Cheer up," Nolitye says. "We wished for money, and this must be the way in which the stone sent it to us."

The queue waiting for a taxi to Phiri is long. Some of the grown-ups regard their school uniforms with suspicion. "Shouldn't you be in school?" a man carrying an umbrella like a walking stick asks.

Bheki is first to answer. "We had to come to the library."

"But doesn't your school have a library?" the man asks.

"Ja . . . but it doesn't have a lot of books," Bheki says, sounding less confident.

Four Eyes, happy to have thought of another excuse, helps Bheki out. "It's kind of a field trip. Our teacher wanted us to come to the big library in town to see what a real library looks like."

This answer seems to satisfy the man. He takes a newspaper from his briefcase and starts reading it. Nolitye smiles when she sees the name. When the minibus arrives, she, Bheki and Four Eyes squeeze inside it with thirteen other people. The man with the many questions is so interested in what he is reading in The Star that he misses the taxi.

They sit squashed up, but at least they sit together. Their neighbour, a plump woman, takes up most of their space, but she has the good humour to say, "At least two of these three are as thin as broomsticks and I'm big as a rhinoceros, so the average is good."

Phiri is in the heart of Soweto. Nolitye is sure it's no coincidence that Phiri means "secret". The three get off at a bus stop next to what looks like a small business area. They look around. They don't have to ask for directions, because Four Eyes spots Vilakazi's Butchery straight away. It is not far to walk.

"Let's first check at the back," Nolitye suggests. "That is where the dog is supposed to be."

They find a small dusty parking lot behind the butchery, and from a distance already they are met by the sound of a dog barking.

Nolitye stops in her tracks. It is a German shepherd, an Alsatian, just like the dogs the police use to sniff out and control criminals. It looks vicious, barking fiercely and pulling on its chain. When the chain drags on the ground, it stirs up dust. Pale, muddy bones lie scattered beside its wooden kennel.

Nolitye approaches the dog very slowly. "Now what?" Bheki whispers. Nolitye checks to see if anyone is nearby before she opens her mouth and says as bravely as possible, "Hey, Mister."

The dog stops barking and limps forward, careful not to step on his right front paw.

"I believe you called my name," he says in a very posh accent, very unlike Shorty's way of talking, even though Shorty looks very much like him, except for the short tail.

The three stare wordlessly at the dog.

"Well, are you just going to stand there and look at me?"

"My friend here has something to ask you," Bheki says and nudges Nolitye.

"How very boring. I thought you'd have delicious bones to offer me."

"Actually, I was wondering if you have the stone," Nolitye says.

"Aha!" remarks the dog rather smugly and sits back on his haunches and gives his right front paw a slow, gentle lick. "And what stone might that be?"

"The magic stone, of course!" Nolitye feels annoyed by the dog's arrogance. Here he is chained up in an awful place and he behaves as if he's a big chief.

"Ah yes, the precious stone," the dog muses and lies down, his head on his paws.

"Please, Mister," Nolitye pleads.

"You'll have to do a lot better than just pleading."

"So what do you want us to do then?" Nolitye says, getting really exasperated.

"I've always wanted to know what boys and girls do while I'm guarding this place."

"Well . . . we go to school."

"School? What's that?" asks the dog, pricking up his ears.

"It's a place where you go to learn things."

"What kind of things?"

"Like writing and stuff."

"Stuff?" the dog says, sitting up.

Nolitye sighs. "Like adding and subtracting sums and reading books."

"Sounds terribly boring, if you ask me," the dog says and lies down again.

"Actually, school is quite fun," Bheki remarks and cringes when he realises that he sounds like a real cheese boy. Four Eyes and Nolitye give him a strange look.

Mister gets to his feet in a flash and starts barking ferociously. The three look around. A man in oil-streaked jeans is standing next to his car, about to get inside. He pauses to look at them.

"So what do you do all . . . Hey, come to think of it. Were you kids talking to the dog?" the man asks, a puzzled frown on his forehead.

The three feel embarrassed. "We weren't seriously talking . . ." Bheki blurts out.

"We were just playing around." Nolitye pokes him in the ribs and thinks, Bheki always talks too much when he is in a tight spot.

"You should be in school instead of fooling about."

"And you look like you could use a shower, quite frankly," Mister replies, sniffing the air.

"What did you say?" the man asks.

"Nothing!" Four Eyes says at once, but he and Nolitye and Bheki cannot suppress their laughter.

"Then why are you laughing? I clearly heard the word 'shower'. Do you imply I am dirty? You little brats!" He takes off his belt and gives a furious step in their direction.

Mister starts barking as if he has gone mad, straining at his chain. "Pretend you are coming to untie me!" he growls to Nolitye. And launches into a new fit of barking.

Nolitye hesitates for just one second and then says to the man: "Our watchdog has just instructed me to untie him so he can have you for lunch. So stick around." And she takes a few steps towards Mister.

The man stops dead, the hand with the belt still in the air. He looks from the dog to Nolitye and then quickly straps his belt back on, gets into his car and drives out of there as though his tyres are on fire.

The three fall about laughing. Bheki is so delighted with the clever dog that he punches Four Eyes on his arm, so hard that his spectacles slip right off his nose.

"So that's what I do all day. Terrorise unruly people," Mister says.

"But you wouldn't actually hurt anyone, would you?" Nolitye is still shaky, not sure that she would've gone any closer to Mister if the man had not driven off.

"Yes, well . . . Where were we? I believe you were asking me for a stone."

"A stone that will save my mother from a woman who pretends to be my mother when she's not. She's just a fake. A Night Rider," Nolitye adds.

"Oh yes, Night Riders. Dreadful creatures, of course." Mister sounds as arrogant as when he opened his snout for the first time.

"So would you please . . ."

"On one condition only."

"You just name it."

Mister puts his right front paw forward. It is very swollen. "Would you be a darling and remove this terrible thorn?" he asks. "It's been hurting me for days."

Nolitye is suddenly nervous. A big German shepherd seriously asking her to take out a thorn from his paw. Is it another trick, like the suggestion that she untie him when the man threatened to use his belt on them? Not knowing what to say, she tries to see if she can see the thorn from where she is.

"Don't worry, you're much too thin even to be considered for lunch. I have my eyes set on tastier things, such as the delicious bones the butcher always leaves out for me."

Nolitye looks at the other two. Bheki shakes his head; Four Eyes shrugs. She takes a deep breath and takes a few slow steps towards Mister. Mister puts his head down. He has the most beautiful coat, Nolitye notices. She kneels next to him, takes his swollen paw in her hand and cautiously feels around for the thorn. Pinching it firmly between her forefinger and thumbnail, she pulls it out in one quick movement.

"Ah, that's better. Thank you," Mister says in his best private-school accent.

"By the way, why do they call you Mister?"

"I used to be an ancestral spirit from the land beyond death, rather like Nomakhosi," he says.

Feeling much more relaxed, Nolitye runs her hand over his lovely glossy coat and says, "So you know her?" And then she whispers in his ear: "Don't mention her name again, because they don't know of her." When Nolitye turns her head to indicate to Mister that she is talking about her friends, she sees, to her relief, that the two are admiring a flashy red car that has just pulled into the parking lot.

"Do I know her?" Mister chuckles. "Of course I do. We were best friends until the day I got terribly bored and was tempted to help a silly man who was playing around with the black arts. Actually, he was a Renegade who talked me into helping him with a spell he tried to use against a Night Rider. This Night Rider was making him grow shorter day by day." Mister sighs, rests his head on his front paws and twitches his tail before he continues, "To cut a long story short, I ended up using a few tricks to reverse the spell. Of course it's considered a crime to meddle actively in other people's affairs. So I was booted from being an ancestral spirit and made a Renegade. And now I'm here, but that's an even longer story and it seems you're pressed for time." And he moves to the back of the kennel.

"Yes, unfortunately we are."

With his left front paw Mister scratches at something in the narrow space between his kennel and the wall. After a while he rolls out a piece of mud. He prods it with his snout and sniffs at it before he takes it in his mouth and drops it at Nolitye's feet.

"Sorry about the spit. One has to do the best with what one has," Mister says. "Take my advice. Wise words coming from a so-called dog."

Nolitye puts her arms around Mister's neck and gives him a hug. Then she scoops up the stone and slips it in the side-pocket of her school bag.

"Thank you!" she whispers and calls, "Bheki, Four Eyes! Come on, we have to go."

"Do be careful," Mister says as they walk away, their school bags slung over their shoulders.

The three catch a minibus taxi back to Mogale; it is too late for anyone to worry about them not being in school. They go to Bheki's house firstly. His mother is baking one of her famous batches of biscuits. Little Khaya is playing with his toy truck on the kitchen floor.

"How are you, Mfana?" MaZwane asks, stroking Bheki's hair. She gives him a smacking kiss on the cheek.

"Ma, I'm getting too old for this," he says, trying to sound firm.

"You're never too old to get sugar from your mother," she says, embarrassing him even more by wiping something from his nose.

"Come on, you two." She puts her arms around Nolitye and Four Eyes, holds them close to her bosom for a second and then squeezes.

"Alright, go on, I know you want to get up to mischief," she says and pushes them out the kitchen door with a plate of biscuits.

They go straight to the bottom of the garden. Nolitye takes out the stone Mister gave her and runs back to the tap near the front stoep. She comes back beaming.

"Let me see," Four Eyes says anxiously.

Nolitye lays the wet stone on the grass in the sun. Like the other pieces, it too is blue and purple and sparkles in the light. Then she takes the bigger stone from her gym breast-pocket and lays it next to the new stone. Like the previous time, the stones start to glow and a small spark flies into the air the moment they join together.

"Soon it will fit into the side-pocket of my school bag," Nolitye says, weighing the stone in her hand.

Chapter Twelve

A PLEASANT SURPRISE

THE next Monday morning, Moeder tells the class she is giving them a surprise Maths test. Everyone except Nolitye moans because no one likes a surprise test, but they nevertheless all take out their Maths books. Moeder starts writing the sums on the blackboard. When Nolitye starts copying down the sums, she discovers that weird scribbles appear on the page. She stops writing and watches as the page fills with weird marks that turn into words.

Hello, Nolitye, she reads at the top of the page.

Taken aback, she pokes Bheki in the side. But Bheki is too engrossed in the test to want to be disturbed. "Stop it," he whispers, "Moeder will think we're cheating."

Nolitye keeps watching the page and again *Hello, Nolitye* appears across the top. She decides to respond and writes 'Hello'.

Immediately the words *I finally get to meet you appear*.

Nolitye writes 'Who are you?'

The answer follows at once: *First you must find the last stone. It is not important who I am. To find this stone you must confront Rotten Nellie. She knows the person who has the stone.*

After that the strange writing fades from the page until only Nolitye's own writing is left. She quickly erases the 'Hello' and 'Who are you?' and resumes writing the Maths test. After a while she stops and looks behind her, directly into Rotten Nellie's eyes. Rotten Nellie looks bored, as if her thoughts are far away from the Maths test. When she notices Nolitye looking at her, she sticks out her tongue.

"Ma'am, Nolitye's staring at me," Rotten Nellie says, disturbing the near-silence in which only the sound of pencils on paper can be heard. Nolitye quickly turns back. Just in time, because when Moeder looks up she is engrossed in her sums.

"Nellie, please get back to your work and stop fibbing!" Moeder tells Rotten Nellie.

"But Ma'am, Nolitye -"

"Do you want to be given detention?" Moeder cuts her short, and after that Rotten Nellie keeps quiet. Everyone suspects she was making a fuss because she doesn't know how to do her sums.

After half an hour Moeder tells the class that time is up. She collects their Maths books. Bheki and Four Eyes look satisfied with themselves. They are confident that they did well. Nolitye, on the other hand, fears the worst, because right through the test she couldn't stop thinking about what she has to do confront Rotten Nellie!

During lunch break Bheki and Four Eyes go to buy fatcakes and dried fish from Mamani, who has put up her umbrella just outside the school gates. Nolitye told them that she was going to the toilet, but instead she marches up to Rotten Nellie who is sitting with the Spoilers in the quadrangle.

"What do you want, Mop?" Rotten Nellie sneers when she sees Nolitye coming towards them.

"I thought maybe we could talk."

"I have nothing to say to you, you disgusting little twit."

This isn't going to be easy, Nolitye thinks. "Don't you think it's time we stopped fighting?" she says.

"No. That's the only thing I look forward to all day - picking on you." S'bu and Thabo snigger.

"Come off it, wimp. What do you really want?" Rotten Nellie says. "You usually avoid us."

Nolitye doesn't know what to say. All she knows is that she's got to get the next stone from Rotten Nellie.

She follows Rotten Nellie's eyes which have turned towards the school gate. A woman who walks in a comical lopsided way is coming towards them. She's rather tall and has fat cheeks, like she's stuffed her face with marshmallows. Rotten Nellie draws in her breath sharply. To Nolitye's surprise, she blushes. Only then Nolitye recognises the woman: it is Rotten Nellie's mother. She still remembers the scowl on her face from the time Moeder called her in.

"Nellie, what did I say to you this morning?" the woman screams. "Ma, I uh—"

"Don't 'Ma' me. I told you to take this package to MaMtonga!" Rotten Nellie's mother grabs her by the ear and twists it. And for good measure she gives the ear a yank before she lets go.

"Eina!" Rotten Nellie cries out in pain. S'bu and Thabo look away.

"Now go and deliver this package immediately if you know what's good for you, you little brat. Otherwise there'll be no supper for you tonight!"

Without a word, Rotten Nellie takes the brown-paper parcel from her mother. S'bu and Thabo stare at Rotten Nellie's mother. Never before have they seen Rotten Nellie obey anybody like this.

"What are you little swines looking at?" Rotten Nellie's mother screams at them. "Have you never seen me before?"

The two turn their heads away immediately. Nolitye pretends to be cleaning her nails so that she won't have to talk to the horrible woman. From the corner of her eye she sees Rotten Nellie's mother grabbing her daughter by the ear again.

"Now do as you've been told!" she shouts, and walks off, waddling like a duck. But then she stops. "No, you better take the parcel after school otherwise you'll be in trouble with the teachers. You're not the brightest of students!"

Rotten Nellie cringes as if her mother had slapped her across the face. Nolitye coughs with embarrassment.

"What are you laughing at, Mop?" Rotten Nellie demands, but not quite as rudely as before.

"Hey, I was just coughing," Nolitye explains.

"Ja, well just get out of my way because I'm in a bad mood."

The stone must be inside the parcel! Nolitye realises. If only she could figure out a way to get hold of it. "If you want, I can take the parcel to MaMtonga," she offers. "She stays next door to us."

"I know that, Balloon Brain. But do I look stupid enough to trust you with this parcel?" Rotten Nellie snaps. "Now get out of my face."

Nolitye leaves without saying another word and goes in search of Bheki and Four Eyes. She finds them on the playground behind the school. They are excited when they hear about the parcel, but agree that getting the stone from Rotten Nellie is going to be very difficult, if not impossible.

After school Nolitye and Four Eyes go home with Bheki. They play cards at the bottom of the garden, while the magic stone draws energy from the sun.

Nolitye plays very half-heartedly; her mind isn't on the game but on the stone in the parcel Rotten Nellie is taking to MaMtonga.

Just as she is losing another game of rummy, Nolitye hears her name being called from the other side of the prickly-pear bushes. She looks at Bheki and Bheki looks at Four Eyes. There is no mistake: it is Rotten Nellie's voice.

"Yes?" Nolitye answers. "Can we help you?"

"Yes. I want to talk to you."

"Okay, go to the front of the house and come in through the gate and past the side of the house. We'll wait for you here."

They are so amazed at Rotten Nellie having spied where they go in the afternoons that they forget to put the magic stone away. All eyes are on the side of the house where Rotten Nellie appears in record time, an urgent look on her face.

"Hi," Four Eyes says.

"Shut up, Peanut Brain," Rotten Nellie says. "I'm here to see Nolitye."

"There's no need to be rude," Bheki points out.

Rotten Nellie ignores him, partly because her eyes are fixed on the stone on the grass. Without warning, she takes the brown-paper parcel which her mother gave her at school from her bag. She unwraps it, still staring at the magic stone. A purplish-blue stone slips from her hands.

"What are you doing?" Four Eyes cries out.

"I'm giving you the stone, stupid," Rotten Nellie says, picking up the stone she brought along.

"But why?" Nolitye is completely perplexed. Just a few hours ago Rotten Nellie didn't even want to see her.

Rotten Nellie doesn't reply, only holds out the stone to Nolitye, who takes it from her and studies it closely. It is much bigger than any of the other pieces, but it is of the same unearthly purplish-blue crystal that sparkles whenever light falls on it.

"This is the last piece of the puzzle," Nolitye murmurs.

"So do you want the stone or not?" Rotten Nellie asks gruffly.

"Of course I want it," Nolitye says eagerly. "It's just that ... well, we haven't exactly been friends."

"Don't get soppy on me, okay? Let's just say I wasn't feeling well. The truth is—"

"You've never been nice to us, so what's the catch, Nellie?" Bheki interrupts her, convinced that she is up to something.

"That's for me to know and for you to find out." Rotten Nellie turns and walks away.

"Come back here!" Bheki calls angrily. He feels much more confident and safe in his own backyard than in the playgrounds at school or in the street.

Rotten Nellie just ignores him.

"Hey, Turnip Face. I'm talking to you!" he shouts, trying to provoke her. He shouldn't have said that because no one calls Rotten Nellie names and gets away with it. She turns around, fury in her eyes.

"What did you call me?" she hisses, striding back towards Bheki.

"You heard me."

"He said, 'Could you turn around please'," Four Eyes says, trying to calm Rotten Nellie down.

"Shut up, stupid!" she yells at him. "I heard what the idiot said."

"Can I just say thank you for the stone, Nellie?" Nolitye quickly interrupts. "You have no idea how much easier you've made my life."

But Rotten Nellie isn't listening. She has clenched her right hand into a fist and is about to punch Bheki in the face. Bheki is saved by his mother who, not suspecting any tension among him and his friends, shows up with a tray of orange juice and four glasses.

"Oh, who's your new friend, Mfana?" she says when she notices the newcomer. No one responds and MaZwane hands out orange juice to everyone. When she offers Rotten Nellie a glass, she takes it without saying thank you and starts drinking like a thirsty horse.

"By the way, this is Nellie, Ma, but everyone calls her Rotten Nellie," Bheki says.

Four Eyes gets such a shock that he chokes on the juice. He knows that when MaZwane isn't there Bheki will have to answer to Rotten Nellie.

"Nice to meet you, Sisi," Bheki's mother says. "But what kind of a name is Rotten Nellie? Did you do something bad?"

Rotten Nellie is too angry to speak and only grunts something nobody can understand.

"Not much of a talker, are you?" MaZwane says. "Bheki, don't forget to water the garden before sunset." And MaZwane walks back to the kitchen.

"Listen, Pumpkin Face!" Rotten Nellie finally explodes and then stops, a defeated look on her face.

"What?" Bheki says.

"I didn't come here to fight," Rotten Nellie says, unexpectedly calming down.

"You didn't?"

Rotten Nellie looks uncomfortable. She opens her mouth to say something, but then keeps quiet. Staring at the empty glass in her hand, she finally simply says, "No, I didn't. I came to warn Nolitye."

Rotten Nellie turns to Nolitye and looks at her with a kind of gentleness they've never seen on her face before. "I was supposed to give this parcel to MaMtonga, like my mother said," she explains holding the brown-paper wrapping in her hands. "I don't like the old woman, she gives me the creeps. But anyway, I went there after school. I just wanted to drop off the parcel and go, but she said I should stay. She wanted to tell me something. So I stayed. And you know what she told me?"

The three shake their heads and look at her wide-eyed with expectation. "She said together with my mother and some other people she was working to make things better," Rotten Nellie continues.

"What do you mean, make things better?" Four Eyes asks.

"That's what I also asked. And MaMtonga said that Ncitjana had promised to make them rich if they stole your stones. She said Ncitjana wants to use the stones to have power over all the neighbourhood children, all the children except me. And then she opened the parcel and showed me the stone. You should have seen her, she was laughing and saying that . . ." Rotten Nellie looks embarrassed and casts her eyes down, something no one has ever seen her do.

"Saying what?" Four Eyes asks after a while.

"She was saying that my mother stole the stone from a woman who was supposed to give it to Nolitye." Rotten Nellie is quiet for a moment. Then she snarls, "There, are you happy now?"

Four Eyes scratches his head and says nothing.

"That's when I knew I had to do something. So when MaMtonga stepped out to go to the toilet, I took the parcel and came to you."

"And once Ncitjana's got the power what does he want to do with all the children?" Bheki asks, nervously chewing on his thumbnail.

"She wouldn't say," Rotten Nellie says, shaking her head. "All I know is that I don't want to be the only one left behind. That's why I came to give you the stone, Nolitye, because MaMtonga said you're the only one who can stop Ncitjana."

Four Eyes and Bheki look at Nolitye gravely, as if she is the only one who can save the neighbourhood children. "Just one thing, though," she says to Rotten Nellie.

"What?"

"Truce?" And Nolitye puts out her hand.

Rotten Nellie looks at it as if it is the first time she sees an outstretched hand. "Okay, truce," she says and takes Nolitye's hand firmly. "But if you tell anyone about this it's off. This is our secret. Okay?"

"Fine with me. My lips are sealed," Nolitye says.

"Mine too . . ." Bheki says. "Huh, Four Eyes?" Four Eyes nods.

"Right, then do what you have to do," Rotten Nellie says to Nolitye.

"But you'll get into trouble when MaMtonga discovers that she doesn't have the stone after all," Nolitye warns.

"It's either that, or all the neighbourhood children are in trouble," Rotten Nellie says and walks away, past the house and out the gate, almost slap-bang into old MaMkize.

A surprised silence hangs in the air. After a while Four Eyes looks around and says, "Did we just make peace with Rotten Nellie?"

Bheki and Nolitye nod. Bheki and Four Eyes start smiling and soon they are laughing helplessly. "Yes! Yes!" they shout.

But Nolitye is distant in her thoughts. She puts the new stone next to the magic stone. A gentle wind stirs as sparks start jumping from the stones. A hue of purple light surrounds the crystals as they fuse. Nolitye gets goose bumps when she realises that she now has all the stones, that the sacred stone is in one piece again, just like it was a long time ago. She picks up the stone and puts it in her bag and clutches the bag to her chest. It has become too big to fit in any of the pockets on her clothing, not to mention the little patchwork bag. "Hey, we got the stone!" Four Eyes rejoices, but then he looks at Nolitye.

"I thought you'd be overjoyed, Nolitye."

"I am . . . I mean, I can finally confront that woman who pretends to be my mother. I was just thinking of my real mother and father. We first have to rescue them from the underworld."

"How do we do that?" Bheki asks.

"I've got a plan, but I'm going to need your help. I was thinking of rescuing them tonight."

"Tonight? You know my mom won't let me go out after dark."

"Not if you say that you'll be staying over at Four Eyes's place," Nolitye says and winks. "And Four Eyes, you can ask your dad if you can stay over at Bheki's place."

"Why would I do that?" Four Eyes asks, confused.

"So that you can both come over to my place and help me rescue my mom and dad."

"Oh. So you mean I won't actually be staying at Bheki's place?"

Bheki sighs. "You know, for a smart guy you can sometimes be really dumb."

"Shut up," Four Eyes says, sticking out his tongue at Bheki. Bheki swallows his smile. "What if we get caught out?"

"We won't," Four Eyes says, ready for the challenge.

"So are we really doing this?" Nolitye looks hard at the boys. They nod. "That's the spirit!" she says, smacking her hands against theirs.

They proceed to put the plan in action: Bheki leaves the other two at the bottom of the garden to go and speak to his mother. He stands with his fingers crossed behind his back when he asks her if he can spend the night at Four Eyes's place so they can do homework together.

"I don't understand why you suddenly have to go to a friend's place to do your homework," MaZwane says while she takes another tray of hot biscuits from the oven.

"Because . . . because we're working on a project, Ma. We have to work together." Bheki can't resist a biscuit and puts out his hand.

His mother smacks his hand before he can take one. "They're hot. You'll be up all night with stomach-ache."

"So may I go?"

"Okay, fine."

"Thanks Ma, you're the best!" Bheki kisses her on the cheek and fetches an overnight bag.

MaZwane packs his clothes in the overnight bag. "Have you remembered your toothbrush? No one likes bad breath in the morning."

Bheki has to take his toothbrush from a side-pocket of the bag to convince her. "There," he says, not able to keep the irritation out of his voice.

"Don't you give me cheek, young man, or I'll smother you with so many kisses you'll wish you were Khaya."

"I'll just tell Nolitye and Four Eyes," Bheki says, dashing out of the kitchen.

"Well, how did it go?" Nolitye asks nervously when he flops down between them on the grass. "You stayed away for a long time."

"Packed and ready to go," Bheki says. Nolitye smiles. "You mean she said yes?"

"Which part of 'packed and ready' didn't you understand?"

"He's getting too cheeky these days," Four Eyes tells Nolitye and clucks his tongue.

Nolitye and Four Eyes gather the cards and the plate of biscuits and follow Bheki to the kitchen, Nolitye's schoolbag slung over her shoulder.

"Thanks, MaZwane," Nolitye says, putting the plate in the sink and her bag on the floor. She rolls up her shirtsleeves and starts running water.

"Don't worry about that, Sisi. It was a pleasure." MaZwane says, and adds, "Four Eyes, if Bheki doesn't wake up in the morning just blow into his ear. That always works."

"I'll remember that," Four Eyes laughs wickedly. Outside the gate he tells the other two that he'll quickly go home to ask his father for permission to stay over at Bheki's house and that he will meet them later at Nolitye's place.

Nolitye and Bheki approach the shack carefully. He quietly wishes her luck as they stand in front of the door. Now that the moment of confronting the woman who pretends to be her mother has arrived, Nolitye feels nervous, a hard knot in her stomach. She takes a deep breath before she turns the door handle.

They find Thembi inside, crouched over the bucket with Nolitye's stones. "What are you doing with my stones?" Nolitye asks, rushing forward.

"Good afternoon, Nolitye," Thembi says.

"Sorry. Hi, Mama."

"Sawubona, MaDube," Bheki says a little embarrassed.

They stand about feeling uneasy, not knowing how to confront Thembi with her real name.

"I'm going to throw these stones away. Really Nolitye, they take up too much space and we could use the bucket for something else."

"No, you can't do that," Nolitye protests.

"I'm tired of your silly stones!" Thembi gets up and heads for the door with the heavy bucket.

"It's taken me years to collect these stones, one by one, and now you want to just throw them out! Well, you can't!" Nolitye glowers at Thembi. Bheki doesn't know what to do, so he looks at his shoes.

"That's it! I've had it with you. You think you can just shout at me in front of your friends, showing off. Well, I'm your mother and I won't stand for it!" Thembi lifts her hand to smack Nolitye.

Suddenly unafraid, Nolitye says, "You're not my mother!"

Thembi's hand drops to her side. "Are you mad!" she says.

"I know who you are. You are Sylvia."

First Thembi's eyes narrow and then they grow big. "What did you say?"

"You heard me. We know who you are, Sylvia." Nolitye pronounces each syllable of the name clearly.

"Yes, Sylvia," Bheki repeats, equally brave.

The woman who said she is Nolitye's mother lets out a terrible scream, so loud that the corrugated-iron walls shake. Her face starts contorting. She tries to cover her face with her hands, but Bheki and Nolitye nevertheless see her features changing as her face takes on another shape. She lets out another agonised scream. Her body starts shuddering violently and shrinks in length. Her hair shrivels until only a bald scalp remains. The woman in front of them looks haggard and clumsy in a dress that is now far too big for her.

"You evil kids. How did you break my spell?" the new woman howls in a coarse voice. She runs out of the shack shrieking like a hyena. Nolitye and Bheki can't believe their eyes. Nolitye looks at the beads and cowrie shells that Sylvia gave her to wear. Realising that they were just a trick to trap her and keep her under the spell, she tears them from her arm and throws them on the floor. To her utter amazement, the beads and cowrie shells turn into a small snake.

Bheki jumps on the bed and watches the snake slither out the door. Nolitye tiptoes after the snake to see where it is heading. It slides in under MaMtonga's door. They still need to deal with the old woman, but she is so powerful they will need the strength of the stone.

Four Eyes arrives as the two are still reeling with shock from what has just happened.

"You should have seen her, man. Eish! When Nolitye called her Sylvia she just began to change into this horrible old woman with a bald head," Bheki says, and jumps off the bed.

Four Eyes is disappointed that he missed out on the action. "Actually, it was rather scary," Nolitye confesses. "I thought she was going to start spitting fire."

Nolitye takes the broom from the cooking corner and sweeps the room. A strange smell lingers in the air, so she opens the window to let in some fresh air. With Four Eyes's help Bheki puts her bucket of stones back under the bed.

Nolitye opens the cupboards and from the shelves she was never allowed to touch, she removes dozens of small packets and throws them in the bin outside. She doesn't even look because she knows the packets are full of Sylvia's strange herbs. Soon she is changing the bed linen. Bheki and Four Eyes help her. Under the mattress they find a dried bat, a chameleon's tail and a snake skin, all covered in clear plastic. Nolitye throws them in the bin too. Then they take out all Sylvia's clothes and put them in a heap on the floor to be washed.

On top of the wardrobe, hidden behind the two suitcases, they discover a black plastic garbage bag. Inside, Nolitye finds the clothes

Sylvia wore the night she saw her with MaMtonga and the other Night Riders at the Amanzi Mnyama river. She dumps the clothes in the corner with the rubbish bin and starts mopping the floor.

"So how do we get to the underworld?" Bheki asks.

Nolitye rubs her forehead. Only Nomakhosi knows the way, but Nolitye still can't tell them about her special ally. While Nolitye is trying to think up some solution, Four Eyes says he is thirsty. She points him to the kitchen cupboard where their two glasses are kept, and to the bucket of water on the kitchen table. When Four Eyes opens the cupboard door, a glass tumbles out. But it doesn't crash to the floor; it remains suspended in the air.

This can only mean one thing, Nolitye thinks excitedly. Nomakhosi must be in the room! She looks around to see in what shape Nomakhosi could have hidden herself this time.

Four Eyes's gaze is glued to the suspended glass and Bheki stands there gaping.

Nolitye turns around when the door creaks. Nomakhosi stands there, still dressed in her traditional blue-and-red-striped Shangaan skirt with flounces, edged with white beads. When she steps forward, Bheki steps back, afraid that it might be Sylvia in a new guise. He taps Four Eyes on the shoulder.

"Guys, I want you to meet someone," Nolitye says to them.

Without saying a word, Nomakhosi takes Nolitye's hand. Bheki relaxes. Four Eyes still can't keep his eyes off the suspended glass.

"Guys, this is Nomakhosi," Nolitye says proudly, glad that finally her friends can meet this wonderful being who can slow down time and change shape. "She's an ancestral spirit-kind of my guide."

Four Eyes and Bheki are drawn by her green eyes. They stare stupidly.

"I see you've been busy," Nomakhosi says as she looks at the heap of laundry on the floor and the table pushed back so Nolitye could mop the floor.

"We finally got rid of that woman," Nolitye announces.

Four Eyes has only one thing on his mind. "Please, how did you make the glass float?" he asks.

Nomakhosi smiles. "Life is full of mystery. Don't be fooled by what you think you see."

Nolitye has more pressing things to talk about. "So how do we rescue my mother and father from the underworld?" she asks urgently.

"You'll have to go to the Amanzi Mnyama river after sunset. But this isn't going to be easy, Nolitye," Nomakhosi warns them.

"I know, but I've come this far." The thought of seeing her father and her real mother gives Nolitye all the courage she needs. "Don't worry," she tells the other two. "We have the stone on our side."

"You have to be careful, though," Nomakhosi warns them again, and then explains: "There's a big hole in the ground near the reeds where you hid the other night. It's not easy to find because it is well concealed. That is the entrance to the underworld."

"You mean we have to crawl down a hole?" Bheki looks extremely doubtful.

"I'm afraid so."

"Will you come with us, Nomakhosi?" Nolitye asks hopefully.

"The underworld is not for people like me. If I go there I may never return."

Nolitye bites her lip when she realises that she will have to rescue her mother and father with only the help of her friends.

"You better catch that glass before it smashes to the ground," Nomakhosi says. "I am about to leave." And with that she is gone, leaving the boys to wonder at her powers. Four Eyes catches the glass just in time.

To collect her thoughts, Nolitye makes the bed and takes her school books from her bag. She puts the sacred stone in a side-pocket where it will be safe. Four Eyes, the most eager for adventure of them all, has brought a pocket torch with him. Nolitye tells them to put on their jerseys as it might be cold. They make some sandwiches. For some inexplicable reason the woman who said she was Nolitye's mother for the first time in a long while brought home some fresh bread, jam and peanut butter.

They eat in a sombre mood. Doubt and fear start nagging at Nolitye. What if they don't find her mother and father? Who will look after her? Unlike Bheki and Four Eyes, she doesn't have any relatives.

"Hey, everything is going to be alright, you'll see." And Four Eyes, who senses that she is worried, takes her hand. Nolitye gives him a skew little smile.

She locks the door before they set off. With Thembi-Sylvia gone, she doesn't have to ask anyone for permission. She doesn't even bother to take off her school uniform, she just puts on her old jersey.

Chapter Thirteen

THE TRICKSTER

AN icy wind is churning up dust outside. The door to MaMtonga's place is ajar. She must have noticed the threesome's shadows as they pass and, trying to scare them, she screeches, "The night will eat your flesh for what you did to Sylvia, you horrible rats!"

But they pretend not to hear her. The only thing that Nolitye can think about is the journey ahead.

It is a long walk to get to the Amanzi Mnyama river. Not wanting to draw attention to themselves, they walk down the back alleys, not past MaMokoena's spaza shop and the clinic as they would normally do. The last person they want to run into tonight is Ntate Matthews.

As they cross the soccer field, they notice Rex and his pack scavenging near a rubbish heap. They bark at the three, but there is no time for a chat, so Nolitye, followed by Bheki and Four Eyes, quickly sprint across the unusually quiet freeway.

On the other side they are met by the unmistakable stench of stagnant water. Nolitye stands quietly for a while, trying to retrace her steps of a few nights ago when Nomakhosi brought her here. She spots the faint footpath down to the river. Near the water the reeds grow tall, but still she manages to follow the path leading to the spot where the Night Riders made their fire. The three-quarter moon doesn't give enough light, so Four Eyes takes out his pocket torch.

"Do we really want do this?" Bheki asks. He is getting cold feet.

Four Eyes shines the light in his face. "You're not scared of the dark, are you?" he teases.

"Of course not," Bheki is quick to say, but his voice shakes too much to be convincing. Just then something scurries in the reeds and Bheki clutches onto Four Eyes, breathing hard.

"Chill! It was probably just a rat looking for a boy called Bheki to eat."

"Very funny."

"Shush, you guys. I'll go in front," says Nolitye.

Four Eyes hands her the torch. It makes only a small circle of light, but it is enough to be able to follow the path which now seems well tramped. It runs past a big rock and some prickly bushes. Something makes Nolitye stop and peer under the thorny bushes. She shines the torch to make sure. Yes, there is a large hole, but it is completely overgrown and covered with branches.

They stand there, staring at a hole. A rat crawls out of the dark and disappears in the reeds. Bheki grabs Nolitye by the arm, but he doesn't make a noise. Taking a deep breath, Nolitye starts pushing and breaking the bushes out of the way. Bheki and Four Eyes help her. Their hands and arms get scratched, but they keep at it. Spiders and crickets crawl up their legs but they persist and shake them off. Seeing how diligently Four Eyes works, Bheki stops complaining.

"Okay, guys, this is it," Nolitye says once the mouth to the path into the depth is clear. She silently counts to ten to calm her nerves and touches the side-pocket of her school bag to make sure the magic stone is still there.

Nolitye crawls in first, shining the torch just far enough ahead of her to be able to see where to put her hands down. She would rather not look too far down the tunnel. The other two follow close on her heels. Bheki has made sure that he is safely sandwiched between Nolitye and Four Eyes. They move forward in silence, crawling on all fours. Their progress is painfully slow because there is hardly any space and it is stuffy.

They concentrate so hard to see in the dark that their eyes get dry. To see nothing while crawling down an endless, narrow, musty tunnel plays havoc with the imagination, and Bheki begins to believe he sees a big snake just beyond the small spot of torchlight. He shudders to a stop when he hears something scratching in the dark; Four Eyes bumps into him. "What was that?" Bheki whispers.

"Probably a mole," Nolitye answers. She too stops and shines the torch ahead. There's nothing to see.

"What if it's a snake, a python?"

"Cool!" Unlike Bheki, Four Eyes sounds calm.

"What's so cool about that? I want to go home, guys. This is not for me," Bheki whimpers.

"Don't be a wimp," Four Eyes says. Bheki is getting on his nerves.

"I can see light ahead," Nolitye whispers, and Bheki crawls faster, eager to get out of the tight space.

Slowly the tunnel widens, and crawling round a last corner, they are blinded by light and almost overwhelmed by fresh air. Dizzy with exhaustion and anxiety they straighten up to survey the scene.

It is morning in a remote, boulder-strewn valley. A river gurgles nearby. Bheki dusts off his knees and Four Eyes blinks his eyes against the glare. It is so quiet that the distant cry of a fish eagle can be heard. Nolitye hands Four Eyes the torch. They look around silently, in awe of the valley's beauty.

"Where are we, do you think?" Bheki asks after a while.

"I don't think we're in Phola any more." Nolitye looks around for signs of people but finds nothing. Empty veld stretches as far as the horizon.

"Well, you did say it was going to be an adventure." And Four Eyes looks at Nolitye with two sets of shiny eyes.

"One I'd rather get over and done with quickly," Bheki whines, sitting down on a boulder.

Quite nearby they hear a rustling in the grass. Bheki shoots up, alarmed. They all turn their heads in the direction from where the sound came. Behind a boulder a pair of long ears protrudes and hides again. Bheki steps back. Four Eyes and Nolitye watch closely. The ears protrude again, slowly revealing the head of a hare.

"Nogwatsha!" Four Eyes whispers.

"Actually, my name is Vundla," the hare corrects him with an air of importance.

"And I am Nolitye. These are my friends Bheki and Four Eyes," she says, pointing them out to Vundla. He nods at them and gently hops onto the boulder. For a while no one says anything as Vundla stares at them and they stare back. He scratches behind one of his long ears.

"City slickers," he concludes. "How did you get here?"

"Through the hole in the ground." Nolitye turns round to point out the place, but the hole isn't there any more. "It was here just now, I promise," she says, searching around. Bheki and Four Eyes also look but find nothing. Dumbfounded and embarrassed, they give up the search and look to Vundla for an answer.

"I suppose it doesn't matter how you got here," Vundla says nose in the air. "But tell me, what are you doing here?"

"We're here to rescue my mother and father."

"They've been trapped by Ncitjana here somewhere." Nolitye swallows.

"The Mean One." Vundla shakes his head, his ears flopping from side to side.

"Do you know where my parents are being held?"

"Uhm . . . yes . . . I do, as a matter of fact." Vundla hesitates. "Your mother, she's like you, right? Only taller, isn't she?"

"Yes, yes," Nolitye says, excitement making her talk fast. "But she has a beautiful face."

"And your father . . . well . . . he's like any father, right?"

"Yes, yes!"

"Suppose I help you find your mother and father, what would you do for me?"

The three look at each other and whisper among themselves. Four Eyes scratches in his back pocket and takes out fifty cents.

"We have fifty cents for you!" Nolitye says showing him the money.

"And what is the use of money here?" Vundla says. "We're in the wild, not the city."

"Oh, sorry." Nolitye looks sheepish.

Vundla casts his eyes on Four Eyes. "What's that strange thing your friend has in his hand?" he asks Nolitye.

"You mean this?" Four Eyes holds up the torch. "We use it to see in the dark. It's called a torch." Four Eyes presses the ON button. Vundla leaps from the boulder and takes shelter behind it.

"It's just a light," Four Eyes says turning it off. "It can't hurt or harm you."

"Oh, really? I knew that!" Vundla steps from behind the boulder, his floppy ears standing upright again. "May I touch it?"

"Sure, here." Vundla hops over to Four Eyes and gingerly takes the torch from him. He examines it, giving a delighted squeak every time he succeeds in switching on the light.

"So will you help us find my mother?" Nolitye asks.

"Of course I will." Vundla hands the torch back to Four Eyes. "We'll have to ford the river below, but first I must go back home to tell my wife that I will be helping you out."

Nolitye nods. "We understand."

They follow Vundla as he makes his way up a slope. He hops easily over the rocks and boulders, laughing to himself when the others are not looking. Every once in a while he turns back though, to make sure that they are still behind him.

Bheki, not frightened any longer, tags along at the back. He tires quickly and after a little distance they have to wait for him to catch his breath before they can move on. Four Eyes seems delighted with the scenery and whistles as he walks. Nolitye concentrates on the rock-strewn path.

Vundla stops at the mouth of a deep cave. "Are we there yet?" Bheki, breathing heavily and his face wet with sweat, asks. He wipes the perspiration from his forehead with the back of his hand and collapses on a rock.

Vundla nods. "As a matter of fact, we are."

"But I thought hares lived in burrows," Nolitye points out.

"They do . . . but not all of us. I prefer living in a cave because when it rains you don't get wet."

"Fair enough," Four Eyes says, feasting his eyes on the vista in front of them.

"Come!" Vundla invites.

"Where's your wife?" Nolitye asks as they enter the cave.

Vundla does not reply, but quick as the eye can travel he leaps across to a low-hanging part of the cave. Pushing hard with both front paws against the roof he pretends to hold it up. "Quick! Quick! The cave is falling in!" he shouts, straining every muscle.

"What? Where?"

"Help me hold it up before it crushes us all!" Vundla shouts to Nolitye.

As one, Nolitye, Bheki and Four Eyes place their hands against the rocky roof, panic on their faces.

"Push, or it will crush us!" Vundla shouts.

They push upwards with all their strength. Bheki starts breathing hard again. After a while Vundla says, "My friends, I think my wife ran in there because she was scared she would be crushed. I am frightened for her. Please lend me that light-thing of yours so that I can find her and together she and I can find help before the cave collapses."

"You mean the torch? It's in my pocket," Four Eyes says. "Here on the left," he instructs, his hands still pressed against the roof of the cave.

Vundla reaches inside his pocket and takes out the torch. He switches it on and shrieks with delight when he sees how the torch lights up the cave.

Grinning widely, he disappears into the depths of the cavern, leaving the others to hold up the roof.

"My arms are getting tired," Bheki moans.

"Just keep them there!" Four Eyes yells at him.

Shortly after, Vundla comes back alone.

"Well, did you find her?" Nolitye wants to know.

"No. I think she went to visit her sister who lives in another cave not far from here. I'll go there and get them to help us. Just keep holding up the roof. I won't be long." And off Vundla runs with the torch.

A long time passes and still Vundla does not return with his wife and her sister. Though their arms are aching, Nolitye, Bheki and Four Eyes have no choice but to keep holding up the roof. Nolitye starts to remember all the stories she heard about the hare's trickery and begins to suspect that something is wrong. Perhaps they have been tricked, she thinks, but doesn't tell the other two.

Faintly they can hear laughter echoing through the valley.

Finally Nolitye, her arms weak with fatigue, stops holding up the roof. "What are you doing?" Bheki shouts.

"I've quit holding up the roof. We've been tricked!"

Four Eyes and Bheki slowly take their hands down. Nothing happens. The roof stays in place.

Four Eyes punches his fist in one hand. "My torch!" he groans.

"They don't call him the Clever One of the veld for nothing," Bheki admits reluctantly.

Nolitye feels bad and apologises. "I'm sorry, Four Eyes."

"It's not your fault."

"What do we do now?" Bheki asks, exasperated.

"We better get down to the river," Nolitye says, moving towards the daylight. The others follow her out of the cave and down the slope, all of them looking out for Vundla. He is nowhere to be seen, but they do stumble upon a path that leads down to the river. Dassies observe them going past without batting an eyelid; cicadas shrill around them.

Near the river the grass is long and brushes their legs. Weaver birds flit in and out of their nests waving on the reeds. The air is scented with wild flowers and the dank smell of the nearby river.

Four Eyes picks a straw of grass and sucks on it. He walks with a bounce in his step, seemingly over the disappointment of having lost his torch, and engrossed in the scene around him. He ignores the gnats and midges buzzing round his face; Bheki swats them full of wrath.

On the river bank, they find the carcass of a buck, scraps of meat still stuck to the bones. Flies and bluebottles dance around it. Bheki stops and looks behind him. "You don't think there are any lions nearby, do you, Four Eyes?"

"It wouldn't surprise me." And Four Eyes walks on as if he couldn't care less.

Chapter Fourteen
THE QUEEN

NOLITYE is staring out over the river, a line of concern furrowed between her eyes.

"How are we going to get across?" Four Eyes asks. "I can't swim."

"Me neither," Bheki says, catching up with them.

"I'm thinking." Nolitye looks around for logs or planks or something that will float. There is nothing of the sort, but something else catches her eye - a ripple in the water. Suddenly a spray of water shoots out. Two tiny ears and two large nostrils lift out of the water before a frighteningly big maw opens, showing a pink lining and four massive white stumps for teeth. The threesome scream as if from one mouth, turn and head for the hills.

"Wait," a low voice calls. "I'm not going to hurt you."

The three slow down and look back. A fat hippopotamus is waddling onto the river bank. It flicks its short tail and ambles to a nearby tree, rubbing its rolls of fat against the trunk. "I heard you saying you want to get to the other side of the river," the hippopotamus says.

The children say nothing, watching the huge beast scratching itself.

"My name is Mvu and I will help you get across if you'll do me a favour," the hippo offers.

"Not that again! I'm not falling for another trick!" Four Eyes says and crosses his arms.

"Vundla just stole our torch so we have nothing to offer you," Bheki says.

"But I don't want anything from you," Mvu says, speaking very slowly. "I thought you could pick these ticks from my back while I carry you across the river. The birds that usually clean them off were caught by the Zim and put in a cage."

"The Zim!" the three exclaim, horror in their eyes.

"You mean he is here?" Nolitye asks.

"Yes, he lives behind that koppie over there." Mvu points across the river with his head. "They say he keeps the birds in a cage and feeds them to Ncitjana's khokhothis."

It is almost too much for Bheki. "Ncitjana is here too!" he groans, throwing back his head and rolling his eyes.

"Yes, he is," Mvu says very calmly. "The Zim lives with him and Ncitjana's khokhothis."

"Khokhothis?" Nolitye asks.

"Slaves. Ncitjana keeps four children that he stole from the city as khokhothis. They tend his cattle and work in his fields all day. They live in his kraal."

The three look at each other knowingly. It must be the kids that were stolen from Phola.

"What about a grown man and a woman?" Nolitye asks, holding her breath. "Are they there also?"

"A man and a woman . . ." Nolitye has stopped breathing altogether.

"Yes, now that you mention it. I saw them once when they tried to run away. But Ncitjana caught them as they tried to get across the river. Their legs and arms were in chains. I don't know what became of them after that."

Nolitye takes a deep breath. Her face shrivels up with sadness.

"They could still be there," Four Eyes says, putting his arm around her. Nolitye, encouraged again, says, "Mvu, we'll help you pick off the ticks." Mvu moves to a boulder and starts grazing on some tufts of grass. Four Eyes steps on the boulder and with ease hurls himself onto Mvu's back. Nolitye crawls up with his assistance. But Bheki struggles and in the end, Four Eyes and Nolitye have to pull him up and nearly fall off Mvu's back themselves. Mvu doesn't budge; he stands stock-still, steady as a rock.

Mvu's skin is soft and delicate to the touch. The three start picking at the ticks as he slowly waddles towards the water, grazing in between. They have to keep their balance when Mvu wades in. The water is cool and comes up to their shins. Four Eyes cups a handful of water and splashes it on his face and grins. Mvu glides forward effortlessly, like a feather floating on the wind.

"Much better," Mvu murmurs as the three get rid of the ticks.

Five sets of small ears and big nostrils appear next to Mvu. "This is my family," he says proudly.

"Dumelang," the children say and wave.

Mvu's family spray water into the air by way of greeting them. The three giggle as tiny refreshing droplets settle on their faces.

"Now take care to keep your balance," Mvu reminds them as they get to the other side of the river. While his family wait for him in the water, he slowly wades out of the water and gets the children on land without them falling off his back. Mvu snorts a warning and kneels on a patch of grass. Nolitye and Four Eyes slide down and land on their feet; Bheki lands on his bum but scrambles up so quickly that Four Eyes and Nolitye don't even notice.

"Thanks for helping us," Nolitye says.

"Thanks for getting rid of those pesky ticks," Mvu replies.

"So Ncitjana is just behind that koppie over there?" Nolitye asks to make doubly sure.

"That's where you'll find his kraal. And you better go right now because he is away with the Zim looking for other khokhothis."

They watch Mvu glide into the water and take his place as head of the family. Then they start walking up the slope in single file, the tall grass stalks on either side coming up to their waists. Bheki tries hard to keep up with the other two. The well-worn path zigzags to the top of the koppie. A little out of breath they stop to survey their surroundings. Aloe trees are scattered around them; in the distance they can see Ncitjana's kraal with three huts and a patch of wheat. Some cattle graze nearby.

"Brace yourselves," Nolitye says before she breaks into a run down the hill, Four Eyes on her heels. "Wait for me!" Bheki shouts from behind.

At the entrance to the kraal, Nolitye and Four Eyes stop to wait for him. Camel-thorn trees line the fence around the huts. From a big tree next to the middle hut a wire-mesh cage with white birds hangs. There are too many birds crammed into the cage and their distressed calls can be heard from afar.

Bheki arrives, sweating and breathing hard. He bends down to tie his laces. "What is this?" he scolds them. "Physical education?"

"You heard what Mvu said. We don't have time. The Zim will be back soon." Nolitye walks into the yard, past a fire place built with roundish rocks. The ash in the hearth is cold, an empty three-legged pot lies toppled over. Nolitye goes straight to the first round, ochre-coloured mud hut. The thatch roof is sagging and the hut has no windows.

She knocks on the rickety door and says, "Hello." No one responds. She knocks again and waits patiently, but no sound comes from inside, not even a footstep. Her heart beating wildly, she slowly pushes the door open. She glances back to indicate to Four Eyes and Bheki to stay outside and be on the look out.

Light floods the dark room as Nolitye tiptoes inside. It is empty! She stands on the mud-and-cowdung floor and quickly inspects the hut. There is nothing except for some grey blankets, neatly folded and stacked one on top of the other against the wall. She closes the door behind her and shakes her head.

"Maybe they are out in the fields," Bheki says, keeping his voice low. Nolitye casts an eye on the cattle, idly grazing in the sun. "But someone must be watching the cows." They go to the next hut, only a few metres away from the first one. Nolitye knocks. This door, too, is rickety. She listens, expecting to hear the sound of children and maybe a woman calling them, but all she hears is the crying of the birds in the cage, the sound of flies buzzing over cowdung, cicadas shrilling in the heat and the occasional mooing of cattle. And in the distance a fish eagle's cry, echoing over the river.

Nolitye takes a deep breath and opens the door. A nauseating smell hits her and a horde of flies rush out through the door. She indicates to Four Eyes and Bheki to join her. They have to cover their noses it smells so bad. Inside the hut they are met by a horrible mess. The floor, made of soft sandy soil, is littered with bones. Large footprints run haphazardly in every direction.

"This is where he sleeps," Nolitye whispers, swatting flies.

"You mean Ncitjana?"

"No man, Four Eyes, she means the Zim," Bheki says, holding his nose. They hurry out of the filthy, smelly room and gulp the fresh air outside.

Visibly relieved, Four Eyes closes the door.

Nolitye is deeply worried as they walk to the third hut. What if Ncitjana took her parents and the children away? Or worse, what if the Zim . . . She looks around her and listens for any noise.

There is a padlock on the door of the third hut, but it is not locked. This time, Nolitye doesn't bother to knock but simply opens the door. It creaks horribly. Four children huddling together in a corner cover their eyes against the bright light. Their ankles are bound in chains.

"I found them!" Nolitye calls over her shoulder. Bheki and Four Eyes follow her inside. The children have removed their hands from their faces; now there is only naked fear. Their unkempt appearance makes their faces look gaunt, and they could certainly do with a good wash. Nolitye crouches in front of the first child and peers into her face. "Mbali!" She recognises the girl who also went to Nka Thutho until she was stolen. And then she recognises Vusi. She assumes the two other children must be Sara and Tebogo, who disappeared from Phola earlier. But what Nolitye really notices is the look of terror in everyone's eyes.

"Mbali, don't look so worried, we've come to take you home. Look, we've even come in our school uniforms," Nolitye tries to reassure them. But the children don't look happy to be found, and they don't want to look at the newcomers. Vusi, the littlest one, wipes his runny nose on his arm and points behind them, his hand shaking. Nolitye, Bheki and Four Eyes turn around.

The door suddenly slams shut and darkness fills the room. In the gloom Bheki, Nolitye and Four Eyes make out a tall figure moving about. The figure fidgets with something and a small, bright light comes on.

The three scream. Blocking any escape, a large, hairy man - so tall that he has to stoop to fit in the hut - stands over them. He lets his arms dangle at his side and laughs with a booming voice. The three, barely able to remain on their feet, retreat, almost tripping over the crouching children. The giant of a hairy man holds the light under his chin so that his teeth appear sharp as small razors. Dribble is dripping from his mouth onto the floor. It can only be the Zim.

"Shut up, or I'll eat you!" he hollers. Bheki, Nolitye and Four Eyes have no intention of talking, but they can't keep their teeth from chattering.

"Ncitjana told me that you would be paying us a visit, so I made preparations," the Zim says, coming closer on huge, hairy, bare feet. The three stagger backwards till they hit the wall. They sink to the ground, sitting almost on top of one another.

"Very handy, this little thing. What do you call it?" The Zim waves the light in his left hand, while he brings the pinkie nail of his right hand to his face and starts picking his teeth. The nail is as long as a man's arm and is curved like a sickle-blade.

"It's ca . . . called a torch," Four Eyes stutters, recognising his pocket torch.

"Hmmm. I found it on Vundla . . . before I ate him. But he told me all about you and the trick he played on you." The Zim steps even closer. "So don't be clever with me, because you won't get far."

Nolitye swallows hard. She can't remember ever being as scared as she feels now, not even when MaMtonga sent the two men to find her in the reeds.

"Ha! Ncitjana is going to be very happy when he sees his new khokhothis. All three strong and healthy and one nice and fat." And the Zim bursts into laughter. His booming laugh makes the walls shake; dust particles sift down from the thatch roof. He shuffles to a wooden trunk and takes some chains from it. Bheki is on the verge of tears when the giant moves towards him, drooling and breathing heavily.

The Zim grabs Bheki by the legs and straps the chains around his ankles. Bheki almost wets his pants. He does the same to Nolitye and Four Eyes." Be good so I won't have to eat you," he bellows, switching off the torch. He closes the door and this time he clicks the padlock shut, leaving the hut in darkness. Only thin beams of light sneak through the cracks in the rough door.

Vusi, the youngest one, starts crying.

"It's going to be fine. You'll see," Nolitye says, trying hard to remain calm. "No, it's not," Vusi sniffles. "You've made him angry and now he's going to eat us."

"No, he won't," Four Eyes says.

There is a long silence before Nolitye asks hesitantly, "Was there ever a woman and a man here with you?"

"I was the first to come here," Sara, the oldest girl, says. "In the beginning there were a man and woman here. The woman cooked for Ncitjana while the man worked in the fields all day long. They never spoke much, and Ncitjana made sure that they couldn't speak to us much by keeping them locked up in the other hut. But we did speak a few times. The woman said her name was Thembi and that she missed her daughter terribly. The man said his name was Xoli and that he dreamt about the daughter every night. And then one day I came back from herding the cows and found that they were gone."

"They are my parents," Nolitye says very softly. In the dark Four

Eyes gives her a little hug. It gives her courage to ask, "What do you mean gone?"

"I never saw them again. Next thing I knew the Zim was staying here. Ncitjana boasted that he offered the woman - sorry, your mother - to the river spirits in exchange for having power over the Zim. I suppose that's why the Zim came after your mother left. Ncitjana threatened he would offer me to the river spirits too if I tried to escape."

Nolitye clears her throat. "What happened to my father?" The others can hardly hear the question, she speaks so very softly.

"I don't know," Sara says. "Ncitjana wouldn't say. But I never saw him again."

The lump in Nolitye's throat won't go away, and she has to fight back the tears. For the first time since they have entered the underworld she puts her hand in her school bag and takes out the sacred stone. In the dark she kisses it and thinks of her parents, trying to remember what they looked like in the dream.

It is dead quiet in the dark hut. After a while she starts feeling stronger and in a much firmer voice says, "We must get out of here before Ncitjana comes back."

"But how?" Mbali wants to know.

Nolitye clutches the stone to her chest and closes her eyes. "I wish our chains would come loose and the door would open," she whispers.

As soon as the words leave her mouth there is a dull clattering and clanging as the chains slip off their ankles.

"What's going on? My chains are loose!" There is disbelief in Mbali's voice.

"Mine too," Tebogo says.

"Let's get out of here quickly," Nolitye says and flings her chains across the room. Her heart beats fast as she puts back the stone in her school bag and rushes to the door, Four Eyes and Bheki with her. But the other children don't stir.

"Come," Nolitye encourages them.

"What if the Zim is waiting outside the door?" Sara sounds terrified. "He'll eat us."

"No, he won't. I'll protect you. It's now or never." And Nolitye reaches for the door handle and opens it.

The captured children gasp with wonder. How did she do that? What about the padlock?

Light pours into the hut again. Nolitye gingerly puts her head round the door. "He's not here," she says. "We must move quickly, and right now!"

"I want to see my mother again," Vusi says and gets up and takes Four Eyes's hand. Tebogo, Sara and Mbali look at each other.

"We have to go now," Nolitye says. "While he's not around."

Terrified, the other three join them. "He's probably sleeping in his hut," Mbali whispers under her breath. "He likes to nap in the afternoon before he goes out hunting with Ncitjana at night. So we have to be dead quiet."

Four Eyes carefully closes the door. The children sneak out, tiptoeing past the Zim's hut. They can hear him snoring, making a loud gurgling sound. They cautiously open the gate and are about to leave when Four Eyes turns back.

"Where do you think you're going?" Bheki whispers urgently and grabs him by the arm.

"Those birds," Four Eyes says. "They don't belong in a cage."

"Four Eyes, this is not the time." Nolitye sounds desperate.

"Nolitye, I must release them!"

Nolitye silently throws her hands in the air, but she nevertheless tells the others to wait. They gather out of sight around the corner, while Bheki stays where he is to keep a lookout.

Four Eyes tiptoes back to the tree, past the hut where the Zim snores so loudly now that the walls vibrate.

Nolitye cannot wait. "Well?" she asks from behind Bheki's back.

"He's not there yet," Bheki reports.

Four Eyes, looking over his shoulder to make sure the Zim's door stays closed, doesn't notice the rusted tin in front of his feet and sends it clattering over the ground. The Zim stops snoring and Four Eyes closes his eyes, biting the insides of his mouth. It sounds as if the Zim swallows, and then the snoring resumes.

Four Eyes has reached the cage and unties the wire door. The white birds flutter out in a panic, but as if aware of the danger, they don't make much noise and glide away. Free. With a broad smile Four Eyes tiptoes back to his friends.

"Next time you want to be a superhero discuss it with us first," Bheki scolds him.

When they are far enough from the kraal the seven start running towards the koppie, occasionally turning back to see if the Zim is behind them, but he isn't. When they get to the top of the koppie, Vusi pleads with them to stop, he needs to catch his breath.

Some children shelter behind boulders, others in the shade of the aloe trees.

"How are we going to get home?" Tebogo asks Nolitye.

Nolitye looks him in the eye and says, "I have a plan, but I don't have time to tell you about it." She turns to the littlest one. "Vusi, are you fine?" He nods his head and wipes his nose on his tattered T-shirt. "Okay," Nolitye says, getting up, "let's take the path down to the river."

"Wait! I have an idea," Mbali says. "When the Zim wakes up he's going to come after us. And there's no way we can outrun him. But we can slow him down."

"How?" Nolitye asks.

Mbali gathers a handful of the tall grass that grows in clumps along the edge of the path and ties it to an equal - sized bunch on the other side of the path, making a good, strong knot. The others watch her and then also start making knots. After making several knots, the children move a short way along the path and make some more grass knots.

Mbali, who has kept a count, nods satisfied when Sara ties the twentieth knot across the path. By now Vusi is completely rested and they take off, running with big champion jumps down to the river.

They skirt bushes and boulders. Everything goes flying - small stones, bits of grass, dust. Nolitye's school bag bounces against her back.

"Argh! Argh!" A loud scream suddenly echoes through the valley, rumbling along like heavy thunder. The bellowing cry makes the children stop in their tracks.

"I can smell you! You!" the echo booms. "You won't get away! Away!"

A flock of doves flying in formation dive in all directions when the sound hits them.

"It's him. He's coming after us," Vusi says, his teeth chattering.

"Run!" Nolitye shouts. They muster all their courage and dash for the river. But they don't get far before they hear the Zim approaching. He is thundering up the koppie in long strides, stopping on top only to see where they have gone. Jerking his head from side to side, he waves his sickle nail in the air and roars like a leopard.

"I'm going to eat you all!" he bellows when he detects them running through the shrubbery towards the river.

"Don't stop!" Nolitye says, yanking Vusi to his feet, because he has sat down, paralysed with fear, tears welling up in his eyes.

The Zim comes galloping down the path, brandishing his long nail above his head. And then his toe gets snagged in the first trap. He stumbles but is back on his feet. "Eish!" he exclaims, not seeing that other traps await him.

The children run for their lives.

With the grass brushing his ankles and almost hiding the pathway, it is impossible for the Zim to see the other traps. Once more his foot catches on a grass knot. This time he lands on his knees. "I'm going to get you!" he fumes scrambling to his feet.

The children have been clever enough to leave a good stretch of the path clear before the next lot of knots. The Zim picks up speed again, more determined than ever to catch them. The last few traps are too well concealed for him to see, so, catching first one and then the other foot, he trips and tumbles headlong down the slope.

Thack! There is a sickening sound as the Zim's skull smashes against a boulder with a crashing thump.

The children turn back. The monstrous man lies motionless on the ground. He doesn't breathe; he doesn't twitch a muscle. He just lies there, dead.

Vusi starts crying, dead tired and overwhelmed by the events of the last few hours. "Come. We must go before Ncitjana finds us," Nolitye says, taking him by the hand.

Mvu and his family are waiting on the river bank. They have heard the children running down the koppie. But Nolitye is not ready to leave. "My mother. I must save her," she says to Mvu. "Sara here says that Ncitjana offered her to the river spirits."

"Then you must speak to Noka, the river spirit," Mvu tells her. "You wake her with a stone."

Nolitye scouts around and spots a lovely round stone. With the stone in her hand, she climbs onto a big boulder, half in the water, half buried in sand. She stands on the boulder and throws the stone as far from her as she can into the river. Circles ripple from where the stone has disappeared under the water. "Noka, Noka, please give me back my mother," Nolitye pleads. "Her name is Thembi and Ncitjana offered her to you."

But the water surface remains calm and nothing happens.

"Noka, Noka, please give me back my mother, I beg you," Nolitye pleads again.

The children watch helplessly as Nolitye starts sobbing.

"Noka, Noka, I have come from very far to find my mother. Please help me take her home," Nolitye cries. Her tears fall into the river, tiny droplets that dissolve in the water.

This time a slight disturbance makes the water swirl, creating a small whirlpool. A hollow voice comes from the water: "Follow me, follow my ripples, if you want to find her."

Nolitye wipes her tears, and with a little wave to the other children she follows the ripples up the river. At a very much larger and deeper pool she stops and calls out again: "Noka, Noka, please return my mother to me!"

Once more the river remains silent. Nolitye waits patiently before she repeats her request. Immediately there is a violent eruption of water as a loud voice says, "Come and get her, my child!"

Nolitye takes off her shoes and socks and hands them to Four Eyes, who with the other children and the hippos have followed a few steps behind her.

"You can't just go in," Bheki cautions. "What if you don't come back?"

"She will," Mvu says.

Bheki puts his arms around Nolitye, gives the school bag strapped to her back a pat and whispers in her ear: "If all else fails, use the stone."

Nolitye tells the others not to worry because she will soon be back. She takes a deep breath, expecting to have to hold it. She submerges herself, sinking down, down, down, until she stands on the bottom of the pool. To her amazement she can breathe underwater. Groping in the half-darkness she ends up at the mouth of a large, brightly-lit cave. She enters timidly. To her surprise she finds that her clothes are dry. She glances up at the roof and notices bunches of bats clinging to the rough surface. From a dark corner at the back an ugly old woman, wearing just a simple loincloth, emerges. In large hops the woman bounds towards her. Nolitye is tempted to turn her head away, because the woman's right arm and left leg are missing. In four hops she is at Nolitye's side. The old woman's skin is wrinkled and cracked, peeling at the elbows and knees.

"I know I am ugly and old, my child," she says. "You may laugh, I will not blame you."

"Dumela, Mama," Nolitye answers. "How can I laugh when my heart goes out to you?"

"If the sight of me doesn't put you off, my child, then let the balm of your kind healing tongue heal me by licking my wounds," the old woman says.

Nolitye doesn't hesitate and does as she asks. The old woman starts shivering and shaking. Fascinated, Nolitye watches as she changes. First she grows an arm, and then a leg. Her face takes on a youthful beauty and clothes start covering her body. She stands before Nolitye, an elaborately patterned woollen Basotho blanket draped elegantly over her left shoulder, her head covered by a conically shaped hat of woven grass. Her neck and wrists are decorated with beads only queens wear. She holds a staff with an intricately carved elephant's head at one end - the sign of royalty.

"I am Noka," she introduces herself, "Queen of the River Spirits, and I show myself only to deserving souls.

You have a compassionate heart, my child, and have passed the test. How can I reward you?"

"My name is Nolitye, Mama, and I'm looking for my parents. Ncitjana imprisoned them in his kraal, but they are no longer there. You see, Ncitjana offered my mother to the River Spirits to get more power, and I am trying to get her back," Nolitye explains. "Can you help me?"

"I have heard of what Ncitjana did, my child. He turned your father into a baobab tree that grows near the elephant graveyard, and offered your mother to Kwena, the crocodile, to have power over the Zim. Kwena has hidden her somewhere in these underwater caverns. But I don't know where. You will have to wait for him, my child. The only way you will ever see your mother again is if you are willing to confront Kwena. To find your father, you will have to go to the elephant graveyard." Noka stops talking, turning her head in order to listen, and says, "Kwena is about to return."

No sooner has she uttered the words than a hideous crocodile waddles into sight. Nolitye pulls in her breath sharply when she sees how big Kwena is. His teeth are overgrown with moss and he heaves as he crouches, his body misshapen and ungainly. His brownish scales are loose, covered in slime. His legs are short and stubby, with long curved nails.

"What delicious human flesh awaits me," Kwena says, opening his dreadful jowls.

"The child has come to get her mother," Noka intervenes. "The woman you keep hidden here. I warned you this day would arrive."

"No one will have her! I made my deal with Ncitjana." And Kwena slams his heavy tail on the sand floor.

"Kwena, you know the law," Noka says sternly.

"Yes, yes, you don't have to remind me."

"What law?" Nolitye whispers to the Queen of the River.

Noka explains: "The only way to rescue anyone from the River Spirit world is by answering a riddle."

"But if the young one doesn't answer the riddle correctly she too will have to stay here." Kwena snaps his jaws shut to underline his threat.

Nolitye looks about her, considering the frightening prospect of being trapped here forever. She must answer the riddle correctly! She must get her parents back! "What is the riddle?" she asks.

Kwena moves closer, dragging his body along the sandy floor. His breath smells foul and his prescence fills the cave with gloom. "It is everywhere around you and hides itself in every corner, even in places the size of a pea . . ." The pupils of Kwena's reptilian eyes grow bigger as he looks at Nolitye, sizing her up. "It is only destroyed by one thing and that is light. What is it?"

"Think about it carefully, my child. Or you will be stuck here forever," Noka says.

Nolitye wracks her brains trying to figure out the riddle. She thinks of a bat, but a bat can't hide in a pea. She looks at Noka, pleading with her eyes, but she knows that the Queen of the River dare not help her. And she can't ask the sacred stone, because Kwena would see if she took it out of her bag.

"I'm waiting!"

"Give her time, Kwena!" Noka orders him.

Nolitye tells herself to calm down. She closes her eyes so she can think better. She thinks about her real mother alone in the dark somewhere. A warm feeling of love comes over her as she sees the answer clearly. "I've got it!" she shouts.

"Well?" Kwena edges closer.

"The only thing that can destroy darkness is light. And darkness can hide itself in a place as small as a pea."

"Well done, my child," the Queen of the River says. "I knew you could figure it out."

"She cheated! She cheated!" Kwena says angrily. He snaps his jaws and thrashes his tail about.

"Kwena, you know she didn't cheat. I was right here. Release her mother before I banish you from this river."

"Alright!" Kwena sulks. His eyes become mere slits as he sluggishly drags himself to the back of the cave and starts digging. Nolitye and Noka watch him kicking back the sand and soil with his powerful hind legs. He is slow but with every stroke he moves a whole heap of earth. After a while a large, pale-yellow egg appears. Nolitye steps closer to take a look. Kwena carefully digs around the egg, all the while grumbling that Nolitye cheated.

"Here's your mother," he mutters, cautiously rolling the huge egg towards her. Nolitye goes blank. She doesn't know what she feels; she's excited but scared. And then a memory comes to her: she saw this same egg, just smaller - and a baobab tree! - in a flash of light from the magic stone the day she and Bheki sold fatcakes at Mogale station. She didn't realise then that the stone was giving her a hint as to what had happened to her parents. With a thumping heart, Nolitye looks at Noka.

"Kwena, help her open it," the Queen of the River orders the enormous reptile.

The grumpy crocodile reluctantly, but with great care, cracks the shell of the egg with his huge teeth and starts breaking it open. First Nolitye and Noka see a pair of feet, then as Kwena peels away more shell they see arms, legs and a neck; Nolitye's mother sleeps curled up like an unborn baby. When the egg has been broken open completely, Kwena pokes at Thembi with his long snout. She starts moving, wriggling a bit. Then she rubs her face and yawns as though she has been in a deep sleep. Nolitye can't stand still with excitement. Thembi gets up slowly and stretches. There is a bit of slime on her face.

A flurry of emotion goes through Nolitye. She's so happy that she wants to cry, but she swallows back the tears. She savours the moment of seeing her real mother before her eyes.

Now Thembi is standing up and straightening her dress, a plain mud-coloured cotton dress. Nolitye can't believe this moment has arrived. A thousand times she has imagined how she would feel when she saw her true mother again, and now that she is standing in front of her she can't believe how nervous she is. How shy she feels. It is like meeting a stranger.

"Go to her," Noka whispers to Nolitye.

Nolitye takes a step forward, her stomach doing somersaults.

Thembi looks groggy and confused. She blinks her eyes against the light in the cave. It takes a while before she gets used to it. Kwena moans to himself.

"Where am I?" Thembi says softly, looking at Noka and Nolitye for an answer. They say nothing. Thembi walks towards them and then she stops, a look of shock on her face.

"It can't be," she says, stepping closer.

Nolitye stands there trembling; she doesn't know what to do.

"Nolitye is that you?" Thembi asks, looking intently at her. She utters a low moan and falls to her knees when she realises that she's looking at her lost daughter. Nolitye runs to her mother and flings her arms around her. They both start weeping with joy. Thembi strokes Nolitye's dreadlocks. There is a gentleness in her eyes that affirms to Nolitye that this is her real mother. All the ordeals that she's been through no longer seem to matter; she clings to Thembi, forgetting every hardship.

"Noli, I thought I'd never see you again," Thembi says, holding her tightly.

The Queen of the River blesses them with a benign smile while Kwena waddles out in a huff.

"Mama, we have to save Papa," Nolitye remembers. "He is at the elephant graveyard. Ncitjana turned him into a baobab tree."

Her mother's face becomes clouded with anguish.

"Oh! I knew something terrible would happen to Xoli that night we tried to escape."

"We must go, Mama," Nolitye says urgently but not letting go of her mother.

Thembi disentangles herself from Nolitye and takes her by the hand. "You lead me, I'll follow."

"You have a wonderful child," Noka says to Thembi.

Taking her first careful steps of freedom, Thembi proudly says, "Thank you."

"Come, Mama." Nolitye starts pulling Thembi by the arm. "May the road always be kind to you," Noka says to them.

An important question pops into Nolitye's mind. "Please, Queen of the River Spirits, before we go, how do we get out of the underworld back to where we come from in the city?"

"That is easy," Noka says. "Just follow the Healer of the Road. He will lead you to where you need to go."

"The Healer of the Road?"

Noka, looking incredulous, says, "My, my, you didn't know? It is Nqonqothwane, of course. Dung beetle is the Healer of the Road."

Thembi apologetically pulls up her shoulders and explains: "She grew up in a township."

"I can't believe there are places where children grow up without knowledge of the Healer of the Road," Noka says. "But never mind. All the better that you have learned something new, child. The road holds many lessons." With a little nudge on the nose, she sends Nolitye on her way to the edge of a still pool.

"Are you sure about this?" Thembi says as Nolitye wades into the water.

It is dark and murky, as if it holds many secrets.

Nolitye nods and stretches out her hand to her mother. Thembi approaches nervously, following her daughter's lead. Nolitye squeezes Thembi's hand and wades in deeper until the water comes up to their shoulders. Then they start paddling up the river, Kwena a distant memory.

Chapter Fifteen
THE RACE

WHERE Nolitye disappeared under the water the others are anxiously watching the surface, once in a while casting an eye backwards to see if the Zim has not perhaps revived. But in the distance he lies like a log.

"Look!" Bheki shouts with shining eyes.

The water has begun to ripple, and as they watch two heads pop out of the water. Nolitye's dreads are unmistakable, but the second person they don't recognise immediately.

"Must be Nolitye's mother," Four Eyes thinks out loud.

"Her real mother!" Bheki exclaims.

Mvu grunts relieved and flicks his short tail happily. Nolitye had been gone for so long, that although no one spoke about it, they feared that she might have been forced to join her mother where she was held captive. The children, Bheki and Four Eyes the loudest, cheer and clap their hands as Nolitye and her mother step onto the river bank. They rush to welcome them. "Wow!" Four Eyes exclaims. "Come feel, their clothes are dry!"

In awe of the magical river, the other children can't stop touching Nolitye's school uniform. In spite of her having been in the water, it is still as grimy as ever from crawling down the hole. Nolitye just smiles contentedly and puts on her socks and shoes.

"Who are you all?" Thembi asks, looking at Four Eyes and Bheki who are still just staring at the woman that Nolitye has been yearning for ever since she discovered that Sylvia was not her real mother. The two haven't said a word to either Nolitye or her mother yet. In fact, it gives them goose flesh to look at Thembi because she looks exactly like Sylvia. It is only the affectionate way in which this Thembi looks at and touches Nolitye, and the warmth in her eyes, that tell them she is her real mother.

"My name is Bheki and this is Four Eyes," Bheki finally says, stepping forward and holding out his hand. But Thembi doesn't take it. Instead she gives him a hug and says, "I'm Nolitye's mother and she's the light in my life."

She also hugs Four Eyes and asks, "What kind of a name is that?"

"It's kind of a nickname and it has kind of stuck," he says, peering at her through smudgy glasses.

"Well, do you like being called Four Eyes?"

"I don't mind it. It makes me feel special, you know."

"Then Four Eyes is what I too will call you."

Thembi goes over to meet Sara and Mbali and Tebogo. Vusi enjoys the special attention he gets as the smallest one. Thembi wipes his nose with the hem of her dress and tells him that he has the cutest stubby nose she has ever seen. He laughs, content to be under the care of a warm and loving woman, but probably missing his mother more than ever.

"And this is our friend Mvu, Mama," Nolitye says. "He and his family helped us over the river."

"And I better get you lot back across the river before Ncitjana returns," Mvu warns. His family, none of whom has said a word or made a noise, are already each waiting near a boulder. They are half-submerged, so everyone easily hops onto their backs. Vusi insists on riding on Mvu's back with Thembi and Nolitye. As the hippos wade deeper and deeper into the river, until they start floating, the children splash and splatter water at each other.

Only Thembi is not sharing in the fun. "What's wrong, Mama?" Nolitye asks when she notices the concern on Thembi's face as she looks back. "Kwena's gone."

"It's not Kwena I'm worried about," Thembi says. "Look over there on the top of the koppie."

Nolitye turns her gaze to the top of the koppie and sees a small figure standing there. In his hand he holds a long crook and on his head he wears a hat made of ostrich feathers. The feathers stir in the wind.

"It's Ncitjana. He can't do anything to us now," Nolitye says. "You don't know him," Thembi warns.

Nolitye leans over and shouts in Mvu's little ears, "Mvu, Ncitjana is behind us!"

The children fall silent at once. Bheki, who didn't quite hear what Nolitye said, asks, "What did you just say?"

Nolitye points to the lonely figure on the koppie.

"Kwena, we had a deal! Deal!" Ncitjana's words echo through the valley. "What has happened to our deal? De—"

Ncitjana's words get drowned out by a sudden rapid, repetitive, splashing sound that sends droplets of water shooting into the air. The children look around them at the strange display in the water. "Look, they are all around us!" Vusi notices excitedly.

"Mvu," Nolitye asks, leaning forward so he can hear her amidst the din, "what is this all about?"

"It's the crocodiles, they are marking their territory," Mvu says, speaking as calmly and slowly as ever.

"What do we do now?" Nolitye asks.

Vusi has already clamped his arms around Thembi's neck, almost strangling her in fear. Behind them, Nolitye notices, Bheki is staring into the empty sky, while Four Eyes is hugging his pulled-up legs to keep them as far as possible from the water.

"Normally," Mvu says, "we would fight and they would leave us, but now we have you to think about."

A long snout surfaces to their right and glides towards Mvu. Many other crocodiles also show their heads but remain floating in a circle around the children on the hippopotamuses.

Mbali and Sara, holding each other tightly, start to sing old church songs. Their thin, shaky voices the only sound to be heard for a few seconds.

"Well, well, well," Kwena gloats, close to Mvu. "I think a feast awaits us." He keeps his head straight but turns his evil reptilian eyes from child to child.

"Over my dead body," Mvu says snorting and spraying water into the air. "I'm afraid your little tactics won't work this time," Kwena sneers. "You have your wives to think about. Now why don't you be a good bull and hand over the children and the woman before this feast becomes a bloodbath? There are fourteen of us against the five of you. I don't think . . ." To bear out Kwena's words, the other thirteen crocodiles menacingly snap their jaws shut and throw their tails about aggressively, splashing water everywhere.

Mvu looks at his terrified family. They are so scared that they shut their nostrils hysterically and grunt in panic. Mvu looks at Nolitye. He wants to help her but he has to choose between her and her friends, and his family.

"Cousins! Cousins! They are here! They are here!" a familiar voice shouts from the far side of the river. A pair of long ears peaks out behind a boulder and a hare hops onto the rock.

"Vundla?" Bheki says, just as surprised as the others. "Who's Vundla?" Thembi whispers to Nolitye.

"Nogwatsha, Mama." And Nolitye points to the hare jumping up and down on the boulder.

"Cousins, the herds are here! The wildebeest have arrived on their yearly trek. I've come to warn you," Vundla shouts.

"What are you talking about?" Kwena grumbles. "The grass is still dry."

"Cousins, I'm telling you, they are on the other side of the valley, can't you hear them!?"

"I can't hear anything," Kwena says.

"Then listen properly!" Vundla shouts, signalling to his mates scattered at the top of the valley. A score of hares, carefully concealed behind bushes and rocks, as one start kicking back boulders and rocks with their strong hind legs. The rocks and boulders roll rumbling down the hill, gathering speed as they go and sounding just like a stampede of wildebeest. And since crocodiles have bad eyesight and can't see anything until it is close up, Kwena in a twinkling becomes convinced that the herds have truly arrived.

"Quickly, to the other side where the waters run low!" he instructs his following. In a mad frenzy the crocodiles swim downstream to shallow waters.

Vundla hops out of harm's way as the boulders and rocks come crashing into the water. "Quick, cousins! There's no time to waste," he shouts to Mvu and his family.

The hippopotamuses, who are usually slow, make a concerted effort to reach the river bank as quickly as they can. Exhausted, they waddle out of the water, flapping their short tails urgently. They go down on their knees to let Thembi, Nolitye and the other children slide off. They're not afraid now, because they know crocodiles are most at home in water and are particularly clumsy on land. Luckily it is also a long way for the crocodiles to swim before they would get to the low waters where they think the wildebeest will cross. Ncitjana is nowhere to be seen.

"Thanks, Mvu," Nolitye says, pressing a kiss between his wide nostrils. Mvu, a creature of few words, says no more than: "I hope the road home finds you well." While Nolitye and the others wave at Mvu and his family as they wade into the water and swim upstream, away from the crocodiles, Vundla's mates hop down into the valley and join them on the river bank. The hares slap each other behind the ears and laugh raucously at their ruse.

"Vundla, I thought the Zim ate you after he took away my torch," Four Eyes says.

"He took away the torch, but he certainly didn't eat me."

"So what happened?"

"I was flashing that thing . . . a torch you call it, at everyone and almost everyone ran away in horror, much to my delight. And then I hid behind a bush waiting for Rhinoceros to come by so I could play my trick on him. He's always boasting that he's scared of nothing. So when I heard heavy footsteps approaching, I jumped out and flashed my light - only to be confronted by the Zim. I got such a fright that I dropped the torch." The memory of the Zim suddenly standing in front of him makes Vundla's split lip and long ears quiver, but he continues.

"Well, in one quick movement he grabbed the torch with one hand and me with the other. He told me he was going to eat me and I thought I was done for. But the torch was on and for some silly reason the light irritated him. He tried, but he couldn't get the light to go off. So knowing that if you're not strong you have to be clever, I told him I knew how the thing worked and could make the light go out. So he put me down and was about to hand me the torch when I took off like the wind. Before he knew, I was gone."

"But he told us that he ate you," Bheki says.

"Of course he would! No one likes to be duped," Vundla says proudly. "Do you know why we've got split lips? And why crocodiles bury their eggs? Because of a trick Hare played on Crocodile long ago! The first clever hare stole the first female crocodile's eggs and replaced them with stones. When Crocodile realised that her eggs weren't hatching and that they had been stolen, she became so angry that she swore revenge. One day while our troublesome ancestor was having a drink at the river, Crocodile ambushed him. Due to his quickness and agility he managed to escape the attack, but unfortunately not without Crocodile biting his lip. So you see, once a hare, always a trickster!"

"We're pleased he didn't eat you, Vundla, and grateful that you saved us from the crocodiles," Nolitye says. "But I have a question: do you know where the elephant graveyard is?"

"Of course I do. Nobody knows the forest better than a hare." And Vundla pushes out his chest.

"Well, could you take us there, please, because Ncitjana turned my father into a baobab tree that grows near there."

"Ah yes, the big tree near the graveyard. I have seen it. But I'm afraid I can't help you. Part of the fun of playing a trick on someone is laughing at them. I can't leave this spot, I want to see how long it takes the crocodiles to figure out that they have been tricked once again," Vundla sniggers.

"But Vundla, this is urgent," Nolitye pleads. "I have to save my father." Thembi, standing patiently at her side, gives her daughter an encouraging hug.

But Vundla has already turned his back. "Sorry, but I have better things to do."

Nolitye thinks fast. She can't let Vundla get away that easily. "What could be so complicated about this forest anyway?" she says loud enough for everyone to hear. "I'm sure I can find my way around as well as any hare . . . if not better."

Vundla's floppy ears perk up when he hears this. "What did you say?" he asks turning around.

"You heard me."

"There's no way you can know the forest better than me. Ha! Ha!" Vundla says, turning to his mates to laugh with them. "The idea is preposterous!"

"If you took me there I could show you," Nolitye says. "But what does that big word mean?"

Hare, doing his best to sound even more clever than usual, says. "Outrageous, unthinkable, incredible, impossible, non–"

"Sounds like she's challenging you," one of his mates interrupts him and tips his head to Vundla.

Vundla dislikes being challenged because he believes he is the cleverest. "I'll tell you what," he says to Nolitye, "I'll challenge you to a race. If you win I'll show you around the forest."

"Actually, I just want to see the elephant graveyard," Nolitye interrupts him.

"Fine. I'll show you where the elephant graveyard is. But if you lose the race you'll have to apologise to me and say that I'm the cleverest animal in the forest," Vundla says.

"Sounds fair to me."

Nolitye and Vundla seal the deal with a handshake.

"What do you think you're doing?" Bheki whispers in Nolitye's ear. "He's going to beat you."

"Don't worry, I have a plan."

"You can still pull out and save yourself the embarrassment of losing and having to apologise," Vundla says confidently.

"No, it's fine. I still want to race you," Nolitye says.

All the while Thembi doesn't say anything. She obviously has faith in her daughter who succeeded in finding her in the underworld.

"We will run as far as that ridge over there where the first aloes grow," Vundla announces, pointing the place out. "It's only two hundred metres away."

Nolitye ponders the proposition and says, "You know, when I run, Vundla, I prefer kilometres and not metres. Why don't we race for two kilometres?"

"You really want to embarrass yourself, don't you?" he says with a smirk. "But it's fine with me. There's a path to Modjadji's Pan. It's about that distance from here; we'll race there. You see that third ridge over there in the distance?"

Nolitye nods.

"Well, behind it is Modjadji's Pan. But first I must go home and tell my wife to call all her friends so that they can all see for themselves how clever I am, that I can even beat a human child." Vundla chuckles softly. "I'll meet you here on the river bank at noon."

"How can you challenge Vundla to a race?" Four Eyes asks as soon as the hare and his friends are gone. "Of course he's going to beat you."

"Not if I use this," Nolitye says, taking the sacred stone from her bag.

It glows splendidly. Thembi and the other children gasp. They gather around Nolitye, ogling the purplish-blue shimmering stone.

"What are you going to do with that?" Mbali wants to know.

"I'm going to make sure that I win that race. Now here's what I want you to do." And Nolitye instructs the girls and Thembi to place themselves at regular intervals along the path to Modjadji's Pan, and at noon to start running towards the Pan. At the same time she will ask the stone to turn them into her likeness, so that when Vundla passes anyone of them he will think he is running past Nolitye.

Mbali, who can't quite believe what she hears, asks, "You mean that stone is going to turn me into you?"

"It is not an ordinary stone," Bheki explains to Mbali. "It's magic and powerful."

"Trust me, it will turn you into me," Nolitye assures her. "But only for a while. As soon as Vundla has passed you will turn back into your normal selves again."

"I hope so," Mbali says, still looking sceptical.

Nolitye asks Mbali, Sara and her mother to hold hands. The boys watch intently as Nolitye holds the stone in front of her and says, "Spirit of the Stone, I ask you kindly to turn Mbali, Sara and my mother into me. And when Vundla has passed, to allow them to become themselves again."

In a flash, a blinding light surrounds Mbali, Sara and Thembi. They all cover their eyes as the light swirls around them. The light disappears as suddenly and to everyone's delight four Nolityes stand next to each other. They are identical; they look like quadruplets. It is so uncanny that the boys can't distinguish the real Nolitye from the others. Only their behaviour betrays who might be Nolitye: one girl, Mbali, looks at herself with her mouth hanging open; two others, Sara and Thembi, keep looking at their hands and touching their dreadlocks; the fourth girl is rubbing her hands together, very pleased with herself.

"I told you the stone was powerful," Bheki tells the girl whose mouth is hanging open.

"Wow," Vusi says. "Wow."

Thembi's eyes do not leave the real Nolitye's face for a moment.

Certain that everyone understands the plan, Nolitye, Sara and Thembi set out in the direction of Modjadji's Pan. Bheki, Four Eyes, Tebogo and Vusi walk with them, but they will walk on and wait at the finishing line to see if Nolitye's plan has worked. Mbali will wait for Vundla on the river bank.

Vundla arrives at the starting point on the dot at midday. "Where are your wife and her friends?" Mbali-who-looks-like-Nolitye asks.

"They'll be at the finishing line to celebrate my victory," Vundla boasts. They shake hands and the race begins. Vundla chews up the path and in a few moments is out of sight. To her delight, Mbali changes back into her normal self and sets off towards Modjadji's Pan, quietly laughing to herself.

Vundla too runs along laughing, until he comes across Sara-who-looks-like-Nolitye at the top of the first ridge. Vundla's eyes nearly pop out of his skull as he sees her running in front of him.

"But I thought—"

"You thought what?" Sara says, trying to keep a straight face.

Vundla puts on extra speed and races past Sara, a huge frown on his forehead.

At the top of the second ridge, Vundla is astonished to see Thembi-who-looks-like-Nolitye running in front of him. He races past her, now convinced that Nolitye can fly. The sun is boiling hot and Vundla breathes hard, his throat is dry and his muscles ache and sweat is pouring down his flanks. He doesn't even spare Thembi-who-looks-like-Nolitye a word. He approaches the last ridge determined to win when crash! he trips over himself and falls head over heels. He looks behind him but can't see Nolitye. Exhausted he gets up and tries to run, but he simply can't carry on; his limbs are trembling with fatigue. So he decides to take a short nap to recover his strength.

Vundla doesn't sleep long and when he awakes he feels refreshed. He takes off like the wind again and passes the third ridge. No sign of

Nolitye. On the other side he catches a glimpse of the winning post. The Pan, shimmering with water, waits on the plain below.

But what is this? Vundla gasps when he sees the real Nolitye strolling towards him. She shakes his hand and says, "Nice try, Vundla. I know you did your best." The clever hare is so shocked that he faints. Vundla's wife and friends have to carry him to the pan and sprinkle water over him to revive him. But Vundla is out for the count.

Mbali, Thembi and Sara stealthily join the boys at the finishing line while the hares fuss over Vundla. After a long time Vundla finally stirs. When he opens his eyes and sees his wife and their friends gathered around him, he turns his face away to cover his embarrassment. But the other hares aren't laughing at him and only his wife has a word of caution: "At least next time you won't be so quick to challenge everyone."

The boys giggle while Vundla staggers to his feet, a defeated look on his face.

"So now you have to show me where the elephant graveyard is," Nolitye reminds him.

Chapter Sixteen

THE JOURNEY

NOLITYE and her gang follow Vundla through the dense forest, teeming with colourful birds and strange crawling insects. As they get closer, they can hear the babbling sound of water running over stones. Vundla stops at the stream and explains to Nolitye: "This is where the elephant graveyard starts. If you go through that prickly bush over there you will find a clearing, and not far from there the baobab tree. I cannot go beyond this point. The indawas on the opposite bank are always looking for hares to eat."

"Indawas?" Nolitye asks.

Vundla's eyes become mere slits as he speaks, his ears trembling slightly. "They're supposed to be cousins of the Zim - hairy and fierce, human-looking creatures that walk on their hands and knees. So be on the lookout."

"Well, thanks for showing us this place," Nolitye says. "For what it's worth."

"Good luck is all I can say." Vundla doesn't sound nearly as arrogant as when they first met him.

Bheki pulls on Nolitye's sleeve. He has noticed a group of vultures circling high above them. Vundla only shakes his head when Nolitye asks him what this ominous sight means, and with that he bounds away.

Nolitye hesitates just for a second before she leaps over the little stream. The others follow. "Noli," Thembi asks, "do you know what we have to do when we get to the baobab tree?" She has picked Vusi up and is carrying him on her back.

"I'm not sure," Nolitye says, her immediate concern being how to get through the dense prickly bush. Four Eyes has joined her at the front, and they pull branches and other obstacles out of the way as best they can to let the others through. They nevertheless get scratched, especially the four children in their old, tattered clothes. But they all persist and finally come to a clearing, just as Vundla had said. No one says a word as they gaze on the gigantic carcasses - rib cages, shoulder bones, spinal columns, tusks and scraps of tough elephant hide - scattered over a stretch of land the size of a soccer field. The soil is a dull grey and nothing seems to grow in it.

When Nolitye lifts her eyes she sees the baobab tree on the far side of soccer field. It stands alone as though stranded, its branches reaching into the empty sky like roots. She walks ahead, carefully skirting and stepping over bones. The other children, also having seen the tree, are quiet as they follow in single file behind her.

Nolitye glances back at Thembi who brings up the rear. Thembi nods, her face taut.

There is a gloominess about the place that makes everyone nervous. She looks around her cautiously. No one says a word as they make their way through the graveyard, trying not to breathe in the smell of rotting carcasses that hangs in the air. The further they walk, the more intense the feeling of dread becomes. A few times they have to shoo a vulture or a clutch of crows out of their way.

When they get to the tree, Nolitye takes her mother's hand. "Now what do we do?" Thembi asks.

"You stay here forever," a gruff voice replies.

Nolitye turns to see where the voice came from. Everyone heard it but no one saw from whom it came.

"I've been watching you, Nolitye," the voice continues.

"MaMtonga, I know it's you!" Nolitye says, recognising the familiar voice.

"You are a clever girl. But now it is time to be a good girl."

MaMtonga's cackle sends a chill down their spines. Vusi slides from Thembi's back and runs to Nolitye, clutching her close to him as if to protect her. Overhead a crow squawks.

"Give me the stone, you horrible girl," MaMtonga shrieks.

"Never. You hear me. Never," Nolitye says defiantly. She looks around her, like everyone else, but still they can't see the old woman.

"Then I will have to set my friends upon you."

Loud moaning noises start up. The bush rustles; birds frantically flutter away. From the bush behind the baobab tree a face drooling with saliva emerges as a dreaded indawa proceeds to crawl forward. Four other indawas follow. They are shaggy with patches of hair clotted with mud. Their teeth look like small knife blades - sharp and long, but covered with brown moss. The children stagger back a few steps as the indawas advance, growling ferociously. The creatures are surprisingly fast on their hands and knees, leaping effortlessly over bones.

Nolitye, remembering the trick she played on Rotten Nellie not so long ago, stops retreating and plants her feet a little apart so as to be able to stand firm. She slips her hand in her school bag, takes out the sacred stone and wishes: "Please, Spirit of the Stone, let an invisible wall surround us."

When the fierce indawas are close enough, they leap up and pounce on the children. But they hit the invisible wall. They look dazed, attack again, but the same thing happens: they hit an invisible barrier. They don't give up though, but with every attack they injure themselves more, bruising their heads and limbs. When finally they realise that they cannot break though the wall, they run off in a panic.

Inside the magic wall the children cluster behind Nolitye and her mother. "You're ruining everything as usual!" MaMtonga shouts. And a cloud of mist descends upon them. As it gradually clears they begin to make out the figure of MaMtonga a few metres away, her green-and-brown snake coiled around her neck. So quickly that they could almost not see, she grabs the snake by its tail and turns it into a stick, pointing it straight at Nolitye. A ray of light shoots from the stick, right through the invisible wall. It knocks the stone out of Nolitye's hand. Bheki tries to reach for it but MaMtonga emits another bolt of light from her stick, which throws Bheki against the baobab tree. The stone hovers in the air, but MaMtonga pulls it to her with her magic stick. It drops at her feet with a dull thud.

"There's no need to hurt the children," Thembi says sharply, helping Bheki up. There is a small cut on his arm.

"Thembi, your little brat will pay for the trouble she has caused," MaMtonga says menacingly. Then, pointing her stick to the sky and falling onto her knees, she shouts, "Master, I have the stone!"

A bolt of lightning strikes the graveyard even though the sky is cloudless. Ncitjana, the dreaded Mean One, appears from nowhere, wearing a loincloth and his strange hat made of ostrich feathers. Holding his crook firmly in his hand, he walks up to MaMtonga. She kisses his feet before she rises.

"You are doomed to share your husband's fate, Thembi," Ncitjana says.

"I will turn you into a baobab tree too, while the children will become my khokhothis." And he breaks into high-pitched laughter with MaMtonga.

A thousand thoughts flash through Nolitye's mind. She thinks about all the effort it took to get this far. I didn't come all this way just to fail now, she says to herself. What can I possibly do to get rid of MaMtonga and Ncitjana? She wishes she could just talk to her father again. But to hope for so much is like carrying something too heavy, like carrying a huge suitcase stuffed with stones. She gets scared that her wish might not come true and that all that weight of hoping would just spill out.

"Nolitye, do you remember what Gogo used to say?" Thembi whispers in her ear. "It was her favourite saying."

"Yes," Nolitye nods.

"I think it's time to act on Gogo's wise words."

"Do you have anything to say before I send you to your fate?" Ncitjana asks Thembi.

"As a matter of fact I do," Thembi says. She looks at Nolitye and they both say, "You mess with a woman, you mess with a stone." Together they repeat: "You mess with a woman, you mess with a stone."

The children pick up the words and start repeating Gogo's saying: "You mess with a woman, you mess with a stone."

"Shut up! Shut up!" MaMtonga shrieks.

"You mess with a woman, you mess with a stone," they continue to chant.

An enormous shower of light starts pouring onto the sacred stone in MaMtonga's hand. She and Ncitjana try to get away with their booty, but struggle as they may, their feet seem stuck to the ground.

"You mess with a woman, you mess with a stone," the chant swells on, louder and louder.

"Stop it!" MaMtonga shrieks. "Stop it!"

Ncitjana tries to use his crook to cut his feet loose, but it has no effect. Instead the ground around him and MaMtonga starts sinking as the light continues to pour on them.

"You mess with a woman, you mess with a stone," Thembi and the children keep chanting.

"Thembi, I will get you for this!" MaMtonga shouts as she struggles to move.

"What is happening?" Ncitjana panics as they sink deeper and deeper into the ground. In vain Ncitjana tries to use his hands to set himself free. The ground is slowly but surely swallowing them in spite of MaMtonga shrieking like an injured vulture. When she realises that they are irreversibly being eaten by the earth, she hurls the magic stone away from her, in a last, desperate effort to try and save herself.

"I am the Spirit of the Stone," a gentle voice suddenly says. "Ncitjana, MaMtonga, you have stolen from the land and never given anything back. You will reap what you have sown by paying with your lives."

As the words are uttered, MaMtonga and Ncitjana disappear completely, taking their witchcraft with them. The earth completely covers them. Not a trace remains.

Thembi and Nolitye hug each other when they realise that MaMtonga is gone forever, along with the wicked Ncitjana. The children jump around with joy and cheer.

Nolitye turns to the stone which is still surrounded by a bright light. "Spirit of the Stone," she asks. "How do I save my father?"

"You must smear the trunk of the tree with mud from the stream," comes the answer.

If MaMtonga and Ncitjana can disappear forever, anything can happen, Nolitye says to herself, and because only she among the children and Thembi can hear the Spirit, she calls them together and tells them that they all have to go back to the stream to fetch mud. Without complaining, the others follow her, first crossing the graveyard of the elephants, and then struggling through the prickly bush. At the stream they scoop out handfuls of mud and trudge back to the graveyard. Everyone joins in. They plaster the trunk of the baobab tree with mud, and then return to get more mud. They have to make the strenuous trip several times before the thick trunk is covered.

They stand back. With growing fascination and excitement they watch as a head and then a pair of hands emerges from the tree. At first these human parts seem to be made of wood, but then they lose their hard texture and become flesh. Slowly but surely shoulders begin to form. There is a murmur of wonderment and awe as the children see Xoli coming to life before their eyes.

"Smear some more mud!" the Spirit of the Stone commands.

Nolitye, who hardly dared to breathe as she recognised the figure emerging from the tree as her father, repeats the order and hurries back to the stream to get more mud, her heart thumping wildly.

"It's working," Thembi says as she dashes after her daughter, laughing joyously. Light-heartedly they, with the children at their heels, run back to the stream for more mud.

Four Eyes winks at Bheki; they have never seen Nolitye happier. "Once more! Once more!" the Spirit of the Stone encourages them.

The baobab tree seems to come alive under their hands as they continue to smear its trunk with mud. Xoli's face, his eyes closed, appears. Then a human trunk, arms and legs.

It takes unbearably long before Xoli opens his eyes. Smiling faces glowing with wonder and joy fill his field of vision. Nolitye trembles, she is so happy. As Xoli steps forward from the tree trunk the baobab tree vanishes behind him. He blinks his eyes slowly to get used to the light. Then he takes a deep breath, filling his lungs with fresh air.

Speechless with joy, Thembi takes her husband's hand. "My wife, I thought I would never see you again," Xoli says. Thembi embraces him, her eyes brimming with tears of gladness.

"My bubu," Nolitye's father says when he recognises her. "I knew you would find us."

Nolitye leaps into his arms even though she is not a little girl any more. She puts her arms around his neck and rests her head on his shoulder. Bheki is so pleased to see Nolitye so happily reunited with her parents that he punches Four Eyes so hard on his arm that his spectacles slip off his nose. He readjusts his glasses - just in time to shake hands with Xoli, who is shaking hands with all the children to celebrate the success of their journey.

"Shush," Nolitye tells everybody, and solemnly whispers, "Thank you, Spirit of the Stone, for your kindness. We will never forget this journey, not as long as we live."

"You took up the challenge and found what your heart was aching for," the stone replies. "And I'm whole again. Now it is time for the different tribes to come together as it was meant to be from the beginning of time."

A burst of light shoots up from the sacred stone like a comet. It streaks across the sky until it forms a rainbow, leaving a magnificent arch for every living thing to see.

As soon as the different animals, big and small, see it, the forest, mountains and plain come alive with activity. Every creature recognises it as a message from Nkulunkulu the Great One: birds sing in the trees and baboons shout from the tops of hills; elephants trumpet on the plains. From the depths of the forest and the wide open plains a strange procession starts to make its way to the elephant graveyard. In a peaceful and orderly fashion elephants, lions, zebras, fish eagles, crocodiles, wildebeest, ostriches, monkeys, baboons, bats, duikers, hares and many others gather at the elephant graveyard. Even the slow chameleon manages to show up in time.

Enthralled, Nolitye, Bheki and Four Eyes, Xoli and Thembi, and Ncitjana's former khokhothis watch as the collected animals stand before the sacred stone, silently paying their respects to the gloriously shimmering purplish - blue crystal.

Everyone in the gathering pricks up their ears or turns their heads to hear when the Spirit of the Stone begins to speak for, unlike the humans, they can understand every word: "Now that you have come together as it was meant to have been right from the beginning of time, Nkulunkulu the Great One wishes for you to return to your tribes and deliver his message to them. Grow and be strong, for the light of wisdom has been shown to you again. Knowledge that had been obscured, like a hidden star, has been restored to you. But those dark days are to be no more. The ancestor gods have spoken: the tribes shall once more gather and live in peace." After a brief pause, the voice adds, "And as for you, Nolitye, be well and may the road always be kind to you. My gratitude to you: I am back where I belong." Then the Spirit of the Stone falls silent.

A loud joyous trumpeting echoes throughout the forest and plains as the animals cry out in praise of the stone. Grass starts sprouting all over the elephant graveyard. Soon bushes and shrubs, majestic trees and creepers fill the once barren land. The elephant bones crumble away and the pungent smell of decaying flesh clears. The scent of wild flowers and ripe berries fills the air. As soon as the elephant graveyard has been transformed into lush greenery, the animals once again scatter, leaving the children and Nolitye's parents marooned in the middle of a dense forest.

Unnoticed by them, the sacred stone is loosing its purplish-blue glimmer. Just as Nolitye is wondering whether she will ever see Nomakhosi again, a magnificently coloured sunbird flies into view, flashing the deepest of purples and greens as it hovers in front of them. Nolitye smiles. Only she knows it is her faithful mentor and friend Nomakhosi. The bird soon shoots back into the sky and disappears over the forest.

With a lost expression on his face, Bheki looks around them at the dense forest. "Now how do we get out of here?" he asks.

Nolitye too looks around. A small dung beetle pushing a ball of dung across a patch of clear ground catches her eye. Just follow the Healer of the Road. He will lead you where you need to go. She remembers Noka's words.

"Look!" she says excitedly.

"So what? It's just a beetle." The others, like Bheki, look at Nolitye strangely.

"It's not just a beetle," Thembi, the only other person who heard what the Queen of the River said, explains. "In actual fact it is the Healer of the Road and it's going to lead us home."

Behind his smudgy glasses Four Eyes's eyes are wide with surprise. "What do you mean?"

"She means the dung beetle is going to help us find the hole through which we entered this place," Nolitye says.

With everyone staring at the dung beetle, Nolitye turns toward the sacred stone. She gives a gasp. The stone, which has already taken on the ashy colour of the soil, is sinking into the earth, disappearing from her sight. She quietly bids it farewell and then turns and follows the beetle as it rolls its ball through the undergrowth, over sand and grass, and later through gaps between boulders. Sometimes the ball rolls off course, but each time the persistent Healer of the Road scuttles after it and retrieves it.

The group of children and two adults crouch under thorny trees and jump over boulders as they follow the beetle. A strange silence has settled over everyone. Even the cry of the fish eagle is no longer heard. In the profound silence which makes them aware of themselves and of each other, Thembi starts singing Unqonqothwane, a Xhosa folk song that honours the dung beetle. The children listen to the words of the song, to her voice, to the melody caressing their ears, and soft memories of their homes and loved ones come back to them.

They follow the dung beetle as far as a dry ravine. Here the ball rolls down the slope, the beetle scurrying after it. Both disappear under tufts of long, dry grass. Eagerly the children follow. Bheki and Four Eyes get on their knees and with their hands carefully clear the grass. And there, hidden under the grass, a large hole becomes visible. Not paying the humans behind him any attention, the beetle unperturbed continues rolling his prize down the hole.

Four Eyes sits back. "This must be it. It's big enough for us to fit."

"I never thought I would see myself out of this place," Thembi says. Xoli gives her a hug. "Neither did I," he says.

"At last we're going home," Nolitye says gratefully. "Together."

Suddenly in a rush to get home, they enter the hole: Nolitye, Bheki and Four Eyes in front, Thembi and Xoli at the rear, behind Sara and Mbali, and Tebogo and Vusi, who can't wait to see their families again, to enjoy a wholesome home-cooked meal. But most of all they can't wait to be in familiar surroundings again. They've missed the township with its dusty streets. They've missed MaMokoena's spaza shop, the shebeens and other small corner stores with their dilapidated roofs, even Rotten Nellie and her gang, moaning Mandla, Rex and the rowdy stray dogs. They've missed the squeezed-in shacks that leave little space for anything else, and the train that makes the tracks hum as it passes by.

They've missed the township, because it is home. And home is never far away when you believe in it.